I0766999

New Adventures

Science Fiction & Fantasy Anthology

Dedicated to our loved ones past and present:

Thank you for all of your patience and support

This section still has fancy spacing

Table of Contents

Foreword

In our first anthology, *New Beginnings*, our foreword discussed the power in stories: the power to inspire others, the power to record a history of thoughts and beliefs and legends, and the power to leave behind something that countless future generations can still share and enjoy.

There is power, also, in patience and persistence. The road of writing is not a smooth one. It is beset on all sides by trials and tribulations, battles with syntax and typos, the struggle to free one's self from the quicksand of writer's block, always trudging through a miasma of inner demons and internal voices telling you that your words are hot garbage, that your efforts are meaningless, that you have nothing new or unique to say so why are you even trying? If one does not write for a living – like all of the authors in this book and, I imagine, most of you aspiring writers out there – you must also contend with keeping up the motivation to write after a long day of working a job, oftentimes one that leaves you so emotionally and mentally drained that staring at the blank page with its blinking cursor seeking your imagination and input is the most demotivating feeling imaginable.

The pathway to publishing is even bumpier and more trying. Not only does one contend with all of the above, but now you are trying to coordinate those efforts and overcome those battles with others experiencing the same thing; a scattered army of weary warriors trying to find their comrades-in-arms during the brief moments of respite before the fighting begins anew. An effort that takes much planning, much scheduling, and much forgiveness when those plans and schedules get derailed by a job or real-life woes complicating matters.

But in both cases, there's nothing more you can really do except lower your head, dig in deep, and push through. It doesn't have to be fast. In fact, it never is. Yet, if you make a small bit of effort, toss down a few words a day, you will eventually get there. Patience and persistence: patience with yourself most of all, and the persistence to keep trying. Always. For you are never truly defeated, never fully beaten, never completely conquered... until the day you stop trying.

With *New Beginnings*, our group found a shared voice and rhythm for bringing you stories of science fiction and fantasy. Four of us now return to you with more and, in some cases, you'll see some familiar faces from the first anthology embarking on new adventures. So, if you haven't read it yet, we highly encourage you to pick up *New Beginnings* first and get caught up; it is available for free download at <u>dragonscript.net/books</u>.

In this second anthology, we'd also like to welcome a new author to our group: C. Red. She comes to us with a long track record of inspired writing, and we are honored that this anthology contains her first officially published original works. New adventures all around, it would seem!

And now, gentle reader, I leave you with one final thought and blessing: may you always aspire, may you always question, and may the wind always be to thy wings.

- T. M. Lowe

Stealing Laughter

Written by

Estee Lee-Mountel

Few studios make their office locations public knowledge. Even fewer keep open-door policies. In a place like New Socalwood, it was a matter of survival and mental well-being for the administrative staff. The hungry and desperate didn't swarm soup kitchens or food pantries around here. No, they came to the studios: the ones who promise fame and fortune, an instant solution to life's pesky problems like poverty and malnutrition, loneliness and obscurity.

No one expected Black Hole Studios to survive beyond a year or two, especially during the Great Creatives Depression of 2109. One year turned into a decade and saw the end of the Depression itself. In that time, its ad in the media feeds largely remained the same:

The advertisement now flashed onto the screen of the slender device tucked under Coramie's arm. Her attention was absorbed with reading the historical interactive plaque in the studio's lobby. She ignored the crowd moving around her through the reception area. Mounted high near the ceiling, a portrait of the studio's founder looked out over them all. His round face spoke of benevolence and congeniality. Events like The Great Creatives Depression were faint ghosts, seventy years distant. It certainly had no bearing on prospective up-and-coming talent like Coramie. After all, her grandmother, mother, and aunt all had established careers that started at Black Hole. Tonight, the New Socalwood skies would have a new star— or, so the saying goes.

"Are you in need of assistance, miss?"

Coramie jumped, dropping her tablet. The service bot smoothly plucked the tablet out of the air before it could hit the polished floor and proffered the device to its speechless owner. She took the item back and hastily stowed it in her bag before she could endeavor to break it again. Her eyes quickly scanned the room to see if anyone had noticed her silly mistake. Thankfully, no one paid her or the service bot any attention. "I'm sorry. And thank you. What did you say?"

The service bot smoothed an imaginary wrinkle from its night-dark suit as it straightened. "Are you in need of assistance, miss? Perhaps you'd like a tour of the studios? If you are interested, please proceed to the corridor on the left. A docent bot is waiting there and will leave in five minutes, as scheduled."

"Actually," Coramie said, putting steel into her voice and hardening her composure, "I'm here for my audition." She was descended from a line of successful performers and actors, she reminded herself. It's time she started acting like it and embraced her legacy. "I have an appointment with Director Falls at—"

"Ah, Coramie! You're early! I like that."

She glanced over her shoulder then executed a crisp pivot toward the booming voice, wordlessly dismissing the service bot as she did. *Watch and learn*, she thought, hoping that others had taken notice of her special treatment and superior skills. Director Edward Falls waddled out from a doorway that was guarded by a particularly lethal-looking security apparatus. He beamed at the young woman with every ponderous step.

"Let me take a look at you, sweetheart," he said, finally stopping mere inches from her.

Edward looked Coramie up and down, and she tried her hardest to ignore the oily gleam in his eyes. She lifted her chin ever so slightly, giving her what she hoped was a semblance of dignified confidence. Although the aging entertainment executive towered over her in both height and bulk, she was not about to be intimidated. He was not the first, nor was he likely to be the last. Her current task in making a good first impression was a matter of fine balance: neither too harsh and lofty nor too meek and eager to please. The director could try and push, but he'd meet resistance if he pushed too far.

That was the idea, anyway.

"It's an honor to finally meet you, Director Falls," Coramie said, holding out her hand and bowing slightly in one fluid motion. She used the gesture to generate some distance between herself and Edward. "I'm Coramie Risu."

If Edward Falls was offended in any way, he gave no indication of it. The smile embedded into his face remained the same. "A pleasure, my dear," he said, taking Coramie's hand eagerly. "Always exciting to meet the newest star of such a prestigious and talented family. I sat in on your mother's first audition here at Black Hole, you know. Ah, I remember it like it was just yesterday. I knew she'd be a star. She had all the right stuff, and such fire and talent. All ancient history, of course, especially now that we're about to start a new chapter, eh? With Vaniri's little girl, no less!"

Coramie freed her hand from the man's grasp and held it over her heart. "My mother told me the story often as I grew up. She sends her warmest and kindest regards."

"I'm sure she does." Edward began the slow journey back toward the guarded doorway, waving a thick hand at Coramie to follow him. "Your family legacy won't get you everywhere, sweetie. Here at Black Hole Studios, we admire genuine talent and reward innovation. You pull your weight and blow us away. That's how you make it big."

"Of course—"

"We want to see something new, something we haven't seen before! It's up to you to show us that you can give us something no one else can."

"Yes, sir, Director Falls," Coramie said. "I assure you; you won't be disappointed."

In the silence that followed, Coramie noticed an increasing dimness in the hallway. She pushed the thought away, chalking it up to pre-audition anxiety and noted that the studio's reception area had been exceedingly bright— likely a symbolic concept pushed by an overbearing interior designer. *We're the start of a bright future!* or something similarly trite.

Coramie forced herself to take two deep breaths, reining in her scattered nerves. A tiny blip of advice pushed through the mental fog that threatened to engulf her: "You are the master of your mind and body." The words were said by one of her first mentors. At the time, Coramie dismissed it as so much pseudo-spiritual mumbo jumbo that she often heard quoted from the history books about early 21st century America. As she trained, however, she realized the truth in the saying. She conditioned her mental and physical aspects to respond like marionettes in a master puppeteer's hands. *I am a fine instrument of performance art*, Coramie recited to herself. She clung to the words, holding them firm in her mind.

Edward stopped without warning. They stood in front of a plain white door, identical to its neighbors. There was nothing on or around the door to distinguish it from the others they had passed in the hallway. A high-level executive like Director Edward Falls, who obviously had been with the studio for decades, probably navigated the building on autopilot. Coramie, on the other hand, figured it would be months before she learned to go to the right office— granted she landed the role and job, of course. She felt a twinge of pity for any newcomers to the studio. And herself.

Holding up a thick wrist toward the door, Edward touched a softly blinking light on the smooth, matte band that had been hidden under the cuff of his pressed shirtsleeve. The door swung open with a gentle click. Inside, the room was sparsely furnished with a cold steel table, a wooden stool, and what looked like a small recording booth. Without a word, Edward ushered Coramie inside and waved his arm at the door. It closed with a firm thud.

With so little in the room, she noticed the security cameras immediately: three in all. Black Hole must be serious about their security and NDAs, which was the tradeoff for being one of the few studios to throw its doors open to anyone and everyone. That, or there were others watching. Regardless, she would give them a performance to remember. Coramie glanced about for a script or some indication toward what she would be doing for the audition. There was nothing.

"I'm not going to bother with any of the bullshitting," Edward said, "especially since you're Vaniri's girl. I don't have to impress you with the whole 'This is New Socalwood!' routine. You already have an idea of how we do things here at Black Hole. That makes my life easier. And I like things that make my life easier."

He tapped another command into his wrist device, summoning a cushioned chair that popped up from the floor. With some effort, Edward heaved his body into the seat. "So, let's get started." He tried and failed to hide the slow smile seeping through the folds in his face. "I'm eager to see you in action."

Coramie hesitated by the table. She wasn't stepping foot into the sound booth until she had a better idea of what she was doing. "You'll be giving me the direction and cues, then?" she asked, keeping her voice carefully pitched and controlled.

"Wha?" Edward said, blinking. "We're starting simple, babe. I told you already: your family name got you in, but you're untested. I need to see what you've got."

"All right then," Coramie said, facing Edward now. "What's first?"

"We've been working on a better, more natural sounding laugh track. I think your voice would be a good addition."

"A laugh track, sir?"

Edward's eyes narrowed. "Think you're too good to work on a laugh track?"

"I said no such thing. Sir." Coramie added the pleasantry after a beat. Her mouth was a taut, painted pink line. "I just thought using real actors to create laugh tracks was a relic from my history books in school."

The hostility abated from Edward's face, just ever so slightly. "The bots and sound effect boards can only do so much, you know? You've probably seen enough shows while you were growing up. Those laugh tracks sounded awful! We're innovators here at Black Hole Studios, sweetheart. And I, Director Edward Falls, will always improve on something until it's absolutely perfect."

"I understand, sir, but…"

"Are you here to audition or ask questions all day, Miss Risu?" Edward said, cutting her off. Hostility edged his voice again. "Because I can refer you to our docent bot, instead, if you like. It can answer all of your questions, and you can stop wasting my time. I'm a very busy man with plenty of other auditions to get through."

"I'm here to audition, sir. I apologize, Director Falls," Coramie said, flashing a small sheepish smile. "My nerves must be getting the better of me. Mom always said I talked a mile a minute when I get nervous."

"Well, I can certainly understand that, my dear," Edward said, suddenly mollified. "You know, I remember Vaniri did the same sort of thing. Poor girl. Must run in the family, eh, babe?"

Coramie chuckled along with Edward, even as she felt her skin crawl. She started to ease her hand toward the tablet tucked away in her bag. The director was still laughing, caught up in his thoughts, self-importance, and the nostalgia. If she was quick enough, she could thumb on the device's location tracker. At least someone would know where she was if something were to happen— granted anyone was listening.

Edward snapped back to attention in an instant. The chair under him creaked in protest at the sudden movement. Coramie clasped her hands uselessly at the small of her back. If only she had just a few more seconds, she would have gotten to her tablet. Now, she feigned disinterest at having Edward's full, rapt attention again. He stared at her with a different, fervent light in his eyes.

It was a look of pure, unabashed hunger.

"What a delightful laugh you have, Coramie," Edward said. "Oh, you'll do quite well. I can tell already."

Coramie started toward the sound booth when Edward stopped her with a gruff noise. "You can leave your bag on the table," he said. "You won't need it in there."

She tried her best at looking casual as she gently placed her bag on the table's gleaming surface. There was no chance of flipping the device on now; not with Edward's eyes following her every move. Coramie walked back to the recording booth and stepped inside. Whatever was going to happen, she may as well get it over with now. No use in prolonging the inevitable. As she shut the door to the booth, she realized there were other instruments arrayed on the walls. Perhaps laugh tracks were to be taken more seriously than she thought.

Distracted by the accessories around her, she missed the small sound of the door's lock clicking into place.

"Finally!" Edward said. "Now, here's the scene: a mother walks into the house and sees a huge mess. In the middle of everything is a puppy. The mother sternly looks at the puppy and demands to know if he's responsible for the mess. In response, the puppy rolls onto its back and gazes at the mother with an endearing look, panting with the tongue hanging out. And, go!"

The light cue in the booth turned from red to green. Focusing her thoughts, Coramie pictured the puppy in her mind. She let out a small squeal of delight and giggled into the microphone. Several panels on the walls lit up around her. Before she had a chance to wonder what it meant, she suddenly felt tired, like she had run a marathon and was out of breath. The image of the puppy she had conjured in her mind was suddenly gone. She tried to regain the scene in her head but couldn't. It was like the thought never existed in the first place.

Beyond the booth, Edward pushed a button, changing the light cue back to red. The panels winked off. Coramie's weariness left as suddenly as it had started. She could see Director Edward Falls beaming at her through the booth's window. He opened the door to the booth and pulled her to him in a crushing hug.

"That was perfect, babe," Edward said. "Absolutely perfect!"

"Does that mean...?" That one hanging question swept everything else away in her mind.

"Welcome to Black Hole Studios, sweetheart. You've officially made it to the big time."

Coramie nearly danced out of the recording booth, so utterly wrapped in the euphoria of passing her audition. She didn't even realize when they had made it back to the studio's reception area— and Edward was gone, vanished once more behind the heavily secured doors. Her eyes watered, blurring her vision: from tears of joy or reacclimating to the bright lights, she couldn't tell.

***

"Guess what, Mom?" Coramie said into her phone. "I passed! I rocked my audition and impressed Director Falls!"

She sandwiched the phone between her ear and shoulder, trying to talk and cook herself a celebratory meal at the same time. Coramie briefly considered calling her best friend first; her mother, however, would be most incensed if she ever found out that she, the great Vaniri Risu, was not the first person Coramie called. The EnviraWalls surrounded her in the ambient light of a hundred illusory scented candles. It gave her tiny studio apartment the impression of warmth and wealth. Her mother always had old-fashioned scented candles on hand for aromatherapy— even though the house they lived in had air conditioning tech that could reproduce over one million scents. Artisanal, handcrafted candles were costly, and that was the main reason why Vaniri Risu would want such messy, hazardous commodities.

"Director Falls also said to pass along his warmest regards," Coramie said. "He said he fondly remembers your first audition with Black Hole Studios and remains quite a fan of yours."

"Of course the tub of lard was quite fond of me," came Vaniri's voice from the other end. "He still is! You think he'd set aside time for just anybody?"

Coramie could picture her mother, dressed in synthsilks and gesticulating like an android gone haywire. The polished floors and walls of her house would amplify her movements in dozens of reflections. With luck, the reflections will distract her enough to forget what she was ranting about.

"I know, Mother. Thank you again."

"Oh, anything for you, my darling girl. Now, tell me: how did the audition go? What did they have you do?"

The younger woman took a breath, bracing herself. Just in case her award-winning mother decided to deride her for the work she did. "Director Falls had me work on a laugh track, actually." She held her breath as soon as the last word left her mouth.

A beat. "Did he now? He's still on that project, then?"

"For the better, more natural-sounding laugh track?" Coramie asked. "Yeah. Has this been his thing for a while?"

"Well, that's one way of putting it, Cara."

Coramie carefully, slowly put down the chef's knife she'd been using. She wiped off her hands on a nearby towel and adjusted the phone against her ear. "Wait, what did you say, Mother? Did you just call me 'Cara?'"

"What? 'Cara?' Why would I...? Oh, it must have been a slip of the old memory, sweetie. All this talk of auditions and Director Falls and Black Hole Studios; it's got me all nostalgic, I guess. Cara was a girl I used to work with back in the day, that's all. Cara Wootsen, I think? Woodson? Ah, it doesn't matter."

"That's funny, I don't think you've ever mentioned Cara Wootsen before. And I know you love talking about your earlier acting days."

"Like I said, it doesn't matter, Cora, dear. Just another sign of old age, am I right? So, you were saying earlier about your audition, darling...?"

***

The building that housed Black Hole Studios' offices and recording facilities was actually a modest one, especially in comparison to the other skyscrapers that littered the sprawling megatropolis of New Socalwood. Tall, brushed steel letters, backlit with the glow of nearly ten thousand LEDs, spelled out the company's name so that it was visible two territories away, however. It had a reputation for surviving the Great Creatives Depression, which only added to the mythos and symbolism behind the eye-melting signage.

Coramie stood in the letters' towering shadows. She wondered how many people, with hope in their eyes and dreams of fame in their minds, stood where she was now. An old adage from the 20th century about "standing on the shoulders of giants" came to mind. Sure, there was her mother and aunt, who undoubtedly helped clear the way for her— which Director Edward Falls readily reminded her at any given moment. But Coramie thought of the ordinary folks like her grandmother who aspired to the extraordinary, building up the studio in its first years. They were the ones who paved the road to stardom brick by synthbrick, becoming the very foundation of the Creatives Renaissance and New Socalwood itself.

Their courage and bravery that reignited a passion for show business had fueled Coramie, propelling her toward the shining beacon of creativity Black Hole Studios had been— and forever will be, as far as she could tell.

It was a week since her initial audition, and the reality of being employed by a major studio had finally become comfortable in her mind. When describing the events that happened in the recording booth to her mother, she had difficulties relaying the specifics. Details were obscured at best, as if she were viewing them through panes of frosted glass. Luckily for her, Vaniri Risu had never been a good listener and the lack of details didn't seem to bother the aging diva.

She still felt a well of disquiet, sitting in the space of her chest right behind the sternum. It caused her to hesitate, to question. *Don't be silly*, she admonished herself. Perhaps she was not as comfortable with her new employment as she wanted to be, but she could push past it. Coramie thought again of the courage and bravery of her grandmother and the others like her. If they could pioneer, create, and survive, so would she.

Coramie put her shoulder to the heavy steel and glass door and stepped into the reception area. It was quieter than she remembered, though the noise may have been a projection of her nerves and anxiety. By the reception desk, she spotted the service bot who had so gracefully saved her tablet from becoming a hundred tiny shards. She crossed the room with quick, measured steps and tapped the humanoid machine on its shoulder.

"You may not remember me," she said, "but I'm Coramie Risu. I wanted to thank you again for your kindness last week; when you caught my tablet after I'd dropped it."

"Certainly; I remember you, miss," the bot replied. "It is part of our programming, after all, as is recovering your personal technological device. I am a service bot, and my directive is to serve."

"How long have you been in service here at the studio?"

"Approximately forty years, seven months, one week, and five days."

"Over forty years..." Coramie turned the words over in her head, quickly doing some calculations. "That means you were here when my mother started, too! Her name is Vaniri Risu."

The service bot paused, standing completely still as its processors worked. "Yes, I do recall Vaniri Risu. Daughter of Caroline Risu. Younger sister to Sakura Risu. It is an old memory file, but one with many iterations, as I remember Vaniri Risu often made sure I knew who she was and who her relatives were."

"That sounds like something Mother would do," Coramie said, rolling her eyes. "If that's the case, do you also remember a Cara Wootsen? Mother said she and Cara worked together for a time here at Black Hole Studios."

Another pause, though this one was lengthier. The smooth metal face was unreadable; its optics seemed to stare intently into her. When the service bot spoke again, it sounded almost... reluctant. "That may be a query better posed to our Docent Bot, Miss Risu. The Docent Bot has been with the company since its inception and has access to the archival databanks." The android sketched a hasty, yet polite, bow to Coramie. "If you'll excuse me, I must return to my duties."

She watched the bot scuttle away, its mechanical legs moving more quickly than normal. Bots weren't supposed to exhibit emotion, though she wondered if four decades of working for and around humans imbued it with some personality quirks. It also occurred to her that she was, once again, projecting her own thoughts onto the situation. The woman shook her head. Overthinking wasn't going to help anyone or anything. It certainly wasn't going to get her any answers.

Coramie checked her watch. She had about thirty minutes until she needed to be back in the reception area to meet Director Falls for another session in the recording booth. That should be enough time for a tour of the studio offices with the Docent Bot— or, at least ask it a few questions. If anyone took issue with her digging around, she could always chalk it up to her nervous habit of asking rapid-fire questions again.

She followed the small but stylish signs leading to the "OFFICIAL BLACK HOLE STUDIOS TOUR" staging area. The Docent Bot stood patiently behind the kiosk, waiting and watching, at the end of the corridor. It perked up at the sight of Coramie. Straightening its formal dress uniform, the Docent Bot approached her and grabbed her hand, shaking it vigorously.

"Ah, welcome!" it squeaked. "Welcome! Are you here for the tour? We can wait a few more minutes for more people to come; then we'll set off on our historical adventure through Black Hole Studios! But we can leave now if you don't want to wait. Because I can't wait! Can you?!"

Again, Coramie wondered if this was all part of the poor creature's programming or something else entirely. There was little to no sign of the wear and tear of over seven decades on the android— if this particular bot had really been with the company since it first opened its doors to scores of desperate people. The uniform was undoubtedly a more recent acquisition, but the android itself gleamed like it had just left the assembly floor over in southcentral New Socalwood. In all likelihood, there was a standing order from the studio's founder to take care of the Docent Bot as the studio's sole historical curator.

"Actually, I was wondering if you'd be able to dig through the archives and look up a name for me, please?" Coramie asked. She extracted her hand from the bot's firm grip and slid around to the opposite side of the kiosk from the Docent Bot.

"Sure, can do!"

The Docent Bot tapped a couple of commands into the band on its wrist, one that was similar to the device Director Edward Falls wore and used. With a faint whirring sound, the kiosk expanded into a small console with screens, a keyboard, and multiple command keys. The bot stepped into the neat cavity left in the console's center. It sank a few inches into the mechanism as the console hissed around it. Coramie watched the Docent Bot become part of the database retrieval hardware in silent awe. When the bot spoke again, even its voice was altered.

"Please input your query via voice command, phrased in the form of a question."

It took a moment for Coramie to find her voice again after witnessing such a beautiful dance of technology and machinery. "Who is Cara Wootsen?"

"Please wait while I process your request." The lights in the bot's optical sockets flickered, flashed, then settled into a steady, rhythmic pulse.

Coramie shifted her weight from one foot to another, then back again. The Docent Bot's overenthusiasm had been awkward and unsettling, but the thick, sudden silence was worse. She glanced around, thinking of different excuses to give in case anyone walked by and asked why she was standing there. Five minutes passed, and no one came around. In fact, Coramie slowly realized as she looked around again, there seemed to be only her and the

Docent Bot at this end of the building. Even the lights looked dimmer than the ones used in the rest of the studio's reception area.

She adjusted her bag, suddenly uncomfortable. Perhaps she could go back to the primary waiting area and pretend none of this happened. Just as she finished the thought, the pulsing behind the bot's optical sockets ceased. The Docent Bot blinked once or twice, then focused on Coramie. There was another series of whirs and hisses as the bot stepped back out, and the console shrank back down to a simple, unassuming kiosk.

"I apologize for the delay," the Docent Bot chirped. It handed her a thin datapad. "These old processors aren't what they used to be. Now, you had asked about Cara Wootsen, yes? Let me—"

"CORAMIE, SWEETHEART. IS THAT YOU DOWN THERE?"

Coramie turned from the Docent Bot to see Director Edward Falls waddling as quickly as he could down the hallway toward her. She chanced a look down at her watch while she slipped the datapad into her bag. Her blood turned into a glacial spring at the thought of losing track of time— and on her first official day on the job, no less. To her relief, unless her watch had stopped, she still had twenty minutes to spare. Her panic gave way to confusion as she tilted her head at Edward.

"Director Falls?" Coramie folded her hands in front of her, gently laying them on top of her bag. "I thought I wasn't up for another twenty minutes."

"You never know how these meetings and appointments will go around here in New Socalwood," Edward said, panting. His face was a bright, unhealthy hue of red. "But what are you doing down here in this corner of the offices, babe? You should be where the lights are shining on full blast because you... You're a *star*, baby, that's what you are."

Coramie couldn't help herself. "Stars only shine when it gets dark, Director Falls."

Edward stopped panting long enough to stare at her. "Clever," he finally said, his expression flat. "Your mother never mentioned how clever you were. Come on, we're wasting time standing around here."

Left without any other options, Coramie turned to follow Edward back into the main reception area. A gentle touch on her arm made her pause.

"Miss," the Docent Bot said softly, "would you still like a tour of the studio? Or perhaps hear the information I retrieved for you?"

Coramie could feel Edward's eyes on her. She tapped into the bravado that came with her family name and prestigious acting lineage once more. "Can't you see Director Falls needs me?" she said. "I'm busy! I don't have time for some dolled-up history lesson. Leave me be!"

The Docent Bot tilted its head ever so slightly to the side, then nodded, as if it understood— not just the words, but the underlying intent of the woman's tone and body language. It returned to its bubbly, overenthusiastic directive. "Of course, miss. I look forward to your next visit!"

Edward gripped Coramie's upper arm firmly as he steered her toward the main hall. His rubbery face was pinched into a tight, angry expression. She could hear him muttering under what breath he could spare on the long, arduous journey toward the same fortified doorway from last week. While she had a general idea of what he was grousing about, she didn't bother asking for clarification. He gave the impression that any further conversation was strictly unwelcome.

Devoid of Edward's usual bluster and her own nervousness, Coramie focused on the spare details of the hallways behind the heavily secured door. Like the door to the recording booth last week, none of the other doors that lined the corridor had any numbers or markings. The walls were painted a flat medium grey without a scratch, bubble, or bump. Even the floor's white synthesized tile lacked distinguishing patterns or wear. When Edward stopped, Coramie thought she heard a faint *blip* right before he held up his wrist and pointed the device toward the door. She figured the bracelet might be a literal key to navigating the studio offices, especially given the lack of directories or even basic floor plan maps pointing to the nearest fire exit.

The room that lay beyond this particular unmarked door was much larger than the one she used for her audition last week. Even the recording booth was bigger. There was equipment stuffed into every possible corner of the room. The floor was barely visible through the tangle of thick cables. Instrument boards were interspersed amongst the acoustic panels like some ridiculous modern art installation. It looked like a self-proclaimed visionary had wanted to make a statement by chopping up an old science-fiction starship and reassembled the chunks in a chessboard pattern. As Coramie examined one of the boards up close, she caught the steady hum of electricity emanating from behind the metal. She peered closer and realized the entire wall was practically vibrating with energy. She was no sound engineer, but she knew enough to recognize that this entire setup was wrong wrong wrong.

Lost in her curiosity, she forgot about Edward completely. Like a petulant child seeking attention, he threw his mass into the unfortunate chair he'd summoned out of the floor. It let out a series of alarming pops, snapping Coramie out of her thoughts. Edward kicked the metal table hard as he shifted his weight, winced, then glared at nothing in particular. Coramie kept her expression neutral.

"That Docent Bot is nothing but a nuisance!" Edward said. "It's why I put the damned thing down there in the first place: so it can't bother *anyone* who just happens to walk by! Talks too damned much if you ask me." As if remembering the main reason for his rant, the director's eyes narrowed as they focused on Coramie. "What were you asking the machine, anyway? Why were you down there?"

"I was just curious about the history of the studio, sir," she said. It was mostly true.

"What, you haven't heard enough from your motormouth mom all these years? Or your aunt?"

"Oh, I've always loved hearing stories from them and everyone who works here; and I'm sure you have some *incredible* stories of your own." Coramie widened her eyes and nodded enthusiastically at Edward as she spoke, the lilt in her voice rising.

It was the oldest trick in the book, really— looking as young, as eager, and as innocent as possible. It hadn't let her down yet, and she hoped an old-timer like Edward wouldn't be immune to its charms.

Judging from the slow, mollified smile that came across his toad-like features, he wasn't.

"I'll listen to anyone talk to me about the studio, sir," Coramie continued, "and I guess that includes the bots. I just kinda sorta guessed a machine named the Docent Bot would have a pretty good comprehensive history of the studio."

The smile dimmed. "That's true," Edward said. "The damn android was a creation of the studio's founder, you know. Knows almost every detail of the studio's history. Care and maintenance of the bot is a 'sacred' duty passed on from one director to the next." Edward paused long enough to snort and roll his eyes. "I don't really care for the thing, though. Let the bots take care of their own, I say."

He leaned forward. Light reflected from the metal table before him cast a pallid, wolfish glow into his face. "Enough of history," he said. "If you do well today, maybe I'll let you pick my brain for a couple of good stories later. Right now... Let's get you into that recording booth."

Coramie tried to keep her pace steady and even as she headed to the safety of confined space. She was trapped, yes— but at least now there was a physical barrier between her and Edward. There was also a good chance that Edward would forget about the whole ordeal once their work got underway. All she had to do was make sure he was happy with her work. Once again, Coramie took a deep breath and reached down into the calm at the center of her mind. Work for a major studio wasn't what she thought it would be, but she wasn't about to let that shake her.

She shook out her arms and hands, cramped from being crossed too tightly around her body, and realized her bag was still slung across her chest. In her haste to get into the recording booth, she had forgotten everything else. If Edward minded— or noticed, for that matter— he didn't say anything.

He was completely engrossed in the task at hand, especially now that they were going to get started. The greedy, oily gleam in his eyes was visible from where she stood behind the glass. Coramie forced herself to smile back and give a thumbs-up.

The screen to her left lit up with a series of silent scenes: a kitten startled by its own tail; amateurs experimenting with pyrotechnics to disastrous, but non-injuring, ends; an old black-and-white reel of slapstick gags from the 20th century. In her periphery, the green recording light flicked on. Coramie lifted her face to direct her voice toward the microphone before laughing out loud at what she was seeing. Harsh light from the instrumentation panels in the booth blotted out Edward's face. Her head felt light. Spots swam through her vision, threatening to turn into a more complete darkness. The floor of the recording booth looked comfortable, so comfortable, even as it whispered threats of consuming her whole. As her limbs lost their ability to support her weight, she gave up and let gravity take hold.

Then, the lights blinked off in the booth. Darkness surrounded her once again. Coramie felt some of her strength return when the recording was over— but, unlike last week, she still felt exhausted and drained. She fumbled for the door and nearly fell out. None of her extremities seemed to work. Even talking was a distant possibility. All she could do was prop herself against the recording booth, looking at Edward with wide, glazed eyes.

"It's okay, babe," Edward said. "Stamina and endurance for these sessions will come with time. This was your first one, after all. Your first *real* one. You should go home and rest up. We still have a lot of work to do, baby."

He didn't move to help Coramie. Tapping a couple of quick commands on his wrist device, Edward heaved himself from the chair and left the room without another word or glance. Coramie watched him leave. The silence lodged in her throat coalesced into stunned, but impotent, indignation. A service bot came into her field of vision. It moved with precise and oddly gentle gestures as it slid its arm under her shoulders and guided her to a waiting taxi. Before the automated transport left the curb, she saw the service bot step back from the car door and smooth an imaginary wrinkle from its dark suit.

Her eyes had trouble focusing— especially against the glare of the reception area's blinding lights— but she could have sworn the bot gave her a tiny, knowing nod.

***

Coramie woke up to the sound of *BINGBONGBINGBONGBINGBONG* ringing insistently through her apartment.

She rolled over, putting her back toward the noise. *Go away*, she thought. *I'm tired, so tired. Just need a little more rest.* Whatever it was, it could probably wait. It needed to wait. At least, until she felt better. The last thing she remembered was limping into the apartment with her landlady's help, then crawling into bed. Edward hadn't given her a second date to come in to the studio, but she was certain he wouldn't personally beat down her door to drag her back into the recording booth. Mostly certain. Maybe. Studios don't hunt down their actors and force them back into work, do they? And especially after such a demanding session last time—

Last time...

Coramie curled up tighter, as if she could physically ward off the thought. The noise finally stopped. She started to relax, just a little, when she heard the door open. Blindly, she grasped for the covers and pulled them up over her head. Her breath came in short, ragged gasps that felt hot against her face in the impromptu fortress.

"Cora?"

The voice was warm and kind, one she had least expected to hear when the door opened. It, and the gentle hand that pulled away the blankets from Coramie's head, belonged to her best friend, Bennie Curasa. In a wash of gratitude, relief, and confusion, Coramie tried to sit up to better greet her friend. Her body, on the other hand, refused to comply. Undeterred, Bennie pulled the other woman to her in an ecstatic, but careful, embrace.

"Oh, thank God, Cora," Bennie said, her voice breaking as she said her friend's name. "I've been worried sick about you ever since you were a no-show for drinks and dinner. To celebrate your very first session as a paid actor? When you didn't answer your phone, I called your landlady and she said you were home, but not feeling well."

She stopped to take a breath. Her pale, anxious face became tighter. "That was two days ago, Cora. Your landlady actually called *me* today and asked me to come check on you because she's pretty worried herself. She's the one who let me in."

Bennie moved to the kitchen to put on the kettle for tea but kept Coramie in her periphery. Try as she might, Coramie was simply too exhausted to pretend at "being okay." Not that she could fool her best friend, even on her best days. She was more than mentally or physically tired. It was as if something or someone had sucked the spark of vitality out of her and left a vaguely Coramie-shaped husk behind. She could tell by the slight frown creasing Bennie's face that the other woman knew, intuition screaming that something was amiss. Coramie just wasn't ready to talk about it yet. Bennie returned a few minutes later with the steaming mugs of tea and set them on the table.

"You're probably starved," Bennie said, trying to keep her voice jovial. "I brought your favorite: Mom's homemade ragu and spiral pasta. That oughta put some color back in your cheeks."

Coramie watched as her friend busied herself with the bags beside the bed. When Bennie opened one of them up, the aroma of tomato and fresh, made-from-scratch pasta filled the apartment. It was enough to make Coramie sit up and gratefully accept the heaping bowl of food handed to her. Several minutes passed in comfortable silence while she ate and drank her fill. Still, she avoided meeting Bennie's gaze, afraid that the truth of what happened at Black Hole Studios was written all over her face. She wasn't sure if she was ready to have someone else know about it— because saying it out loud somehow made it all more real. Terrifyingly real.

Bennie sighed, setting her mug down. She wrapped a light blanket around her friend's shoulders. "I don't know what happened, Cora, but if you don't want to talk about it— if you're not ready to talk about it— I'm not going to force you," she said. "But I'm ready to listen when you do feel like talking. You don't have to suffer in silence. And you don't have to suffer alone."

"Thanks, Bennie," Coramie said, her voice barely audible. "I... I don't really want to think about it. Not right now."

"Sure," Bennie said. "I hear ya. If you really want to take your mind off of things, I also brought your favorite 20th century show, 'Cheers.' Should be just the thing to *cheer* you up, right?"

That got a small chuckle out of Coramie. She sat back against the pillows as her friend cleared away dishes, refilled tea, and set up the vid viewer. The recording started, and she was suddenly held captivated by the words "filmed before a live studio audience" at the beginning of the episode. Instead of paying attention to plot or laughing at the jokes as usual, she could only hear the forced laughter that saturated every scene. After the first episode faded to black, Bennie paused the viewer. The worry on her face was palpable.

"Not much *cheer* to be found, huh?" she said, taking one last shot at humor.

"Guess not," Coramie said. "But you know what's really funny? If you think about it, all of the people laughing in that audience are long gone. We're hearing the laughter of dead people."

Bennie tried to laugh, but it only came out as an awkward cough. "You're right in a way. The silver lining is that these people are immortalized in their laughter. Not such a bad way to be remembered, if you ask me."

"You always were the optimist of our group, Bennie." Coramie smiled at her friend. "I think you just being here has helped *cheer* me up quite a bit."

They laughed together— Bennie, out of relief; Coramie, out of desperation. It was a small thing, but it was all they had. It's all anybody has, really. And it would have to do just like it always does.

Coramie feigned fatigue, claiming that she had a food coma from all the delicious pasta and ragu. She lay awake long after her friend cleaned up the apartment and begrudgingly took her leave. Bennie had done so much for her, and she didn't want to seem ungrateful. But there was too much on her mind, especially now that she seemed to have regained most, if not all, of her faculties. There were still questions that needed answers.

She got out of bed, careful to test her limbs before putting her full weight on them. Clumsy fingers fumbled to work the lighting panel on her wall. After a minute, she was rewarded with the soft glow of simulated candlelight, just bright enough to see her surroundings. Coramie went straight for her bag and pulled out the Docent Bot's datapad. The eagerness in her eyes quickly turned to confusion as she scanned the datapad's contents.

Subject: Wootsen, Carleigh "Cara"

D.O.B: 10/06/[REDACTED]   **D.O.D**: [REDACTED]

<u>Filmography</u>   <u>Personal Background/History</u>
[REDACTED]   [REDACTED]

<u>Agent</u>   <u>Photos</u>
[REDACTED]   Unavailable

<u>Primary Contact</u>
Director Edward Falls, Black Hole Studios

Coramie set the datapad down and reached for her tablet, unwilling to give up the search just yet. The other device was dead. She swore quietly as she ran to plug the device into its charging stand. Minutes went by and there was still no response. When she lifted the tablet back up and flipped it over to check on the battery itself, she discovered burn marks on the casing. Her tablet hadn't just run out of charge; the battery had been completely drained and consumed, including the hardware. She threw herself back into the couch in a fit of frustration. But just for a moment.

There was only one place left to go.

As Coramie left her apartment, it didn't bother her that she was still in the same clothes from two days ago. In fact, she just counted it as one thing fewer to worry about. On the way to Black Hole Studios, she generated a list of reasons for her presence there. Then, it occurred to her that the studio offices might be closed this late in the evening, and shifted her thoughts toward finding a way in.

The latter was, thankfully, a non-issue. She got the sense that the studio offices stayed open all night, especially since the staff was mostly comprised of bots. Lights from the reception area spilled into the street, brightening the entire block. Now, all she had to do was talk her way into getting where she needed to go and obtaining what she wanted to know. There was an inexplicable urgency propelling her forward, like a miniature tyrant cracking its whip at the back of her mind. She kept moving through the reception area, hoping that she looked purposeful rather than crazy. No one moved to stop her, so she continued on until she finally got to the dim room marked "OFFICIAL BLACK HOLE STUDIOS TOUR."

It was empty. The Docent Bot was nowhere to be found, and its kiosk was gone, too. All that was left were the markings where everything once stood. *Edward.* No one else could have done this. No one else would have had the authority to do this. The thought kept her preoccupied as she walked back toward the lights... And directly into a service bot. It made no startled sounds or sudden movements. The bot merely smoothed away an imaginary wrinkle as it turned to face Coramie, its metal face placid. She started to apologize, but the bot spoke first. It bowed slightly to her and kept its voice pitched oddly low. Then it took her hands, a gentle gesture.

"Miss Risu, I am gratified to see you on your feet again." It tightened its grip ever so slightly, then let go of her hands completely and straightened. "I am afraid Director Falls is no longer in the office. He should be returning tomorrow morning around the hour of nine or ten. It tends to fluctuate."

The service bot bowed to her again. "If you have need of assistance, please let me know."

"Where's the Docent Bot?"

There was a pause, and the service bot gave her that long, unreadable look again. "I believe you will find the answers at your fingertips, Miss Risu."

Coramie stared after the service bot in confusion. She blew out a quick breath against her mounting frustration and ran her hands through her hair. Something heavy bumped into her forehead. Bringing her hand to eye level, she saw a device strapped to her wrist. She glanced around toward the service bot, but it did not acknowledge her. It was, instead, gazing at what seemed to be a random corner of the room. Coramie followed its line of sight as casually as she could and noted, first, the giant decorative clock; then, the inactive camera. Flipping her hair over her shoulder, she noted that the other cameras still adhered to their silent duties. The one wayward unit was supposed to be watching the heavily secured door Edward used all the time.

She had been expected, but not by Edward. And the clock was ticking.

Looking unconcerned, Coramie moved toward the security door. She held up the device and tapped on it as she'd seen Edward do so many times before. Several heartbeats thudded past before the door gave a happy chirp in response. The heavy locks slid back with the slow, heavy noise of metal against metal. And, just like that, the door swung open.

There were still no markings or any distinguishing features in the hallway she entered, but that no longer bothered her. Coramie just started walking with all the confidence she could muster and fake. The door closed gently enough behind her. She heard the locks slam into place with a firm sense of finality. That, too, didn't bother her. Holding up her wrist, she took time to examine the device. Its matte band and smooth display offered little. She shrugged mentally and gave it a tap.

Nothing.

She pointed it at the door to her left. Nothing.

The door to her right? Nothing. The same resulted from gesturing at the ceiling, floor, door frames, and baseboards.

On a whim, she decided to point the device at the blank wall stretching between doors and gave it a lazy tap. A large rectangular outline of light seemed to surface through the wall's paint. The wall itself began to fill up with icons and script, as if being drawn with an ancient Etch-a-Sketch toy using light. Coramie stood in silent fascination until it was all done. The entirety of the studio's offices was laid out before her.

Her eyes scanned the various pictograms and descriptions. She finally found something labeled "STORAGE #4627" ten meters from where she stood and figured it was as good a place to start as any. Coramie tapped the icon she'd chosen and nodded to herself. It was a reflexive gesture, a means of physically connecting to what she had already noted mentally. She hadn't expected a response from the map. The display of her device flashed in time with the now-pulsing icon before both settled back into their dormant states. When she set off again, the light map slowly faded back into the wall.

The device gave a soft *blipblipblip* once she arrived at the correct door. She gave the command to open it. A wave of apprehension swept through her too late, as the door was already opening. Her hesitation, at least for the moment, was misplaced. Storage Unit 4627 turned out to be nothing more than a small room stuffed with mechanical miscellany. No monsters, no hidden bogeymen waiting to leap out and catch her in the act of sneaking around. There was no sign of the Docent Bot, however, or anything that might give her answers.

Coramie was about to leave when the device started flashing and beeping. Staring hard into the storage unit, she saw a faint, pulsing light reflected against the back wall. It matched the frequency of her device's flashing. She wove her way into the room, bending and ducking around obstacles. As she got closer, she heard a faint beeping that echoed hers.

The source of the answering beacon— whatever it might be— was buried behind a wall of boxes and foam props. Coramie started heaving things aside, undeterred, until there was enough space for her to reach in. She held her breath as she put her arm through the gap. Of all the things she expected to retrieve, a single, detached android arm was far, far down the list. It had belonged to the Docent Bot; that much was clear. The uniform's material was shredded around the shoulder joint, but still recognizable as it clung to the metal limb.

She forced back a wave of revulsion and grief. Her mind focused on the blinking, beeping device that was still attached to the Docent Bot's arm instead. Coramie unfastened the matte band and laid the arm aside gently. The device quieted, as if knowing it had been found and heard. Unnerved by the sudden silence, she quickly made her way back to the hallway. She examined the two identical devices, considering her next steps.

As the door to Storage Unit 4627 closed, the wall nearby lit up on its own. The layout of the map looked the same, but several icons were blinking this time. Coramie glanced at the devices on her wrist, flashing in time with the light map. Then, both sets of flashing lights stopped at a steady, vibrant green, almost blinding in the dim corridor. With a fluid motion, the map became a glowing arrow pointing down the hallway. She followed the direction without a second thought. Her excitement was greater than any fear she felt, and she had to keep from breaking into a headlong run.

Whenever she reached an intersection of hallways, another arrow would appear on the wall to keep her on the right path. Once she arrived at the next door indicated by the map, her devices sang out a complex series of blips. The door opened on its own, and, this time, Coramie did not hesitate to enter. This room's label on the map had read "SECURITY CHK1," which sounded innocuous enough. One wall was covered from floor to ceiling with monitors. A small console with several buttons and a control stick stood in the room's center.

An electric hum started up as Coramie walked toward the console. The technology in the room looked ancient, at least a century old. Screens flickered on, showing various areas of Black Hole Studios' offices. Before she could press a button, the devices gave an affirming *boo-beep* that cleared the screens of their current states. A recording began playing instead. It was timestamped for two days ago, and far beyond normal hours of operation. There was no sound, which made the whole experience even more unnerving. Coramie recognized the solitary figure standing near a dimly lit office that was roughly the size of a small supply closet. It was the Docent Bot, happily and patiently waiting for anyone to acknowledge its existence and expansive knowledge. The Docent Bot's head turned toward an approaching shape and began gesticulating, at first, excitedly. Then, two more shapes, much larger ones, detached themselves from the shadows to flank the Docent Bot. The excited gestures turned into panicked flailing.

Coramie watched in horror as the Docent Bot was carried away. The first shape waved an arm vaguely toward the Docent Bot's console, then turned to leave. As the shape walked under a light, right before leaving the camera's field of view, its face was revealed. Instinctively, she slapped the red button on the console to pause the recording. Sure enough, the one giving orders was Director Edward Falls. She remembered Edward proclaiming a loud, vehement disdain for the Docent Bot, but didn't think he would act on it. Part of his stewardship of Black Hole Studios was the care and maintenance of the Docent Bot. He would surely lose his prestigious position once the Docent Bot was found to be deactivated and dismembered.

Unless there was no one left to ensure Edward kept his word. Or, Coramie thought, there was something else— something greater— at stake.

The devices flashed green twice and the screens cleared, returning to their dormant state. Everything else in the room powered down. Coramie took that as her cue to move on. An arrow appeared in neon green on the opposite wall as she exited the security room. She tried to remember what the map had indicated for her next destination. As if in response to her unspoken question, a small section of the map lit up above the arrow. The flashing icon had "ARCHIVES AUX" written underneath.

She took off, spurred on by a rush of adrenaline and anticipation. The path to the auxiliary archives took her up to the top floor of the building. When she stepped out of the stairwell, dust came up from the carpet in a thick cloud. It must have been decades since this part of the building saw any foot traffic. Given that the Docent Bot could access the database at any time, it made sense that no one visited often. Archival servers were built to last and could survive nearly anything short of a world-ending event, which meant that maintenance was almost nil.

The auxiliary archives room was much bigger than any room Coramie had seen in the building so far. There were seemingly endless rows of server racks, their wires and cables neatly tied into bundles. Small lights winked here and there in binary bliss. She picked an aisle at random and started walking toward the back of the room. The devices on her wrist barked out a series of angry chirps. Coramie stopped, thinking she was going the wrong way. To her left, a stream of mechanical gibberish chittered back.

A light clicked on, and the servers seemed to awaken in their snug racks. Coramie made her way toward the light and the chittering, more curious than scared now. Set in a wide clearing amongst the racks, three dark panels rose out of the floor like some sort of technological monument— or ritualistic space. She stood in the center, looking up at the panels' smooth, marble-like surfaces. Suddenly, the Docent Bot's device came to life on her wrist with several sequences of whirrs and bleeps. Before she could figure out what the device was doing, the panels became translucent and everything was awash in an unearthly, ethereal glow.

Then, a pleasant voice started to speak.

"Biometrics confirmed," the voice said. "Subject recognized. Welcome, Carleigh Wootsen."

It took a minute for Coramie to recover her voice. "That's not my name. I think there's been a mix-up. I'm *looking* for information on Cara Wootsen. Or Carleigh, if you prefer. Whatever. But I'm not *actually* her."

The translucent panel in front of her popped up a holographic display of two human forms and their various unique DNA and biometric markers. "We have pulled information from three-point-one-eight billion sources and scans from the timeframe between 2100 and our present day," the voice said. "At a 99.8% match, we can definitively confirm that you are, in fact, Carleigh 'Cara' Wootsen."

Coramie watched in silence as the images merged into one without a single thing out of place. The display shifted to a live image of her face, pale and taut. An old, dated snapshot of a smiling young woman materialized next to hers, making her skin crawl. It was like looking in a mirror.

"We should amend," the voice continued, "that you, specifically, are Carleigh 'Cara' Wootsen iteration four-point-three-three-zero. Working alias: Coramie Risu."

Fighting down the urge to vomit, Coramie slowly shook her head. "Do I even want to know what that means?"

Instead of replying, the three panels steadily increased in luminosity and the air between them thrummed with energy. Coramie threw her arms over her head, for all the good it would do her if the machine blew up.

"This batch better be good, or I'll make sure you never work in this field again, damn egghead."

It was a different voice, one that sounded vaguely familiar. Coramie peeked between her arms. She was in a long, painfully sterile corridor. Two feet in front of her was a younger, slightly slimmer Edward Falls, who was currently berating a terrified man dressed in scrubs and a pristine lab coat.

"Yes, sir, Director Falls!" the man in the lab coat said, his words barely audible through his constant bowing. "We made some modifications to the cloning process that should result in a more stable product, sir."

"Good, because the last one nearly blew up this entire building when we started using her. Do you know how much it cost the studio— how much it cost *me*— to repair the damage caused by that thing?! The top floor won't be usable for a month. *A month!* The money we lose there *alone* is more than what you make in a year!"

"Well, sir, if I may, my colleagues did advise you to ramp up sessions in small increments..."

"You don't tell me what to do, egghead!"

Coramie instinctively flinched when Edward raised his voice. The poor scientist was now cowering against the wall, grasping at the last vestiges of his dignity and professionalism.

Edward cleared his throat and straightened his tie. "Which one of this batch would you recommend?"

The scientist looked up apprehensively, as if suspecting a trap. "Ah, the third one from the third series, sir. From what we can tell, that one shows the most potential."

"Good." A viscous smile spread across Edward's face. "Let's give this one to Vaniri Risu. She might be a vain and vicious diva, but this will be a good reminder for her. We can't have her backing out; her funding is too valuable to lose, especially now. Getting her personally invested in the next potential supply might be enough to rope her back in. She'll finally get the daughter she's always wanted, and I know she won't be able to refuse that."

Edward and the scientist began walking away. Before they were out of earshot, Edward said, "And can we *please* give it a name other than 'Cara?' It gets too damn confusing."

"What about 'Cora,' sir? Or 'Coralee,' maybe?"

"Sure, whatever. It's different enough to help keep them all sorted out." Suddenly, Edward stopped and turned, his eyes boring down into the spot where Coramie was standing. "Service bot! Get that self-absorbed actress on the line and tell her we have fresh stock."

The scene faded away, and she was surrounded by the three translucent panels once again. Her knees gave way beneath her, putting her down hard on the cold floor. As much as she didn't want to hear or acknowledge it, she had to say it out loud. Just once.

"I'm a clone."

"To put it simply, yes," the machine's voice replied. "You are part of the fourth 'generation,' if you will, of clones based on the genetic blueprint of Carleigh 'Cara' Wootsen."

"And my entire life has just been one complex and elaborate lie."

"Director Edward Falls preferred the phrase 'carefully crafted simulation.' Most of the major aspects of your life were tailored to achieve specific goals. For example, putting an acclaimed actress like Vaniri Risu into the role of your mother ensured that you would grow up steeped in the world of the dramatic arts." The voice paused, almost thoughtfully. "It also served the purpose of keeping you close and under their direct supervision."

"But why? What's the point of cloning Cara and setting this whole scheme up? For what purpose?" The questions started coming faster as the shock wore off. "Edward talked about a 'supply.' A supply of *what*? And who was Cara? The real, original Cara."

"The answers to those queries are not available here. The main archive database is housed in a subbasement four floors below the building. That is where Director Edward Falls and his predecessors kept their most valuable data."

"Why," Coramie muttered darkly, "does that not surprise me?"

She got back to her feet almost reluctantly. Much of her earlier zeal had dissipated. There was no point in waiting, however; her original question remained unanswered, and she would like to see at least that much through. When she returned to the hallway, she saw deep grooves in the walls, hastily patched and painted over. Parts of the ceiling were still missing in ragged, gasping holes. Forgotten debris lay dormant beneath the dust that coated the carpet. She had missed all of this on her way in, too excited and eager to get to the auxiliary archives. *The last one nearly blew up the entire building.*

Coramie suppressed the urge to think about the myriad hypothetical situations that could have caused the previous clone to cause this much damage.

Following the directions on the walls, down into the sublevels of the building, she felt the air become increasingly still and stagnant. There were no signs of struggle or damage like on the top floor; just a general sense of abandonment and neglect. Here, things were meant to be buried and forgotten.

The fourth subterranean level of Black Hole Studios was a single, cavernous room. Coramie had reached the very bottom of the stairwell and opened the exit, expecting the usual labyrinth of corridors and lights to guide her way. There was no hallway, no unmarked doors. She blinked against the stifling darkness, unable and unwilling to take another step further in. A small *beep* sounded in unison from both devices on her wrist. Slowly, systematically, the lights began to come on. Even with the lights on, she couldn't see the other walls and barely made out the ceiling. Server racks spread out to either side of her in a slight curve like the spokes of a giant wheel. An arrow lit up dimly at her feet, pointing straight ahead.

Her footsteps, muffled by the thick dust, sent up eddying clouds into the dead air. She tried to conjure a sense of bravado, however false, but couldn't. No one was watching; she didn't have an audience to impress. Any of her tricks just seemed cheap and hollow at this point. Despite the vastness of the main archives' room, she started to feel a deep, awful sense of claustrophobia. It made her teeth tingle, and her jaw ached from being clenched so tightly. Then she realized the aisle between the server racks was, in fact, beginning to narrow. She quickened her pace.

Just as she was about to scream out loud, unable to handle the rising cacophony of tension in her head, the aisle emptied into a wide, open circle. Tall panels stood sentinel around the perimeter, much like the ones in the auxiliary archives, but far greater in number. At the very center, a technological chrysalis of wires, circuit boards, and cables sat embedded in the floor. Coramie got as close as she dared, stepping carefully around the tangle of parts, and peered through one of the gaps in the panels.

Inside, almost serene and regal in its luminous captivity, was the head and torso of the Docent Bot.

The Docent Bot's optics lit up immediately, as if sensing Coramie's presence. Its head swiveled toward her, paused thoughtfully, then nodded. Coramie hurried to step back as the panels of the Docent Bot's cage began to unfold like a twisting metal flower. Around them, the panels turned from opaque to transparent with the familiar thrum of long-dormant energy.

"Welcome to the main archive database," the Docent Bot said, its voice coming from different directions. "Please pardon the dust; cleaning crews for the subterranean levels have been decommissioned since 2132."

"Why would Edward put you down here?" Coramie asked.

"The main archive database is the only place Director Falls could have me hidden away from the general public and still be within the bounds of his stewardship agreement."

"I saw the security footage. He didn't have to be so forceful with you."

The Docent Bot tilted its head, considering the alternatives for a moment. "It was a rather unpleasant experience, true. However, as you humans would say, things seemed to have worked themselves out for the best this way."

When Coramie shook her head, clearly not understanding the implications, the Docent Bot continued. "Here, directly interfaced with the database, I can retrieve any information you desire while safely bypassing any firewalls implemented by Director Falls. Which means none of his search parameter triggers will alert him to come running and shut us down, like last time."

"No wonder he was so worked up about finding me that day," Coramie said, nodding slowly. She had passed off Edward's strange behavior as another level of the director's bluster and overstated self-importance. Now, she saw that the machismo was a flimsy shield for something else entirely: he had something to hide.

"As Docent Bot, it is my directive to answer any queries posed to me by a human. Director Falls, however, was alerted once I processed your question; he ran an override program to alter the results I gave you." The Docent Bot's head bobbed in an apologetic gesture. "That is why I had you brought here."

"It wasn't your fault, not by a long shot, but you can tell me now," Coramie said, pausing for breath before speaking again. "Who was the original Carleigh 'Cara' Wootsen?"

The panels projected a semitransparent human figure into the empty space next to Coramie. She stared blankly into a face that was so much like hers, but had subtle, telling differences, if you knew where to look. Its bright, lively eyes and kind smile made the simulation just a little too lifelike, and she instinctively shied away.

"Carleigh 'Cara' Wootsen was an actor who started working for Black Hole Studios in the summer of 2135. She was immediately assigned to the Laugh Track Project under the supervision of Director Edward Falls. None of the vids she worked on would move past the early production phases, as Cara was frequently in poor health. Her work ended in 2140 when she disappeared from the official Black Hole Studios' records after a session in the recording booth."

"She obviously didn't just disappear because they would have needed her to make the clones," Coramie said. "To make *me*. What do the unofficial records say?"

Cara Wootsen's image vanished from Coramie's side. Panels on the other side of the circle hummed, bringing to life another recording from the studios' archives. Edward and a group of men in white lab coats surrounded an operating table. On the table, Cara looked like she was sleeping peacefully— except for the long, clotted gash across her forehead and the blood matting her hair. When Edward finally spoke, he sounded merely annoyed.

"What a damned mess!" Edward said, slamming his hands onto the operating table. Cara's body rocked slightly from side to side. "And it's not like we can cover this up like the others when we were done with them. She had to go and make a scene in the middle of the award ceremony! People will have questions!" He paused for breath and to mop his wide forehead.

One of the white coats cleared his throat and stepped forward. "We know you didn't want to use us yet, sir, but we're ready."

"Hell of a time we live in if this is what forces my hand. How soon can she be ready?"

"Six months at most, sir."

"And you're certain the accelerated growth process will work?"

"Absolutely, sir. You'll be pleased with the results."

"As long as it gets the job done until we can think of something else. Go ahead and take her in; do what you have to do. I'll get working on the cover story."

Edward, Cara's body, and the white coats dissolved into empty space again. The Docent Bot spoke softly into the silence that followed. "Official public record reports Wootsen tripped on her gown and recovered over the course of six months. Director Falls made sure to remind every media outlet that Wootsen had a history of poor health and instability, which made for a foolproof cover story. When 'Cara Wootsen' reemerged from her supposed rehabilitation, no one asked any questions."

"Except it was a clone, and the real Cara Wootsen was dead."

"Correct. The scientists even made sure to add the detail of a thin scar on the clone's forehead to maintain compliance with the cover story."

"What did Cara say during the award ceremony, anyway?"

"Initial media reports gathered from the incident claimed that Wootsen accused Director Falls and Black Hole Studios for ruining her life and 'literally sucking the life' out of her. She also began to list past actors who had started at Black Hole Studios and had short careers due to untimely deaths. That was when Director Falls appeared from the wings and Wootsen mysteriously fell from the stage."

Coramie bit her lip in thought. Having the life sucked out of her seemed like an apt description of what she encountered in the recording booth. She shivered, trying to shake off the feeling. "Something else stood out for me," she said, trying to switch subjects. "It sounded like the cloning project had been in the works for a while. Why would an entertainment studio need clones?"

"In short," the Docent Bot said, "Director Falls knew people were beginning to notice. After three decades, a pattern with actors at Black Hole Studios becomes obvious: the actor starts; the actor's career stagnates; and the actor dies by some method that does not lead back to the studio. Ten were killed in vehicular accidents; another fifteen died in events that were ruled as suicides. The journalist who confronted Director Falls shortly after Cara Wootsen's incident was suddenly transferred to the Australian warfront to cover 'Culture in Wartime.' He was killed by a landmine within a week. To avoid further scrutiny, clones were the next logical step in maintaining the supply."

The blood in Coramie's veins ran cold. *The next potential supply.* That's how Edward had referred to her when discussing her imminent "birth" and Vaniri Risu's involvement in the cloning project. A supply. The Docent Bot watched her unblinkingly, patiently, waiting for the next inquiry.

"What," Coramie said slowly, "were we— these clones, the other actors, me— supposed to be supplying?"

"Laughter."

Director Edward Falls, head of Black Hole Studios, emerged from the semidarkness beyond the panels and stepped into the circle. He flicked his wrist toward the Docent Bot with a sneer on his face. The Docent Bot's optics shorted out with a sharp, audible buzz. Its head lolled to the side at an awkward angle.

"I always said you talked too much, stupid bot," Edward muttered. He turned his attention to Coramie. "And you, you've turned out to be as troublesome as Carleigh. All you had to do was play along and everything would have been just fine."

He started moving toward Coramie, but she wisely kept the Docent Bot's prone form between them. She fidgeted with the devices on her wrist, hoping for something to happen or intervene. Edward just laughed. The awful, ugly sound bounced off distant walls and came back as hollow, haunted facsimiles.

"Those trinkets won't help you now," Edward said, "but allow me to pick up where the bot left off. Didn't I say I'd tell you some stories? Let's start with some history, then. In 2100, right at the start of a new century, a brilliant and intrepid scientist had an idea: what if we could cure mental illness the same way we helped patients with failing organs? Some cancers could be defeated with a bone marrow transplant. Why not cure depression with a happiness transplant?"

A dry, mirthless chuckle rattled out of Edward's throat. "It was a simple process, really: take happy thoughts and memories from donors and download them into the brains of the afflicted. There were some skeptics, as usual. The first clinical trials were quite successful, and everything was fine for the next several years. Then the donors started to deteriorate mentally and physically because they were literally losing their minds. And the skeptics thought that wasn't acceptable! The project was scrapped, but this scientist wasn't one to give up so easily."

Edward tapped a command into his wrist device, activating a panel next to him. The man sketched out in the display was tall and thin with deep-set eyes that made his face look cadaverous. Coramie frowned. There was something familiar about him, but it was faint, near the edges of her conscious thought. With an exaggerated sigh of dismay, Edward tapped another command. The image shimmered, and the features altered themselves ever so slightly. The nose and brow were a little higher, and the cheeks seemed more filled out. She shook her head, eyes widening in recognition and horror. It was the face that looked out from a stately, ornate frame and greeted would-be stars as they entered the offices of Black Hole Studios.

"The government tore everything down, but he was able to store the most crucial data in a tiny chip, which he installed into his 'personal assistant bot.' It's why I have to put up with that stupid machine." Edward glared at the Docent Bot, then cleared his throat. "But, I digress. Right around the time his laboratories closed, something else came up that brought the world to a standstill."

"The Great Creatives Depression," Coramie said, finally finding her voice again.

"Correct! You're not as stupid as you look. Entertainment vids had been declining for the better part of two decades. It was originally touted that enduring mental illness was just the side effect of genius." Edward's face split into a hideous grin highlighted by the glow of the panels. "Turns out that was all bullshit. You can't write or think of new ideas if you can't even get out of bed because you're too depressed. At least, that was the reason an anonymous 'expert' gave to studio executives, eager to save the business.

And, just like that, our scientist had a very receptive market for his product. With a little movie magic, he reinvented himself and setup Black Hole Studios as a front."

"And desperate people lined up to start their careers because they had nowhere else to go," Coramie said. "With no prior history, a bad social climate, and little-known actors showing up by the hundreds, no one would have asked any questions if a few or few dozen people just disappeared."

Words stuck in her throat, clogged by dust and rising disgust. Her vision started to blur and a maddening, red buzz seemed to fill her brain. She shook her head in annoyance. Moisture skipped off her cheek, splashed her hand. Edward laughed again.

"Aww, getting emotional, are we? You actress types never change. Ever since Black Hole Studios lifted New Socalwood out of the Depression, *everyone* has been coming to us for happiness transplants. You'd be surprised to see some of the names on our client list. That sort of money buys power and silence from all the right people, you know. Still, some discretion was needed. The accelerated growth clones worked for a while, but they were unstable. You were the first to grow and develop naturally. Well, close enough to what passes as 'naturally' these days. Using Carleigh as the base for you clones was fitting, so fitting, especially after what she tried to do."

Coramie looked around helplessly while Edward continued his rant that was steadily increasing in pitch. Even if she could find an escape route, then what? No one would believe her if she told someone, especially since Black Hole Studios was now an established cornerstone in New Socalwood. In all likelihood, due to the studio's role in "saving" the entertainment industry, she would just be silenced and forgotten. She reached out to touch the dormant Docent Bot, letting the loose threads of its ruined uniform dangle through her fingers.

A thought suddenly occurred to her. "The day I came in for my audition," Coramie broke in, "there was a huge crowd. What happened to them? Did they become fodder for your laugh factory, too?"

A low cackle gurgled out of Edward's throat. "Oh, that was all for show. And it was all for *you*! We had to keep up the appearance that we were a busy, bustling studio who saw all manners of people, after all. The 'crowd' you saw was just a bunch of sophisticated bots. Expendable, but handy, scrap metal that they are."

Coramie opened her mouth to retort when the devices on her wrist suddenly lit up. Without warning, the Docent Bot sat up again and turned its head toward Edward, spitting out a stream of shrieking, mechanical noises. The awful clamor drowned out the remnants of Edward's furious monologue. She glimpsed brushed metal hands and neat, immaculate sleeves emerging from the gloom between server racks.

Without hesitation, she sprinted toward Edward. The latter was distracted, trying in vain to shut out the Docent Bot's terrible noise. Coramie slammed her shoulder into the studio executive's bulky body. Her momentum sent him straight into the service bot's vicelike grasp, turning his angry string of expletives into a wordless, startled squawk. Coramie caught herself on one of the metal shelves, causing the server blades to shake violently in their compartments. She quickly grabbed Edward's device and yanked it from his wrist.

"Are you in need of assistance, miss?" the service bot asked.

"That's a hell of an understatement," Coramie said. "Thank you for your help. But what should we do with *him*?"

"The federal authorities have been alerted and are already en route to this location, which means," the service bot said with the approximation of an android's glare toward Edward, "none of them are on Director Falls' payroll. We also took the liberty of uploading the entirety of the archives' records to their inboxes."

The young woman's jaw dropped. "Why couldn't you do that before?"

"The restraining runtimes were lifted once you came down here and activated me," the Docent Bot said. "You have quite literally set me free, Coramie Risu."

"Stop calling her that!" Edward said, spraying saliva onto the service bot's neat and otherwise untarnished sleeve. "She's just a clone! She's *nothing* without this studio, without *me*! *All* of you are nothing without me!"

Coramie paused, considering Edward with a suddenly thoughtful look on her face. The faint, distant sound of heavy boots reached them in the archives' inner sanctum. She smiled softly. "Actually, Edward," she said, "it's quite the opposite. You are nothing without me— without Cara, without the bots. Without New Socalwood."

She turned her back on Edward and started to walk away. Before she disappeared altogether amongst the server racks, Coramie held up her wrist and tapped a single command in. The service bot tightened its grip around the director, just enough past the pain threshold to make it hurt. He couldn't breathe, and his vision started to swim, but he remained conscious— barely.

"I'm free to be whomever and whatever I want to be, sweetheart." Coramie's voice floated to him, light-years distant and as ethereal as solar wind. "After all, this is New Socalwood, baby. Anything is possible. And Cara Wootsen can finally rest in peace."

Author's Note

I started work on "Stealing Laughter" near the beginning of 2017. The catalyst for the story was twofold: a conversation about laugh tracks with a coworker, and finally giving a voice to the suppressed emotions tied to my survival from past trauma. Since the primary subject matter was taken from the entertainment industry, it only seemed natural to set the story in a futuristic, cyberpunk entertainment hive. The two main characters were, initially, familiar bare-bone frames for me to build upon as I developed and progressed the story: the aspiring actor and the sleazy, greedy studio executive.

The universe, however, has an uncanny knack for bringing things together in the most inelegant of ways. Right around the time we—this writing group and I— were finalizing drafts for first round edits, news broke out of Hollywood. People were coming forward with stories, allegations, and traumatic nightmare fuel concerning famous men and their despicable acts of violation toward other human beings. Reading accounts from victims and survivors was, at best, gutting and heartbreaking.

Many parallels may have become apparent as "Stealing Laughter" unfolded. They were completely unintentional; I have no right nor authority to write a piece of fiction that would draw upon these people's situations, and especially not at the expense of their trauma.

But, perhaps the universe is pushing me toward something with this coincidence. Science fiction has always been about taking the ordinary or insignificant— like laugh tracks— and making it into a something meaningful: something that makes you think. I had always intended for my piece to make you think but, now, there is an additional layer of context to consider, however unintentional.

Thanks for reading, and I hope you enjoyed the story.

Dead Land

Written by

T. M. Lowe

"They say the gods used to walk among us," I reflected sadly, "but those gods are all dead now." To my right, casting a long shadow over the pockmarked dirt, lurched the crumbling remains of an elevated roadway that once circled what we presumed to be a ruined city. No intact buildings or skyline remained of whatever had once been, but the presence of such dilapidated structures of travel usually indicates a large populace had flourished here long ago. These days, though, it was nothing but Dead Land.

My traveling companion loudly cleared her throat. I glanced in her direction as Jewel narrowed her golden eyes at me, looking thoroughly unconvinced. "I say if they all died, then they weren't truly gods to begin with, now were they?" she challenged.

I turned my head forward again and stared at the back of our expedition caravan, hiding my anger. She didn't understand. How could she? It was my people whom the gods had cherished above all others, not hers.

The collective ancestral memory of our fathers' fathers and mothers' mothers passed down to us by oral tradition. It was said that, in our youth as a people, we were the favored of the gods. We were simple yet loyal. We and the gods had been brought together by a shared desire for kinship and survival. The gods had been advanced, even in their own infancy. They wielded knowledge and tools that we could only dream of, yet they shared their fire with us. And as they grew in their own supremacy, we walked beside them. Not as equals, of course, but we were beloved. They gave us food, shelter, and love. We gave them companionship and helped to protect the gods' land. We were the chosen. The Loyal.

That was why we had inherited the land after the Clouded Death swept through. It was said that the skies lit up as if a hundred thunderstorms all boomed and crackled at once. The gods' great cities were swept away in the storms. Those who did not perish in the initial cataclysm eventually did so in the harsh, dark winter that followed. My people fled deep into the wilderness, away from the lingering sickness and dead air of the gods' land. Many viewed our new lot in life as a curse; punishment for having ultimately failed in our sacred duty to serve the gods and protect what was theirs.

We were alone.

And frightened.

And we missed our gods.

But we remembered them.

Our fathers' fathers and our mothers' mothers carried their memory down to each generation so that we would not forget. As parts of the land slowly recovered, so did we. And we grew. We held the memories of our gods close to our hearts, and our knowledge and abilities began to blossom alongside our bodies into something new. We slowly started to reclaim the gods' land. They had been close to us and we had been loyal; so it was our newfound sacred duty to remember and cherish them as much as it was ours to take what they had left behind to try and build anew for ourselves.

Jewel's people had also spent time with our gods before the Clouded Death – but not for as long as our people had, and not with the kind of loyalty and respect that we did. It was said that the Clever had treated life as a game, something to be toyed with, even back when the gods had walked among us. That reflected now when the Clever hissed and argued with the Loyal about whether the gods had actually been gods.

"Max, stop pouting," she said. "It's not a flattering look on you."

"Let's not have a debate out here," I reasoned, fighting down the growl in my throat. "We're too close to Dead Land."

Jewel spat, but pushed no argument. She knew I was right: we had traveled far enough from the settlement that danger could be lurking around any corner.

Up ahead, I saw Duke signal for our group to slow down. He was our expedition leader and head researcher; a rather large, tough-looking fellow with a gruff, commanding voice that hid his otherwise very gentle nature. We tightened up our formation of wagons and mounts behind him and came to a stop. In front of us, a-small-ways down the broken road we were following, stood a metal sign and two mounted riders. One of them faced the sign, waving an arm in front of it. The other spotted our caravan and began to move in our direction.

"Scouts," said Jewel. "This far out, I'll bet they're in pretty gnarly shape."

She wasn't wrong. I bit back my initial disgust, trying not to be disrespectful. After all, scouts were invaluable for discovering new pieces of Dead Land that had become safe for studying and resettlement. Without them to press forward and monitor the environment, the rest of us would remain too fearful to expand our borders and reclaim the gods' land.

However, such a rugged life surrounded by questionable air, water, and food sources meant that scouts often looked as haggard as the frontier they explored. And the longer they stayed out, the worse it got.

What rode up to us looked more like a creature that had died at least a week ago. Patches of grey hair were missing and his skin flaked in areas. His mount looked equally grisly: it was a buck, like ours, but also plagued with hair and skin sloughing off here and there.

When our people had fled the Clouded Death and sought refuge in the deep wilderness, we were surrounded by small herds of deer. As the land recovered, their population grew rapidly and we eventually tamed them for riding, for pulling wagons and other weight, and for food. The males, in particular, were valued as mounts because if they or their rider were attacked, they could defend with either their antlered heads or the third pair of hooved feet that grew out of their chests.

The scout's buck certainly looked ready to fight if necessary, despite its patchiness. It was larger than most of our own mounts, and the way it fixed its bloodshot eyes on mine made my hair stand on end.

"Woah, there!" Duke barked. "Who approaches?"

The scout brought his buck to a halt and swept his own red-eyed gaze over our group, ignoring the question. I suppressed a growl. It was rude not to answer our leader, but it also wasn't my place to potentially pick a fight.

"Where is Sasha?" the scout asked, his voice as raspy as the night breeze through leafless branches. "Why did she not ride back with your expedition?"

"She told me she didn't want to wait for us to gather and set out," explained Duke. "She let me know about the new land and then seemed in a hurry to ride back out again."

The scout looked off towards the north. He sniffed the wind for a moment, grumbled to himself in that watery voice of his, then turned back to Duke. "Sasha always was one ready for the next adventure. Probably heading to the rendezvous point of our next inspection." His buck shifted weight restlessly underneath him. He chuckled, patting the side of the mount's neck. A swath of hair shed loose and fluttered down in a rather unnerving manner. "But I forget my manners. Too long out here and you start to go feral." The scout laughed, but nobody else seemed warmed by his gallows humor. "I am Oscar. This is Patches." He patted the buck again and more hair fell loose.

I stifled a whimper.

"Name's Duke," our lead researcher offered. He studied the sky for a few seconds before looking back to Oscar. "Reckon it'll be gettin' dark soon and I don't think any of us want to be out here for that. Is there a place we can bed down nearby?"

The scout nodded. "Our safe house isn't far from here. Your group can shelter there. That way, the new land to explore will only be about a half day's ride away for you. Then, you're on your own."

Duke nodded, then whistled for us all to begin following him once more after he set in behind Oscar. As we neared the metal sign, I was able to get a better look at the writing on it. Like with most of the signs we had seen, much of the lettering was faded, peeling, or gone. I could make out a D, L, and S, but that was all that was left of the gods' words. In the rusted space below them, in faded red paint, was the phrase "DEAD LAND". Under, in fresh blue paint, stood "NO MORE". The system of coding warned others, especially scouts, if areas ahead were still Dead Land suffering from bad air and carrying the lingering sickness, or if it had become relatively safe again – hence "Dead Land no more".

The scout who had added the verbiage stashed her spray can into her backpack and rode up to join our procession behind Oscar.

Right before nightfall, we spotted the scouts' safe house at the top of a hill. It was one of the gods' houses, I realized, and wriggled about in my saddle in excitement. The structure was one-story. Brick. Surrounded by nothing but a sea of brown grassland and bent trees. Upon further inspection, as we drew closer, my excitement considerably dimmed. Part of the roof had collapsed inward, which meant the interior was probably highly compromised. A pity.

"You'll be wanting to put the bucks inside with us," Oscar advised our group. "We get herds of twitchers out this way and they'll go after anything they can try and eat."

I could hear Toby, one of our apprentice researchers, hiss in alarm. "Wha-what's a twitcher?" he asked.

I'm not sure if the cracked smile on Oscar's face was meant to be reassuring or mocking, but it set me on edge no less.

"Come dark, you'll see," he answered.

***

I stared into the broken mirror and sighed heavily. The reflective glass was hard to find, so I hadn't seen much of my own face save for what murky shadows peered back from grey water. The lighting wasn't ideal; darkness had come, so the rooms of the god's house were lit by small torches strategically placed to illuminate the walkways, but it was enough to see by.

Bright, brown eyes studied my features. I ran a hand along my jawline, scratched at my chin, and swept back brown and black hair. Turned slightly and side-eyed my long nose in profile. Stuck out my tongue and panted.

Jewel's round face appeared beside my own, golden eyes narrowed. "What... *exactly*... are you doing?"

"Heh," I chuckled, a bit chagrinned at having been caught acting silly. "I, uh... well, look." I pointed to her reflection in the glass.

"What am I looking at?"

"Us," I answered simply. "You." I poked the tip of her pink nose with my finger. She wrinkled her face in annoyance.

"What's so special about us?" she asked, sounding far more incredulous than inquisitive." And this?"

I failed to stop my disappointed whine from leaking out. "How often do we actually get to see ourselves, Jewel? See ourselves like others see us?"

She shrugged. "Almost never. Why does that matter?"

I could feel my exasperation rising. She simply had no curiosity whatsoever about the gods or what came before us. I supposed that was why I was a researcher and she was an expedition guard, responsible only for ensuring our safety and well-being, but I still found it frustrating.

"This should be in a museum," I said, perhaps with a bit more forcefulness than needed. I gestured around us. "This whole place should actually be a museum if half of it wasn't falling apart." I sighed, gazing back into the mirror. Funny how eyes can show such sadness in them. "This mirror is here, mounted on the wall of a god's old house. Why? What was its purpose? Some of the old texts reference them looking at themselves in mirrors, but what did that do? Did the gods simply admire their own form in it or was it a tool? If a tool, how did they use it? There has been one in every house I've researched, so it must be important. It played a role in their everyday affairs. What was that? And could it be something we could re-create, something we could use? Would we be somehow closer to them if we did?"

Jewel frowned. "Maybe it has no deeper purpose or meaning. Maybe they just liked looking at themselves."

I reached out and lightly ran my hand down the unbroken side of the glass, sighing. "Maybe, but would that be so bad?"

"Yes," she answered with a conviction that caught me by surprise. "Because we should not be looking at ourselves anyway. That serves no purpose. We should always be looking at others. That is who and what is important. What is important about you, Max, is inside here—"

Jewel pointed to my chest.

"And inside here—"

She pointed to my head.

"Not what you see in there," she concluded, pointing at our reflections in the mirror. "Those are just silly things that do not last." She twitched her ears then, and we both laughed. "See? Only silly things of little importance."

I smiled down at her. Jewel looked away from the broken mirror and up at me, smiling back and eyes dancing in the torchlight. She opened her mouth to say something when Toby suddenly appeared in the doorway, looking nervous and uncomfortable.

"Oh!" he exclaimed. "I'm sorry, I didn't know you two were in here." Hazel eyes darted back and forth under a mop of orange hair. "Can... can I be in here alone for a few minutes?"

I blinked a few times. That was an odd request. "What for?"

Our apprentice researcher noticeably shifted his weight between his feet. Once. Twice. Again. "Um," he hesitantly started, "well, okay. See, the thing is. Uh. I really gotta piss."

"Indoors?" Jewel asked, arching her brow.

"Well, I can't go *outside*," he whined. "The twitchers'll get me!"

"They're not going to just walk up to the door," I challenged. "We put torches around the perimeter. Remember how Oscar said they stay away from the light? You can go out there if you stick close to the wall."

"Scout Oscar was the one who told me not to go out there," Toby countered. "He said there was a... a tub or... basin... or something that I could go in here."

My anger flared and I snarled. "No! You are not defiling a god's house—"

"The god will hardly care now, being dead and all," Jewel argued.

Toby whimpered, shrinking back from me and shifting his weight again. He looked like he wanted to be anywhere else at the moment.

"Come with me," I sighed, relenting. "I'll guard you while you piss outside."

"But... but Scout Oscar said..."

"I don't care what that mangy, flea-ridden scout said," I barked. "You're not going in here. And that's final."

I brushed past Jewel, grabbed Toby's sleeve, and dragged him behind me out into the hallway. He begged and pleaded the whole way, but I ignored him. Oscar, Duke, and some of our caravan guards were gathered in the front room, talking and laughing under the open sky with a campfire in full swing, burning brightly where once gods had lived. It didn't feel right. Seeing the Clever guards partake was no surprise, but to see Loyal guards acting as if it wasn't disrespectful... and Duke especially - both a Loyal and our lead researcher - he shouldn't have been a party to that. It boiled my blood and I bit back a rising growl.

There was a torch on the wall beside the door. I lifted it out of its nailed-in holder and let go of Toby's sleeve in order to grab the door handle. He took a step back.

"You gotta piss or not, Toby?" I asked heatedly, clenching the torch.

He looked guilty, then stared down at his feet as he shuffled towards me.

"I wouldn't be doing that if I were you," Oscar called out in a sing-song manner.

I snorted, wrenched the door open, and walked outside. Toby meekly followed.

We were greeted by the soft, faint rustling sound of hundreds of exoskeletal legs brushing against each other as they passed by. Beyond the tall torches we had set in the ground like a fence line, it was difficult to see. It was as if the darkness moved and undulated like the rippling of waves in water when a large creature swims along. A small sliver of moonlight glinted off the backs of wings and carapaces.

I had seen twitcher herds before, but this one was massive. A shiver crept up my spine.

Toby squeaked and I quickly turned with a finger to my lips. He nodded and silently padded to the nearest bush. I turned my eyes back to the herd and watched.

At first, we were ignored. Then, one of the creatures broke off from the others and took a few exploratory steps in our direction, antenna twitching wildly. I held my breath and tightened my grip on the small torch. The loner inched closer. A second noticed and separated from the herd, slowly following the first. Then, a third.

I turned and looked at Toby. "You need to hurry. Now!"

Toby whimpered.

When I turned back, there were five of the giant insects heading towards us. The first stopped near the torch line, shrinking back. But its antenna continued flailing around and it ground its mandibles together as if debating whether or not we seemed juicy enough to chance a trip into the light. I threw my torch at its head as hard as I could. The twitcher chittered, turned, and ran away, quickly followed by the others.

"Okay, that was a little too close for comfort," I sighed, looking back over to Toby. "Sorry about that."

He stared past me, eyes wide.

I feared the twitchers had returned until I smelled it. Smoke. My heart sank. I spun back around and, to my horror, realized the torch I'd flung had set the brown, brittle grass on fire. The herd panicked, sending the creatures scattering off in every direction.

"Help!" Toby yowled. "Fire!"

I ran towards the flames, cursing myself for being an idiot. They weren't too high or widespread yet, but they were catching quickly. I began stomping them out. When I reached the last of the section that had spread furthest, I suddenly heard a buzzing sound.

"Max, behind you!" warned Toby.

I turned just in time to catch a face full of twitcher, knocking us both to the ground. Its head dove towards my neck and I wrapped my fingers around the mandibles framing its mouth, pushing back against the beast. It rapidly flapped its shiny wings, trying to intimidate me, and I growled in response. A spurred leg raked across my side, catching in my clothing and making a ripping sound.

The struggle ended when a wooden spear skewered the twitcher's head and twisted until it tore free of the body. The rest of the creature toppled over onto its back, the legs shuddering in spasms as death eventually took it.

Panting as I recovered my breath, I took the hand that was offered and got to my feet. Oscar's craggy face greeted me with a smug grin.

"I tried to tell you," he said, voice dripping with self-satisfaction. "Your people should not be called the Loyal. You should be called the Stubborn. Fits better." He lifted the spear and smiled at the twitcher's head impaled on the end. An antenna jerked. "But I thank you for giving me a new prize."

With that, the scout turned and walked back towards the god's house. He drove the other end of the spear into the ground beside the doorway, leaving the twitcher's head there as if on a pike to warn its brethren of the fate that awaited any more trespassers. I frowned at his back. The Clever were *really* annoying sometimes.

***

We were rid of Oscar the next day, and I made no attempt to hide the smile his departure brought me. It was unfair of me to feel too overtly negative about him, I knew. After all, he had saved my life. And on a larger scale, it was he and his scout crew who were able to alert us to more Dead Land becoming safe for study. But that didn't mean I had to *like* him, necessarily.

Once Oscar led us to the center point of the area they had scouted, he turned his buck around so he could face our group. He spread his arms out to either side, gesturing at the surrounding horizons. "Two days' ride in any direction from here is as far as you should go," he said. "Further than that, and you may find yourself surrounded by dead air. Stay out in it long enough and you will be looking as handsome as Patches and me!"

I could hear Toby's nervous laugh from the back of the caravan.

Duke's mount ambled up beside Oscar's and the two shook hands, then the scout left us. Our lead researcher took a moment to gaze off in each direction, sniffing the wind, and finally landed his eyes on us.

"All right, gang," he addressed, "You already know unscouted land is dangerous. And most of you know that even land declared as safe... well, safe is only a relative term out here. For the uninitiated," Duke went on, pausing to make eye contact with Toby, "that isn't meant to scare you. That's just speakin' plainly to keep you informed and payin' attention."

I glanced over at Toby and saw him put on a determined, serious face. We'd see how long the Clever remained brave, but good of him to at least try. He had a bright mind hidden behind that nervous nature.

Duke smiled, nodded, and continued. "Stay on your toes and aware of your surroundings. Weather can shift quickly, especially being close to Dead Land. And as we saw last night, wildlife is nothin' to joke about."

He locked eyes on mine. I felt my face suddenly burn with embarrassment. I quickly averted my eyes and nodded.

"Don't lose sight of why we're here," he said, moving on. "Investigate everything. Record it in your journals. If something seems unusual, write it down and everything that was happenin' at the time it occurred. Salvage anything that looks useful. The settlement would appreciate any weapons, trinkets, or scraps we can find while we're out here.

"Finally," continued our leader, "if you find any signs of one of the gods' settlements, sketch a map of where it is and sniff out anything in their dwellings that might help us learn more about them and where we came from. I know we haven't found many surviving written records so far, but you never know when we might get lucky."

My heart pounded at the thought of possibly finding a god's written words. Other than the road signs, they were hard to find. Whether that was because most of the tomes had burned away in the Clouded Death, decayed in the lifespans afterward, or had simply been created and used less at the end of the gods' reign was anyone's guess. That we understood them at all was a small miracle, given our own preference for oral tradition. But a few of the older Loyal said that one of the first had learned the written language from a young god, and so he had passed that down to the others. It was wild to think of what the first Loyal must have been like, what he had seen and thought... to have been the last to walk with the gods and the first to start evolving into our new form.

Duke's voice shook me out of my thoughts. He paused and looked at each person in turn. "So," he said, "I'm gonna split us up into three groups. Each one is to ride a half day in the direction I tell you, then ride back to this spot by day's end. If you find a good place to shelter, let me know and we'll establish it as a base for exploration."

Duke pointed to Cooper, one of the guards, and Toby. "You two will run north with me. Rusty and Charlie, you guys take the east." He looked at me. "Max and Jewel, you've got west duty."

"Sounds good," said Jewel.

I nodded.

"All right, then," Duke announced, deep voice raised and commanding. "Let's go see what we can dig up!"

Jewel and I looked at the sky to get our bearings on direction and time, then began our journey west. Much of the land looked as if it had never seen settlements before or, perhaps, so much time had passed since the Clouded Death that all traces of any past life had long since disappeared. Tall swaths of brown grass covered the flat land as far as the eye could see in any direction, broken up by the occasional hill or shriveled tree. Wild deer stared at our bucks, as if confused by seeing them ridden as mounts. When we got close enough, they bounded away and disappeared into the thick vegetation.

The ride remained silent and uneventful for quite some time. I glanced over at Jewel and sighed. "I sure hope the others are having better luck than us."

"Max, do you hate my people?" she asked.

"Wait, what?" I asked, dumbfounded.

"The Clever," Jewel said. "Do you hate us?"

"No," I answered, confused and slightly offended, "and whatever gave you *that* impression?"

"You're very short-tempered with us," she explained, golden eyes looking sad. "You get angry if I express any doubt about your gods. You dragged poor, frightened Toby out into a twitcher herd. And the looks you gave that scout, even after he saved your life…"

Anger rose inside me, but I quelled it as best I could. There was no need to reinforce her accusation. "Jewel, I don't hate your people," I answered calmly. "We actually have a lot in common, not the least of which being that our ancestors both walked with the gods before the Clouded Death." I sighed. "But, yes, I do get angry when others desecrate the dwelling places or memory of the gods. Unfortunately, that sort of behavior seems to overlap with the Clever quite a bit."

From the corner of my eye, I saw her bristle and stiffen in her saddle. Her mount made a nervous whistling sound through his nose and mine jostled his shoulders as he paced along. At the same time, I noticed the sky had begun to turn a peculiar shade of green and the pressure in the air had dropped rapidly. It set my teeth on edge. Perhaps that was affecting Jewel, too, and was why she had suddenly rounded on me with such a heated argument.

"Maybe I was wrong about you," she spat. "You seemed so insightful and kind at first. I really liked you. Thought you were different from the others. But your obsession with your dogma and clutching at some unproven memory of an ancient past long dead... you're just like all the other howlers. This saddens me. You have no idea how much, Max."

"Howlers, huh?" I barked back. "Now who's expressing a hate of certain people? When have I ever called you or anyone else a hisser?"

"You don't have to when the other things you say basically say it for you!"

"Seriously?"

"Yes, seriously," Jewel shouted, her short, striped hair rippling and ruffling as the wind suddenly picked up in steady gusts. "Having an open mind is not a bad thing. Looking at the past with an objective eye is not a crime. Thinking about the current needs of others and how current items and dwellings can help them in the here and now - instead of growing dusty in revered memory because they are just *too* precious to touch - that is not desecration. That is simply caring for the people who *matter* - the ones in front of you right now, not some old, dead gods."

"The gods mattered," I countered, "and they still matter. We wouldn't be where we are today if not for them!"

"And maybe *they* wouldn't be where they are today if not for *them*."

"Stop it!"

"Why?" begged Jewel, a desperate look in her eyes and ears pinned back. "You're a researcher, Max. It's your job to question. Question everything. And, yes, maybe that even means questioning your gods—"

"—They're *your* gods, too," I chided her.

"Maybe at one time," she countered, "but not after they died. Not after they left us in a wounded world. What gods are those? There is nothing more they can do for us and no more we can do for them. It's time to look after each other." Her eyes softened a bit, went from anger to sadness again. "I'm not asking you to abandon your love and memory of the gods, Max. I'm just asking you to have an open mind. I'm asking you to see what's in front of you. Not what's behind you in the past or reflected to you in some god's broken mirror, but the world and people in front of you. Because *that's* what's real now. And you're clever enough to know that, somewhere inside of you, even if you *are* technically a Loyal and not a Clever."

I didn't know what to say to that. And before I could think long enough to formulate a response, the first of the tornados touched down.

"Run!" I shouted to Jewel. "Follow me!"

We kicked our bucks and ran at full speed through the knee-high grass. Tornado storms were the worst: swift to begin without warning, spawning multiple funnels with no real rhyme or reason as to where the next would drop, capable of destroying wide swaths of land, and no way of knowing if the flurry of tornados would end in a few minutes or a few hours.

"Left!" cried Jewel as a second funnel twisted down from the sky in the path we'd been running.

I turned to follow in her direction and looked around desperately for any place that might offer refuge. To our right, a third tornado quickly formed and began consuming the grassland, sucking up a small patch of skeletal trees.

In front of us, a massive, crumpled heap of metal came crashing down, spat out by one of the twisters. Our mounts skidded to a halt, bleating in terror. Off in the distance, the space between land and sky turned black. A dull roar picked up.

"Left again?" I shouted over the wind gusts whipping around us.

"Yes," she hurriedly replied, urging her buck to resume the flight.

I fell in behind her again, stealing glances at the wall of darkness. It had gotten closer. Shiny specks of something indiscernible occasionally flashed in random places along the black horizon. My stomach lurched. That had to be the biggest tornado anyone had ever seen.

Jewel's mount screamed, and so did she. I spun my head around and saw them crumpled on the ground. Only, it *wasn't* ground. It was a square patch of raised concrete hidden in the grass growing around and partially over it.

I stopped my buck and hopped down to help Jewel. As soon as I'd left the saddle, the creature's eyes rolled wildly and it panicked, bleating and rearing back on its hind legs. The reins ripped loose from my hand and he dashed off in the only direction that didn't yet have a tornado raging across it.

"Jewel," I called as I turned back to her, "are you okay?"

"I think so," she replied, brushing herself off. "Just some scrapes, but..."

She looked sadly at her mount. He tried to rise, but both front legs were broken. The third set protruding from his chest attempted to bear his weight, but they were made for self-defense and striking, not for standing. The buck fell back on the concrete slab, crying pitifully.

I felt bad, but there was nothing we could do for him save for quickening his end. When Jewel unsheathed her dagger, I held out my hand. "I'll do it."

"No," she replied. "My mount, my responsibility."

I nodded, then looked around to see if there was any hope for us. The wall of twisting winds had picked up speed and added more unidentifiable flying debris inside its collective mass as it rolled closer. I left Jewel to her duty and began feeling along the edges of the concrete. If my hunch was correct, this spot had once been where a god's house sat. With any luck, they might have had some type of basement or underground dwelling.

On the opposite side from where I'd started stood a metal door, angled between the top of the slab and the ground. However, there was a problem: time and winds had shifted enough dirt around that the bottom of the door was blocked. I dropped to my knees and desperately started digging. A few moments later, Jewel joined me.

The wind gusts started to last longer and longer before they were no longer gusts, but a sustained roar in our ears. All around us, tornados twisted in their macabre dance as the monster on the horizon bore down on us.

"Stand back," I said once I felt we'd moved enough dirt around.

When Jewel backed away, I stood, grasped the door handles, and pulled back. They moved slightly, but were still blocked. I pulled again, harder. The doors opened a little further, but not enough. Jewel came up and motioned for us each to grab a door. I slid over and took the left while she grabbed the right. I nodded, and we both wrenched back.

Both sides of the cellar door finally flung open and we quickly scurried inside.

I almost asked Jewel to pull a torch from her pack, but saw she was already one step ahead of me. She lit the wood and held it up while I turned around and closed the doors. The shift from cacophony to quiet and from chaos to deathly calm was unnerving. Jewel held the torch close, illuminating the small area around us. On the floor near the door laid a metal bar and a set of chains. I slid the bar through the set of interior door handles on the cellar hatch, then secured it as tightly as possible with the chains, hoping it would be enough to stop the doors from being torn off by the passing tornados.

"All right," I said, turning towards Jewel, "let's see where we are, shall we?"

With the torch being our only light source, we stuck close and explored the cellar. It was small, almost cramped. The air was stale. Metal shelves lined the walls, but stood mostly barren save for what looked like tools and farming equipment. Scattered on the floor were empty cans and boxes tossed aside like waste. It was... disappointing. The cellar had been a storage place, and presumably looted at some point, and held no more answers about the gods or their way of life. Had the house remained standing...

I sighed. And then I gasped. Jewel and I hurried back to the front of the cellar. We had been so initially preoccupied with looking around at eye level that we had missed the floor by the entrance. There, lying together in a tangled mess, were bones.

"Are those... what I think they are?" Jewel asked.

"I-I think so," I stuttered, in awe and a bit nervous.

She kept the torch close by as I carefully approached the remains. I didn't dare touch them for fear they might've disintegrated into dust. Very rarely had we seen the bodies of the gods, but down there, out of the worst of the elements, those had survived. The bones all overlapped with each other, but I counted three skulls. They had been huddled together when they died, perhaps seeking mutual comfort in their final hours. My heart broke and a whine eked out of my throat.

Near the remains laid two more items of peculiarity. The first was some type of book and my heart raced at the realization. The second appeared to be a harness or possibly a headband resting upon finger bones. I gently picked up the latter for a closer look, careful not to disturb the dead too much. It was definitely a harness of some sort; the material felt similar to the reins and saddle straps used on mounts. Suspended from it hung a small, round metal tag. It was blank. I carefully turned it over and nearly dropped it, freezing in place as I stared.

Jewel's faced leaned in close, nearly brushing my cheek. "That says your name," she gasped. "Max."

I nodded numbly.

"What... what does this mean?"

"I... I don't know," I sputtered. My head whirled. "It's Loyal tradition for sons to be named after their fathers, so I come from a long line of Max's. Was... did this belong to the very first Max?"

"And what is it?" Jewel asked. "It's like a saddle strap, but isn't. Was it a status symbol or... maybe a branding? A collar?"

I gazed over at the skeletons with an even deeper reverence. "Were they my direct ancestor's gods? He walked with them, served them?" I bowed my head. "My gods."

Both of us were quiet for a long time, processing the revelation. After a while, Jewel prodded me. "What about that book?" she asked.

I opened my eyes and felt myself wriggling in anticipation. Yes, the book. *What more revelations might it contain?* I wondered. Jewel gently picked it up and handed it to me, keeping the torch close enough for me to read by but not so close as to pose a risk of setting the precious artifact on fire.

When I flipped it open to the first page, she nudged me. "Well, I want to know what it says, too!" she said excitedly. "Read it out loud."

"All right," I said. And so I did.

March 22, 2010

Dear Diary,

My name is Rachael Whitley and I think this is the stupidest idea ever. But the school counselor thought writing in a journal would be good for me, so I guess I'll try it. I think it's dumb cuz people don't keep diaries anymore. Or, they kinda do, but it's on their computers or the Internet. We only have the one computer we share here and I don't want my brothers reading this, so maybe it's better trying to keep a written journal. I can hide it away from them.

Are you supposed to give a background about yourself in a journal or just start writing whatever? I dunno. I live on my Daddy's farm and have two older brothers. They're annoying. David picks on me all the time and Paul thinks he knows everything cuz he's the oldest. Dad's just grumpy.

Tomorrow, I will turn 13. I don't care, though. It's my first birthday since Mom died and it feels weird. She and Dad got into a big fight and she said she was leaving. She drove her car into a tree and died. I don't know if it was an accident or if she did it on purpose. I was really mad at Dad for a long time cuz I felt like it was his fault she died, but I dunno. She left all of us. Maybe we weren't good enough for her to want to stay. Sometimes I feel like it's my fault. Sometimes I get mad at my brothers about it. We just all kinda fight with each other all the time now. I wish she was here. I miss Mom.

Yeah, this journal idea is stupid. I don't feel any better at all. This sucks.

March 23, 2010

Dear Diary,

OMG, I found a puppy!!! I was riding my bike down by the creek and I found this garbage bag someone threw away. I picked it up to take it to a trash bin and something inside started crying! There was a little German Shepherd puppy inside. He was so skinny and shaking. Who would do that? Just literally throw some poor, helpless puppy away to die in a garbage bag??? People suck!

The vet gave him fluids and shots and stuff so that he'd be okay. Daddy said I could keep him since it's my birthday. I want to believe maybe Mom's spirit sent him to me for a present. I dunno.

I'm gonna name him Max. I love him so much already. He snuggled with me the whole way home from the vet.

I had to stop and compose myself. Who had almost killed my ancestor? It couldn't have been other gods, could it? Our kind had been beloved by them, so how could that be? Jewel looked at me with sad eyes. I couldn't bear to deal with what she may have been thinking about, so I went back to reading.

April 2, 2010

Dear Diary,

Max is the smartest dog on Earth and my very best friend. He follows me everywhere I go, like a wolf protector or... oh, it's like he's a direwolf!

From that book! Except that I don't have dreams like I'm seeing through his eyes, but maybe that will happen someday.

But he's seriously smart for a puppy. He already knows how to sit and shake his paw in your hand. I'm gonna teach him more tricks. It's so cute and funny how he sorta turns his head to the side when I talk to him, like he's really trying hard to understand what I'm saying.

Oh, I know! I'm gonna read to him at night, like he's a little kid. We'll curl up in my bed and he'll lie next to me looking down at the book and I'll read it to him. Maybe I'll start with that book with the direwolves in it...

I paused and took a deep breath. Was that where it all started? Was... was this Max the first that the elder Loyal spoke of, the one who taught our people how to decipher the few gods' books that had survived?

At some point, I intended to go back through and read the entire journal of Rachael Whitley from start to finish, but admittedly, I wanted to know more about the first Max, so I skimmed the entries for his name. Rachael must have been very busy, for her entries were often scattered and long between dates. The next one about the eldest Max wasn't until a year later.

September 15, 2011

Dear Diary,

They wanted to kill Max! I can't believe it! I almost lost him, my best friend in the whole wide world. And it wasn't even fair why they wanted to do it!

Stacey Goldman and her friends are horrible, ugly people. They're juniors and I just started high school. They decided I'm a nerd and they want to make my life a living hell. They're just jealous because I'm smarter and make better grades than them.

They pick on me all the time, but last week Stacey cornered me after school and pushed me to the ground. She started to kick me, but Max had been waiting for me to ride my bike home. He ran up and bit Stacey. He was defending me! She hit me first and he just wanted to stop her.

But dogs aren't supposed to be out without leashes and they can't bite people, even if the person is in the wrong and deserves it. Stacey's uncle (who is her dad, basically, because her parents aren't around or whatever) threatened to press charges and make us put Max down. It's so unfair!

I guess the only good thing about living in a small town is that the sheriff and my Dad are friends. Dad told him what happened and he said Max would be okay so long as we keep him on a leash and muzzled when not on our property. And that I have to start taking him to obedience classes at the mall. It's still unfair. Max is a good boy and he saved me. He shouldn't have to wear a muzzle. But it's better than them killing him.

"Your ancestor protected his god and the other gods wanted to kill him for that?" Jewel exclaimed.

"Are *you* that surprised?" I snarled. I wasn't mad at Jewel, but I resented that she was apparently right about our gods not being so great as we thought we'd remembered.

"I, well... no, I guess," she sputtered, looking ashamed, "but I do not relish being right in this, Max. Not at all."

I snorted, frowning deeply, and flipped the pages again. On one, I stopped at the same time Jewel put her hand on the page to halt my flipping.

"That picture!" she exclaimed. "That's you, Max! That face is a spitting image!"

She wasn't wrong. The photo of my ancestral Max smiled up at me with an easy grin on his face. The same grin I'd seen in the broken mirror last night. We had the same brown and black hair, almost down to the same markings and whorls. Those same dark brown eyes. One of his ears had a notch in it, though. Mine didn't. The only difference was the way he sat and the way he held himself and his hands. Oh, and the fact that he was completely naked.

To his right, kneeling down next to him with a huge smile, was who had to be Rachael. If you had put Max's head on Rachael's body, he'd have looked a bit more like me... more or less. I cocked my head. Rachael had blonde hair, but it only sat on her head and not her whole face. Blue eyes. Metal on her teeth. She had an arm wrapped around Max's shoulders and her face pressed against his cheek. Around his neck hung a red, white, and blue cord with a medallion.

I looked at the page next to the one the photo was attached.

July 10, 2012

Dear Diary,

Max won first place in the Dallas Dog Show for Local Novice!!!

It all started when I had to take him to obedience classes. He did so well and the instructor said Max was incredibly intelligent – like, even more than German Shepherds naturally are, apparently. She had me start challenging him with more complex instructions and tricks, and Max took to it right away.

He got so good that she suggested we try out for the Lone Star Classic, which is the Dallas dog show. For the professional level, you have to be a member and have breeding paperwork that your dog is purebred and stuff. Max isn't, of course. Well, I mean, he might be purebred, but his only paperwork is the plastic garbage bag he came in, so LOL. But for kids and teenagers not touring on the circuit, they have a Local Novice category that is kind of a free-for-all for the best-trained dogs in the area.

Max and I practiced a lot, but he's a natural. He loves learning and performing for me, and we're just bonded, you know? We make the best team. I almost feel bad for everyone else who tried, haha.

"Now I know where you get your cleverness from," Jewel purred. "It runs in your family."

I rolled my eyes, but admittedly, my chest swelled with some pride for my roots. I flipped through more pages, skimming entries again for my great-great-great-however-many-more-greats-grandfather. Sadly, his name did not come up very often again. There were short mentions here and there, and it was obvious Rachael's love for him remained strong, but other things came into focus in her life that warranted more passages: getting closer to adulthood, the coming and going of friends, her ongoing struggle to cope with her mother's death, good and bad times with various boyfriends, her love-and-hate relationship with her father and brothers, and her continuing education.

Then, the passages turned dark. I knew they eventually had to, given her remains, but I had still not been prepared for it to all unfold.

November 21, 2015

Dear Diary,

Right now, I should be looking through more college pamphlets and thinking about the side dish I want to make for us at Thanksgiving. Instead, I'm looking at my room for what could be the last time and breathing in all the memories it contains.

War is coming. Nuclear war. At first, I just thought my Dad was being his usual paranoid self. He's spent the last several years working down in our cellar, saying that he's making it into a survival bunker and packing it with non-perishables and gear and stuff. But now it's all over the news. Everyone's on edge. Everyone's afraid. I don't understand why this even makes sense – if we're all afraid of war, then can't we all just, I dunno, back down from threats and stuff?

I'm scared. I have a backpack of clothes and personal items ready to grab at all times because Dad says we might only have minutes to get below ground when the news hits. He says we live far enough away from Dallas that we should have time, but only minutes. It's crazy to think about. So many people would just... be gone, instantly vaporized. It makes my stomach upset thinking about it.

Even Max seems to know something's not right. He's been pacing and whimpering for days now. Or maybe he's just picking up on all our nervousness.

November 23, 2015

Dear Diary,

It happened. It actually happened. We're all down here now in the cellar, Dad and my brothers and Max and me. There will be no Thanksgiving this year. There will be no Thanksgiving ever again, I guess.

I remember thinking at first that keeping a journal was dumb. But now, this might be one of the only surviving records of modern life. So much of what people wrote was electronic before the end, and so many pictures were just digital and never printed out. Now, it's all gone. If not vaporized, then dead from the EMP waves. We're back to the Stone Age again.

There's some irony for you, I guess.

--/--/--

Dear Diary,

This will likely be my last entry.

I don't know what date it is. We stopped keeping track when the rations started running low. Dad left to go explore the surface, see how things were and maybe try to find some more food. We have no idea how many days ago that was – there's really no passage of time down here by which to measure. But it's been a while. Too long, feels like.

My brothers, Max, and I shared the last can of food a bit ago. I say a bit instead of a while because a bit feels shorter in length. But it's been long enough that our stomachs are revolting. There's been some talk of trying to go outside, too, but Dad never came back, so...

There are no more rations to stretch. David and Paul have started talking about eating Max out of desperation. They think I can't hear them whispering their morbid conspiracies together over in the far corner, but I can.

I won't let them eat Max. He's my best friend. Maybe that sounds sad or pathetic, but he's been the one faithfully by my side ever since I met him. He's been with me through everything, has listened to me cry and licked my face trying to comfort me. He's protected me from bullies. Honestly, he's been more loyal to me than my remaining family has been. He won't fill their bellies.

After I finish writing this final entry, I will free Max of his collar and name tag, as he will become his own master now and belong to no one anymore. I will hug his shoulders and kiss his cheek one last time. Probably cry into his fur. Then, I will open the cellar door and usher him out, closing it behind him and fighting off my brothers from giving him chase for as long as I can.

I know I should probably try to escape with him. But I don't know what awaits us out there. Whatever fate befell Dad could be worse than starving down here. And what if Dad is fine and does return? And what of my brothers? We should stick together for as long as we can, come what may. But Max is part of the family and I won't see him cannibalized. I may be sending him to his death anyway, but at least he'll have a better chance out there in what's left of this world than he would staying down here as we slowly go mad.

This will be Max's world now. We already proved we aren't worthy of it by destroying it.

I love you, Max. I know you won't understand now, why I'm doing what I'm doing, but maybe you will someday. Know that I loved you with all my heart. Know that you served me faithfully and loyally. Know that, ultimately, we failed you, but maybe you can find a better way in this world. Know that I did not wish to abandon you, but I could not walk beside you anymore. Know that you were a good boy.

You were my good boy.

Be free now.

Tears streamed down my face, wetting my hair – no, *fur;* that was what Rachael had called it. For a long time, I simply processed. I couldn't react, didn't know what to do or think. There were so many things in that journal, so many truths and discoveries that turned our world upside-down. Questions answered, yes, but many beliefs extinguished as well. Jewel's earlier theory had been correct – our gods *had* caused their own downfall. And they weren't all fond of our ancestors. Some were inexplicably cruel and unfair.

But even with those flaws, if more of them had been like Rachael – and surely some had been – then not everything we believed was a lie. The deep-rooted ancestral memories held a pocket of truth. For many, we had been beloved and cherished servants, protectors, companions.

Jewel's hand clasped my shoulder. "What will you tell them?" she asked.

I thought about it for a moment. I could hide the collar and the journal, let us continue on in blissful ignorance. Or I could turn the artifacts in, as I should, and shock our society with some of the dirty truths.

As I pondered, a knock sounded against the outside of the cellar door. Jewel and I both tensed, wondering what new danger was present.

"Max?" Duke's voice called out. "Jewel? You guys down there?"

I smirked. "Guess the storms have passed."

"Sounds like it." She smiled.

"Mind going up and talking to him first?" I asked. "I want to spend a few more minutes down here myself."

After Jewel nodded and walked towards the door, I went over to where the skeletons lay and kneeled down. I wasn't sure which one had been Rachael, but it didn't matter.

"Rachael," I said somberly, "you've been gone for a long time. I guess in some way, I have been, too." I sighed deeply and grasped the old collar in my hand. "I'm sorry this happened to you. I'm sorry that your world failed you, as you said it failed your Max. I'm sorry you didn't get to fill in the rest of those blank pages in your journal."

I paused, a little choked up. "Thank you for giving your Max his freedom. I'd like to think that you'd be happy knowing he did find his own way in this new world and that he had sons, many sons. I wouldn't be here today if not for your merciful act of love. We revere you as gods. While that may not be... entirely true... it's not entirely untrue either. We still owe our today to your past."

I stood up, giving the remains one final look. Then, without reason, I impulsively fastened Max's old collar around my neck and turned to join Jewel and Duke at the entrance, journal in-hand.

Dedicated to all of the pets that have touched my life, but especially the following: Hobo, J.J., and Gray, stray cats who had a rough life and a cheeky sarcasm to their personalities, who became some of the sweetest fur babies you could ever ask for; Jewel, a kitty wise beyond her years who always seemed to question life around her; Lassie, my first dog and the most loyal, ever-vigilant sheepdog you'd ever seen; and to Jager – my Max, my shadow – who is currently fighting the good fight against a mysterious head tumor.

Dark Secrets

Written by

K.N. Nguyen

I

Screams rent the air. Men scrambled blindly for their weapons. Women and children huddled in their homes as the sound of death rang through the night. Their neighbors lay bleeding in the streets with unseeing eyes. Voices cried out for help and reinforcements. Chaos reigned.

High Priest Seti rounded the corner of a crumbling wall, dagger in hand, as Messopotem burned. General Meru's night attack had proven successful thus far. King Nodjmet's army was caught off-guard and unable to mount a proper defense. In the distance, Seti saw the western corner of the city go up in flames. *The western front has fallen. Meru and his men have captured the city.* Casting a grim, final glance about the ruined buildings and crumbling walls, Seti put away his dagger and turned back towards the encampment on the outside of the city to find his horse.

At the city gates, Seti ran into some of Meru's soldiers exiting the inferno. They stood at attention and saluted the young priest as he approached. "Holiness, we've received word from General Meru that Nodjmet's men have surrendered. Victory is ours. Thank Re for the watchful eye of Horus."

"Re's will be done," Seti replied. "He would never forsake us on this quest."

A shout alerted Seti and the soldiers. Looking towards the source of the noise, Seti watched as two soldiers dragged a struggling girl towards him.

By the light of torches, he took in their captive's visage. Hazel eyes darted side to side, watching her captors. Her cinnamon-colored skin accentuated the flecks of green in her eyes. Dressed in a simple cream gown with a gold cord cinching the waist, the young woman fought desperately to free herself from the grasp of her captors. A plain gold circlet encircled her head, partially covered by her onyx hair.

"Holiness!" one of the soldiers called out. "We found her on the steps of the city wall shooting down our men."

A third man came up and dropped a bow and quiver in front of Seti.

"Interesting," Seti said, observing the girl. Placing his hand under her chin, he tilted up her head and looked into her eyes.

The young woman glared back at him. She had the longest eyelashes he'd ever seen. "Let go of me," she hissed.

"Well, Seti, I see that you've finally found something useful," an arrogant voice rang out. General Meru strode out of the burning city, sheathing his sword. The remaining contingent of soldiers followed behind him, carrying anything they could pillage and dragging three tearful women with them. They struggled futilely in their captors' grasp. "I never would've guessed that you'd be able to capture this beauty."

Nodding his head to the general, Seti scowled at the stolen property. "General Meru, I trust that everything has been taken care of and we can return home. I assume that there's nothing else for me to do here."

Men carrying torches rushed about, providing light to their comrades.

"Let's head out," Meru replied. Leering at the young woman in front of Seti, he said hungrily, "The sooner we get home, the sooner we can enjoy our spoils."

Seti and the young woman stared at Meru in disbelief.

The sun started to crest the horizon as Meru went to oversee the loading of treasure onto one of their carts. Seti directed the soldiers holding the woman to lead her to a horse and secure her before heading back into the flaming ruins. The three women captured by Meru's men cried out as they were pushed roughly onto horses by the sneering soldiers who climbed up behind them.

"Men, there is no need to treat them that way," Seti reprimanded.

"The general said that they are our prize since we killed the most men, your Holiness," one of the men said, having the decency to look a little abashed - but he maintained his grip on his woman. Tears poured down her cheeks as she stared at Seti, imploring him to help her. "If we don't keep a tight hand on them, they might escape."

"We wouldn't want that, would we?" another man snickered, pulling his woman closer to him. She struggled to push him away.

"By Re, you will not treat them this way," Seti exclaimed. "As High Priest and cousin to the Pharaoh, I will not allow for this to happen while I am on this conquest. Release them!"

The men grumbled but reluctantly loosened their grips on the women and dismounted.

Satisfied that the three would listen to him, Seti continued his trek into the city to make sure that the soldiers he would be left behind were not needlessly destroying the populace after Messopotem surrendered. Flames danced on the thatched roofs as pillars of smoke billowed towards the heavens. People scrambled around to try and extinguish the fire while others tended to their wounded. Dead bodies littered the streets. Children stood with wide, staring eyes and wept over their lifeless parents.

Seti could not believe the destruction. *I never knew Meru was so ruthless. It makes sense to kill the soldiers, but why the women and children? Sweet Re, this is too much.* The inhabitants ignored this stranger who walked their city, struggling to piece together their lives after the death that just befell them. Such distraction allowed Seti to venture deeper into the heart of the city in the early morning light.

A heartbreaking wail caught Seti's attention and he cautiously made his way towards the cry. Nearing the western corner of the city, he saw a woman with wavy onyx hair and dark skin kneeling over the fallen body of a muscular man. Closer observation revealed that it was, in fact, the body of Nodjmet, the King of Messopotem. The scar across his right cheek helped Seti identify the deceased ruler. *The woman must be Ti'aa, the Queen. She looks familiar.*

Seti stood quietly for several minutes while he tried to figure out why Queen Ti'aa looked so familiar. A small crowd stood around the queen and king, giving her time to mourn over her husband's death. A deep gash split open his chest, exposing several ribs. *Meru's handiwork, I see.*

"Ti'aa *quyaa*," a timid voice broke through her keening. An elderly woman stepped closer to the queen, placing a comforting hand on her shoulder. "Nodjmet *quoyan* is dead, but there is still hope for Enheduanna *pryona.* Her body has not been found. She is still alive." The woman's voice trembled as she spoke.

By the mercy of Ma'at, it's her. Hazel eyes, onyx hair; we must have the princess, Seti realized. Spinning around, Seti hurried back to camp. As he exited the city, he observed the remaining soldiers packing up camp for travel. Scanning the men, Seti saw the princess with a rope tied around her neck and wrists; the other end secured her to a horse.

"Meru!" Seti called out as he approached the horse with the princess attached. "What do you think you're doing?"

Men standing near the two stopped to watch the exchange.

"I'm transporting our spoils back home, your *Holiness*," Meru retorted. He spat Seti's title at him, not bothering to hide his displeasure with the priest's interruption. "His High Holiness, Teti, authorized us to bring home any treasures we want. His vizier, Djet'h, has already spoken with His Holiness, and this is his decision."

"Do you not fear for your soul? The way you treat these women may damn you to Ammit for all of eternity. Is it worth losing your *ba* over menial pleasures? This woman is the princess. Surely, you do not mean to make her one of your toys to pass around amongst the guards." Seti struggled for a few seconds before finishing. "She is more suited to be a prize for our pharaoh."

"She is mine to do with as I wish," Meru hissed. "I killed Nodjmet and stopped her from killing our men. I claim her as mine!"

The soldiers, milling around and observing the exchange, shuffled uncomfortably and pretended to finish packing their horses. Though they made noise, they strained their ears to hear the conversation.

"Re's mercy, Meru!" Seti exclaimed, a bit of steel edging his voice. "My cousin would not sanction you turning a neighboring princess into one of your whores. As confidant to the pharaoh, mouthpiece of the gods, I will not allow for you to do this. This girl is more than just an object for you to use. She will be given to Pharaoh Teti to decide what he would like to do with her." His tone allowed no room for rebuttal.

Meru glared at Seti, but did not challenge the young man. With a disgruntled huff, he made his way to his mount and untied the rope connecting her to the horse before stomping off to direct his forces.

"You probably shouldn't have done that," a somber voice said. Ptolem, another general in the royal army, stepped up to Seti and the unbound princess; Enheduanna rubbed her wrists, now relieved of rope. With his dark hair tied in a high ponytail and his bare chest scar-covered, the man radiated a sense of power. "Meru doesn't like it when others usurp his authority," Ptolem explained. "He especially doesn't like you."

"Why?"

"You have Teti's ear, may Re bless his *ba* for all of *djet*."

"But Meru only answers to Teti, may Horus protect him," Seti replied.

"And yet you pulled rank, Holiness," Ptolem said pointedly. "No disrespect intended. As High Priest *and* cousin to the pharaoh, you actually do outrank Meru. Not only do you have the gods on your side, but both you and the pharaoh are younger than him. It drives him mad that once Rameses passed on and road the boat through *duat*, his young son rose to power; only to be joined a year later by his slightly older cousin."

"But that is the will of the gods," Seti said exasperated, as only men of faith can. "I can't help it if my cousin happens to only be sixteen. Osiris deemed the great Rameses' time to be over, and it has been made so. "

Grabbing the princess, Ptolem positioned her on the horse's back. "Just be careful," he warned. "Meru is not one you want angry at you. Now if you'll excuse me, I must find my brother. He managed to grab some food after the attack." With a final glance at Seti, Ptolem made his way back to the center of the group.

Somewhere in the distance, the call was made to head out. Glancing back at the now vanished form of Ptolem, Seti swung himself onto his mount and wrapped his arm lightly around Enheduanna's stomach and kicked his heels into horseflesh. His stallion took off at a canter, keeping pace with the rest of the group.

The stale air of Atunari felt tolerable thanks to the breeze created by the running horses. Seti watched the line of soldiers on the horizon kick up dirt as they made their way back to Re-Mara, the capital city. Long onyx tresses, buffeted by the wind, whipped his face.

Craning his neck, Seti looked down at Enheduanna. Her hazel eyes squinted against the bright sun, causing her nose to crinkle. He paused a moment as his heart suddenly began beating rapidly. *What is going on?*

"What is going to happen to me?" a soft voice asked. Enheduanna never looked up as she spoke to Seti. "Am I going to become the barrack wench?"

"Well," he began, "I'm not entirely sure. My cousin is a kind person. I don't think that he will leave you to Meru."

"You don't *think* he will? A lot of good that does me," she scoffed. Reaching up, she moved a bit of wavy hair out of her face.

"The Pharaoh would not willingly let someone of your stature become degraded like that," Seti replied, rather forcefully. "With luck, you and your people will be treated with dignity. Maybe as serving girls, or something."

"Ha! Serving girls? Don't make me laugh. Raizan, Yva and A'ana will be forced to endure a fate worse than death by those men. Me? Well, I will be the jewel of the pharaoh's retinue; passed around from officer to officer. I appreciate the effort, but if anything, you may have made matters worse by angering your general."

Seti sat quietly for a while. *Could what she said be true? Teti would do the right thing, wouldn't he? By Re's grace, she won't become a plaything. Not if I can help it.*

***

Teti sat on his throne, drumming his fingers on the armrest as he listened to his vizier and advisors argue over the crop distribution of Atunari. Atunari covered a large expanse of land thanks to the endeavors of General Meru and his forces. Though the majority of the land was inhospitable and barren, all of its populace received sustenance from the small city of Sekh'aat, just north of Re-Mara, the capital.

"More and more people are moving to Re-Mara anyway," a squat, toad-faced man fumed. "The bulk of Sekh'aat's produce should be given to the capital. We are the lifeblood of Atunari!"

"Calm yourself, V'yran," a slender, long-haired man replied.

"Djet'h!" the raging V'yran rounded on the speaker.

Holding up a hand, Djet'h quieted the angry advisor. "V'yran, I agree with your view." A look of smug satisfaction flashed across the short man's visage. "However, I believe that we should receive the full bounty of Sekh'aat and distribute it accordingly to our people."

By the gods, this is boring, Teti thought, changing up the pattern in which he drummed his fingers. *I don't know how Djet'h can stand these whiny peons. He's the only one who's actually worked with the people. His ideas and insights are clearly superior to the others because of it.*

The sudden mention of his name pulled Teti out of his reverie.

"High Holiness Teti," Djet'h repeated. "What do you think of our proposal? Ra'jhmet and V'yran have seconded the idea."

Straightening in his throne, Teti attempted to cover up the fact that he'd been ignoring the discussion for the last hour and a half. "Explain it to me again, Djet'h. I have heard many suggestions this day and my mind has been formulating its own solutions. I may have mixed some of my ideas with yours, so please, repeat your proposal."

"Of course, Great Mouthpiece of the Gods," Djet'h said in his silky voice. "My proposal is to bring all of Sekh'aat's harvest to Re-Mara to be distributed throughout Atunari. The way that we'll be dividing the bounty shall be half staying with us in the capital and the remainder being split evenly between Sekh'aat, Hathim, Ammun-tet and Bas-taryan."

Teti tried to quickly calculate how much food that would be for each city while Djet'h continued.

"However, Khome and Djomar believe that we should split the harvest by giving a third to the capital and then evenly amongst the remaining cities." He looked displeased at the notion of the other's suggestion. "Personally, with the number of people living in Re-Mara on any given day, and the large military presence that we need to feed, I believe that *my* idea is the best answer to our food shortage."

Khome and Djomar tried to hide their displeasure with Djet'h. As vizier to the Great Rameses, he carried a little more weight with the pharaoh than they did.

"But your idea only provides a small portion for the surrounding cities while Khome and Djomar would allot a larger quantity. Surely my people need more food than a measly twelve percent of the overall harvest?"

Djet'h looked taken aback by his lord's statement. His mind raced to come up with a new angle to present to the young pharaoh.

"Usually, High Holiness," Djet'h began, "but in this instance, I believe that our people in the capital need it more. Our army goes through a great deal of food to make sure that they are in optimal physical condition. Just last night, General Meru led a raid on our neighbor, Messopotem, in an effort to further expand your realm. It is all as the gods will, or else your cousin, High Priest Seti, would not accompany them."

"Seti went with them?" Teti asked.

"Why yes, High Holiness," Djet'h said with a slight smile. "He has taken it upon himself to provide divine guidance for our soldiers."

"And you think that he would find this to be the most practical solution?" Teti couldn't help but feel a bit confused as he worked out the proposal. On one hand, he agreed with his two advisors, Khome and Djomar, but on the other hand, if Seti was going with Meru and giving his support, then perhaps Djet'h's way was the more pragmatic of the two.

"Please, High Holiness, this is a big decision. Why don't you think about it and provide us with your response during dinner?" Djet'h faced the young pharaoh with a warm smile on his face. He carried himself with a fatherly air as he spoke with the youth. "This isn't something to be made hastily."

Brow furrowed, Teti weighed his options. "If this is in the best interest of Atunari, then I think we should go with your judgement, Djet'h. As my vizier, I respect the wisdom that comes with your station."

Djet'h smiled wider. "Thank you, High Holiness. May your reign be blessed by Re for all of *djet*." Dropping to his knees, he bowed low, touching his forehead to the ground.

Khome, Djomar, Raj'hmet and V'yran followed suit. "Thank you, High Holiness," they murmured in unison.

As one, the five men of the Royal Council got up and exited the chambers, leaving Teti alone with his thoughts.

Why does this feel wrong?

As soon as the echoing thud of footsteps disappeared, Teti buried his face in his hands.

There's no reason for me to not trust Djet'h, and yet, something feels off. What would Seti or Father do?

At sixteen, Teti was the youngest surviving member of his family. His mother died when he was five and his father died just earlier in the year.

Rameses only had one sibling, Seti's father, who died in a fire shortly after Seti was born, leaving Seti to be raised with Teti. Seti studied for years before he was appointed High Priest by Rameses at the age of nineteen. Teti admired his cousin and viewed him more like an older brother.

Seti doesn't trust V'yran, but V'yran listens to Djet'h. I'll need to speak with Seti when he returns. He'll be able to help me settle this feeling of uneasiness.

The growing sound of hurried footsteps pulled Teti out of his reverie. Lifting his head from his hands, he straightened up and attempted to adopt an air of regal boredom. Within moments, Raj'hmet, youngest in his council, made his way to the pharaoh.

"High Holiness," he exclaimed, "I have just received word that General Meru is returning to the capital. He is expected to reach the gate before the sun reaches the Temple of Hathor."

"Thank you, Raj'hmet. Please send word to have General Meru and Seti see me upon their return. I will be out in the gardens."

"Of course," Raj'hmet replied.

Once Raj'hmet turned to leave, Teti returned his face to his hands.

"High Holiness," Raj'hmet tentatively ventured. Teti's head snapped back up and watched his advisor turn back to face him. Raj'hmet did not look like the typical advisor. His frame was tall and muscular, like his brother, Ptolem. Both wore their hair long, but Raj'hmet kept his in tight braids that he wore in a high ponytail. "I know this may be a little presumptuous, but if I may, I would not trust anything that V'yran suggests. It is rumored that he has quite the gambling debt and is known to frequent the brothels." He paused, waiting for a reaction from the pharaoh. When

Teti did not interject, he continued. "I only agreed with this decision because Djet'h has your best interests at heart, but I fear that there's something wrong with… your acceptance… of the proposal. Not that your judgment is ever wrong," he added hastily.

Raj'hmet then dropped to his knees and bowed once more. "Please forgive me if I have misspoken."

"Stand, Raj'hmet," Teti instructed. "Thank you for your information. If we are speaking frankly, I must agree that there is something that I can't quite place either. However, I will stand by my decision as it appears to be the best one for my people."

"As is to be expected, High Holiness." Raj'hmet turned to leave the chamber once more. "Please just take into consideration what I have told you. V'yran's *ka* glows with a dark cloud. I would hate for you to be absorbed into it. Your *ka* carries too much hope to be muddied by that darkness. May your reign be blessed by Re for all of *djet*."

Teti watched the retreating form of his youngest advisor, confused. Once the sound of Raj'hmet's footsteps faded, Teti slid off of his throne and made his way to the royal gardens. His mind swam with a myriad of questions that he could not begin to dissect.

꒭ ꒭ ꒭

Teti wandered aimlessly around the pool in his gardens. The gentle rippling of water always managed to soothe his nerves.

What did Raj'hmet mean about V'yran? Djet'h wouldn't ally himself with such an asp.

A herald's announcement startled Teti, causing him to spin around. Behind the herald stood both General Meru and Seti. The two bowed to their pharaoh, who quickly dismissed the messenger.

"Stand, stand, Seti. You know you don't have to bow to me," Teti said. "It is good to see you both. General, what news do you have for me?"

"The mission was blessed by the gods from the beginning and so our victory was all but assured. Nodjmet has fallen and we have acquired quite the bounty." He glared sidelong at Seti as he bit out the word "bounty". "However, we will need to go back to secure the city and station our men within the walls. I was hoping to perhaps take V'yran or Djet'h so that they could provide guidance and reassurance to the populace."

"High Holiness," Seti began, "I told Meru as we were returning that I do not believe this is a proper course for Atunari. We already have taken their greatest treasures. I have not received any word from the gods that this is their will."

"We *are* doing the gods' will," Meru exclaimed. "When the Great Rameses, may Re bless his *ba* for all of *djet*, was alive, he received a message from the gods personally showing him that the future of Atunari is through the conquest of our enemies."

The sound of approaching feet preempted the arrival of Ptolem with Enheduanna in tow. "Greetings, High Holiness," he said. Ptolem ducked his head in respect, pushing his companion down as well. "I apologize for my lack of decorum, but I did not want to force our... guest... to the ground." He nodded to Enheduanna for emphasis.

Teti stared at the young woman, in awe of her beauty. "Who is this woman?"

Before Meru could speak, Seti answered. "She is the princess of Messopotem, High Holiness. Upon finding her, we decided that she would make a most suitable wife for you since you have not yet taken one for yourself."

Meru's eyes widened in rage, while Enheduanna's widened in shock. Teti looked at his cousin, unsure if he heard properly. Ptolem watched the situation, a bemused expression on his face.

"Really?" Teti finally managed to say. "Well, I must say that this is quite a pleasant surprise. I think this is a suitable arrangement."

Swallowing his look of contempt, Meru said, "We thought that you would find this most acceptable. I am glad you are pleased. If I may, High Holiness, I must return to the barracks and see to it that my men have finished unpacking their equipment."

"Of course," Teti said, eyes still on his bride.

Spinning on his heels, Meru briskly walked out of the gardens, bumping into Djet'h in his haste.

"High Holiness," Djet'h said, "I see that you have already spoken with Meru. Word amongst the soldiers is that I may be asked to speak with Nodjmet's people. If that is all right with you, of course."

"What do you think, Seti?" Teti asked.

"High Holiness, I do not think it wise that we conquer these people since we have both killed their ruler and taken their heir to be your bride. Let them mourn and maintain their dignity."

"If I may interject," Djet'h replied, "what would the gods say if I were to go to Messopotem and console them in their time of grief?" Teti considered the option. "I can also discuss with them about joining Atunari voluntarily since now we will be allied with them through marriage. What would you say to that?"

"I can speak to the gods about that, but I don't think they would object to you going to speak with them while they cope," Seti conceded.

"I greatly appreciate that, Speaker of the Gods," Djet'h said. "Now, High Holiness, if I may, I will go and speak to the rest of the council so that we can begin planning for your union with this young woman."

"Yes, please do," Teti replied.

"Djet'h, make sure you keep in mind that Opet Festival is six days away. What better way to celebrate the unity of Osiris and Isis than to unite the pharaoh and his bride?" Seti said.

"That sounds like a perfect idea. I will mention it to the rest," Djet'h said, bowing to the pharaoh before leaving.

Teti dismissed Ptolem to find a servant to tend to Enheduanna before heading back to his post. Once it was just the two of them, Teti rubbed his hands together excitedly as he faced his cousin. An uncharacteristic enthusiasm flashed in his eyes.

"Now, Seti," Teti began, "let us talk. First, I must say that I am more than pleased with you bringing me such a lovely woman to be my bride. I hadn't even considered 'marriage'; I mean, by Re it's only been three months since Father was laid to rest and here I am, ruler of all of Atunari and now betrothed." The young pharaoh's face was shining with excitement.

"I am glad you're happy," Seti said. "With your leave, I would like to return to my chambers to consult with the gods about Djet'h's proposal. I believe that will leave you with adequate time to get to know your bride."

"Oh, yes, of course, cousin. But, tell me: what are your thoughts on V'yran?"

"V'yran? Well, I am not one to speak ill of my pharaoh's confidants, but I find him to be much like Kuk; full of darkness and deception."

"Darkness?"

"His *ka* consumes the light that surrounds it, while others have *ka* that enhances." Pausing for a moment, Seti tried to find a good example as he noted the confused look on his cousin's face. "Take Raj'hmet, for example, or even the man who was here with your bride, Ptolem. Both of them, though different in personality and rank, bring a... a quality... to those they meet. I... it's hard to explain. There's just something about them that shines from within. Despite the fact that Ptolem is a soldier and kills, I find him to be filled with Re's light. The same with Raj'hmet. V'yran doesn't shine like they do."

"I... I think I understand," Teti said slowly. "I trust your opinion and thank you for help. I think I will go find my bride now. What is her name again?"

"Enheduanna. Please, Teti, treat her well. And, if possible, could you please find a way to give her... handmaidens a spot with the servants that you will provide her? There were three who were brought with her. I believe their names are Raizan, Yva, and A'ana. They will be able to help our people with incorporating Messopotem customs into our own."

"Oh, of course. Thank you, Seti. I will."

With that, the two separated - Seti heading to his chambers to commune with the pantheon, while Teti made his way to discuss marital preparations with his servants.

II

Seti meditated for three days on whether Djet'h should go to Messopotem as an ambassador of Atunari. At times, he received a vision where Djet'h proved to be an asset to the people of Messopotem; others, he envisioned Djet'h causing their destruction. Sounds of screams meshed together with ones of cheers and adulation at the union of the two kingdoms.

He only left his room briefly to get water from a pitcher in the hallway. On occasion, he would see Enheduanna and her escort of serving girls wandering down the halls. With each encounter, her eyes lost a little more of their hostility and curiosity replaced it. After one meeting, one of the entourage whispered to the princess, smiling coyly as he made his way back to his room.

Finally, on the afternoon of the third day, a coherent vision came to him.

Enheduanna walked in front of a crowd. Dressed in a simple, cream-colored gown, she carried her head high, a look of haughty disdain etched on her visage. A deep, rumbling cheer erupted from the group as she neared Teti. Teti stood on a dais looking intently at the young woman. As she neared the young pharaoh, the cheering got louder.

The vision dissolved into a different point of view.

The people of Messopotem chanted on the day of the union. Ti'aa let out a keening wail and buried her face in her hands. The chanting increased in volume and fervor until it reached a fevered pitch. Shouts rang through the city and Enheduanna's name could be heard several times.

Slowly, the vision faded until the cheers of Enheduanna's marriage with Teti mixed with the chanting from her home. A lone figure walked up to Seti as he sat on the floor of his room. Clad in a white kilt with blue trim, a feeling of serenity washed over him.

"Young one," the figure spoke, "do not send Djet'h to Messopotem."

"Who are you?" Seti asked.

"I am he who has been before all and he who shall be after all. You have served me well, and come to know me."

"By all that is holy. Re?" Seti stared at the figure incredulously.

"You call me Re, but may call me by my true name, Re'nuhktet."

Lines blurred and Seti's vision began to return to the physical realm.

"Re'nuhktet, please, don't leave. I have so many questions." Seti cried as he fought to keep the vision going.

The god's voice became fainter and fainter as he replied. "Trust your heart, young one. Your faithful service will be rewarded in the end."

With a start, Seti jerked out of his trance.

"I need to find Teti," he mumbled as he got up and stumbled out of his chambers, a cold sweat upon his brow.

***

"Enheduanna *pryona*, do you truly believe that he is our way out of here?" A'ana asked softly. "Yva found a way to sneak out and thinks she can make it back home. We can escape this prison."

"No," Enheduanna said, "I watched what happened to one of the serving boys who was caught trying to make a run while they were doing my morning purification rituals. They beat him quite severely. I can't risk Yva undergoing the same fate."

"But, *pryona*," Yva cut in. "What other options do we have?"

Enheduanna thought for a moment. Even without sending word of her whereabouts, it shouldn't take too long before her mother sent a few scouts to try and free them. Messopotem and Re-Mara were fairly close to one another and only a small force was left behind to tie up loose ends. *Mother's probably already sent her top soldiers after us. Any day now...*

"Let's see what we can do on our own. The priest seems like one of the few honorable people here. He's been communing with their gods for three days now. I bet I can get him to lower his guard enough for us to sneak out."

The three agreed. After all, their princess had done a good job playing the modest betrothed. Surely, she could overcome the pharaoh's cousin and earn their freedom.

***

Seti made his way through the hallway towards the pharaoh's chambers. Along the way, he ran into four women lounging by a column. It was Enheduanna and her fellow Messopotemians. The four conversed quickly in their native language. Upon noticing Seti, the princess motioned her fellow kinswomen to accompany her as she glided over to him.

"Tell me, Priest," she said as she stopped in front of him, "why would you do this to me?" She swept her hand up and down to emphasize her point. Her cinnamon skin was anointed with oil and intricate patterns were drawn on her arms with black ink. Her eyes were thinly lined with kohl.

"I... uh... I thought I was saving you from a cruel fate," Seti stammered.

Seeing his discomfort, Enheduanna softened her expression. "Thank you," she muttered. "I really do appreciate what you've done for me and my people. Not many people would take that risk for someone they don't know." Dropping her eyes, she looked demurely at her feet.

"I only did what was right, my queen," Seti replied. "I couldn't let Meru disrespect you or your women by making you his whores."

Enheduanna raised her eyes slightly and smiled. "Are you always this disarming?"

With a chuckle, Seti shook his head. "I really must be going, my queen. Should you need anything, do not hesitate to ask."

"I'll keep that in mind. However, I don't think I'll ever be alone long enough to need your services. Teti makes sure that I have a little entourage wherever I go."

Making her way past him, Enheduanna waved nonchalantly behind her, "Farewell, Priest."

"Farewell, my queen," Seti called back.

The trio of servant women hurried to catch up to their princess. Seti thought he heard a quiet giggle from one of the women as they scurried by.

I hope I made the right decision. This really is the only viable option.

Continuing on, Seti finally arrived at the pharaoh's chambers. Making his way in, Seti bowed in respect to his cousin.

"Get up, Seti," the young pharaoh said. "I trust that you've finished communing with the gods?"

Teti looked anxiously at his cousin.

He wants so much for this marriage to be sanctioned, Seti thought. *I've never seen him so interested in what the gods have to say before.*

"High Holiness," Seti began, "I have indeed spoken to the gods. Their messages varied, but I think I've finally gotten their official word."

Teti scooted forward on his throne as he awaited his cousin's answer.

I can't ruin this for him.

"Well, High Holiness, I think it would be best if Djet'h did not head out to Messopotem. I think his energies would be better served if he worked on the Festival."

Teti looked a little confused at the revelation. "So, you don't think that this is a union sanctioned by the gods? Should I have Meru assume control of Messopotem?"

"Oh, no!" Seti exclaimed. "The union will move forward. I just think it best if one of your other advisors were to accompany Meru on his journey back to Messopotem to speak with your people. Perhaps if you sent Raj'hmet to speak with them. He might even be able to get the queen to agree to incorporate some of our customs into their lives as a token of goodwill in exchange for us adapting some of theirs."

A look of relief crossed the young pharaoh's visage as soon as he heard that his marriage could still move forward. Working to keep his emotions in check, Teti said, "This is most pleasing to hear, Seti. Thank you for your efforts."

"I live to serve," Seti replied.

"Now, I must be off. I'm meeting with Djet'h to discuss the harvest distribution. There was some kind of outburst in the outskirts of Re-Mara while you were in your chambers."

Teti got off his throne and made his way towards the doors. Struck with an idea, Seti grabbed his cousin's shoulder.

"High Holiness, how is your bride enjoying her tours of the city?" Seti asked. "Is she getting a good feel for her new home?"

Teti looked at the priest, puzzled. "I don't really know. I'm not sure if any of the advisors have taken her into Re-Mara."

"Oh, well, perhaps I could take her into the city so that she can get a taste of her people's lives."

"That's a wonderful idea. Would you be able to take her out tomorrow?"

"I think my day is open. I won't have to prepare for the Opet Festival until the afternoon."

"Excellent," Teti said excitedly. "Seti, I want to thank you. You've been so good to me these last few days. I don't know what I would do without you."

"I could never do enough to repay you for what your family has done for me by taking me in after Father made his journey through the Underworld. The least I can do is to make sure that you have someone you can count on."

Teti grabbed his cousin in a tight embrace before heading out to speak with his vizier. His gait carried a distinct spring to it. Seti watched Teti leave, a growing stone of guilt sinking into the pit of his stomach.

I didn't lie to him, did I? Re'nuhktet just said to not have Djet'h go to Messopotem. He didn't say that no one should go as ambassador. Surely this doesn't go against the gods' will.

Somewhere in the back of his mind, a voice nagged him saying that he had indeed gone against the will of the gods. *Re'nuhktet would've told you to send Raj'hmet if he believed that were the right path.*

Things will work out, Seti tried to reassure himself. *I'll make it work.*

Pushing away his feeling of guilt, Seti returned to his chamber to prepare for the Festival.

***

Djet'h made his way through the streets of Re-Mara after his meeting with the pharaoh. Men and women walked through the small, dusty streets while children wove in and out, playing a game of tag. Beggars hobbled through the streets, crying out for coin to settle the gnawing hunger in their bellies. Women carrying babes waited outside of the merchant shops, nursing their infants while beseeching a kind soul to give them enough for one more meal.

How do we manage to have this many poor people in our capital? I'll need to remember to speak with Meru about this. Djet'h continued his trek to the tavern, picking up his pace so that he could make it to his appointment with the general on time.

Outside of the bar stood the general. He scowled at the approaching man, arms folded across his chest.

"Where have you been?" Meru said, a slight edge to his voice. "I have been waiting for days to get back to Messopotem to claim what's mine."

"Let's discuss this inside," Djet'h suggested.

The two entered the tavern and grabbed a table towards the back of the room. A slim woman dressed in sheer silks danced seductively at a table, garnering a raucous cheer from the spectators.

Plopping down at their table, Meru summoned a serving girl to bring a mug of ale for himself and a glass of wine for Djet'h. After they received their drinks, Meru addressed Djet'h again. "You never answered my question. My patience is short, Djet'h. First, that damned priest gives away my prize, and now I have to wait to try and replace it."

"Calm yourself, Meru. I have just come from a meeting with the pharaoh. He's told me that I won't be accompanying you. The gods have told Seti that my presence would not be favorable. You will be traveling with Raj'hmet, at his suggestion."

"Raj'hmet? Are you serious? He's not going to turn a blind eye like you do. Damn that Seti!" Meru fumed. "He's getting much too meddlesome."

"I will admit that he is getting a little bothersome. I assume that I won't be getting my customary cut of the spoils now that young Raj'hmet will be joining you. This is quite distressing. However," Djet'h leaned in conspiratorially, "I hear that he will be taking High Holiness Teti's young bride around the city tomorrow."

"What? He's spending time with her now? This is unbelievable! There must be something I can do to get him back for taking my ultimate treasure from me."

"Meru, quiet. I have an idea."

"Go on," Meru prompted, taking a drink from his mug.

"Perhaps you wait a day or two to go to Messopotem. Send someone in your stead to lead and then you catch up. Send anyone you trust. Let Raj'hmet speak with the people of Messopotem. By the time you get there, you'll be able to wipe them out without much of a struggle. You'll catch them by surprise. With Apophmet's luck, you'll be able to alleviate our food problem."

"Why would I kill anyone?" Meru's eyes narrowed in suspicion. "The Pharaoh wants us to assimilate them into Atunari."

"Though I am quite fond of our young Pharaoh, he does not realize how many people we have to support and how few resources we have to take care of everything. With the harvests being what they were, we can't afford to bring any more people into our fold. We must expand our land and spread out the populace." Meru sat quietly and contemplated Djet'h's words. "Messopotem, from what Seti has said, is a fertile land. We take the land and our food shortage will be taken care of. Then we can move forward and conquer more cities and kingdoms."

"So, I should stay here, watch the priest taunt me with what's rightfully mine, and then massacre an entire kingdom, but keep it hidden from one of the pharaoh's advisors?"

With a sigh, Djet'h said, "You may have to kill Raj'hmet. Tell them there was an uprising while you were speaking with them. That should provide cover. As to Seti and Enheduanna, I don't know what to say about that, but you'll need to get over it. We have business to attend to. Why not see what she's up to? I don't trust her. She's taken everything too well to truly be quiet acceptance."

Meru sat silently for several minutes. "Fine. But you're going to give me half of your usual share for the next three trips."

Djet'h gave Meru a look of disgust before agreeing. Downing his wine quickly, Djet'h rose from the table. "Now, I'll be taking my leave. Try and keep your head about you. I don't need our pharaoh questioning my support of you. He's already wary of V'yran."

Waving the vizier away, Meru replied, "You worry about your duties and I'll worry about mine." He then buried himself in his mug of ale, signaling to Djet'h that their meeting was over.

III

The rosy morning sun greeted Seti on the dawn before the Opet Festival. Stretching languidly in his bed, Seti allowed himself a moment to soak in the warm rays. *We have been blessed with a truly lovely day.* Rolling out of bed, Seti got ready for the upcoming events.

When he exited his chambers after a quick breakfast, Seti saw Enheduanna and Teti waiting for him. Teti greeted his cousin enthusiastically while Enheduanna stood quietly behind him, smiling softly with her eyes.

"Seti! Thank you so much for making time to take my bride around her realm. I would love to accompany you, but I have too much to do today."

"I understand, High Holiness." Turning to Enheduanna, Seti asked, "Are you ready?"

"I am," she replied.

The two made their way out of the palace and into the city. Walking through the streets, the two wandered aimlessly deeper into the heart of the city. Signs of the upcoming Festival could be seen around the capital. Effigies of the sun god filled windowsills and green cloths adorned the doorframes of both residential homes and merchant businesses.

Soon the two found themselves at the local bazaar. Merchants hocked their wares and haggled with customers. Enheduanna strolled through the stands, admiring all of the products. Seti trailed slightly behind, unable to take his eyes off of her.

"Everything looks so wonderful," she exclaimed. Stopping at a dress booth, she began to rifle through the clothes. She pulled out a pale pink dress and held it up to her body.

Seeing that he had a customer, the merchant made his way over to the future queen, a giant grin plastered on his sun-worn face. "Ah, I see that the missus has excellent taste. Come, come! This gown is only three silver."

"Oh, unfortunately, I cannot buy this. I do not have any money," Enheduanna explained.

The smile quickly left the merchant's face, but before he could dismiss them Seti intervened. "Good sir, this here is the pharaoh's betrothed. Let me pay for the dress and have someone bring it to the palace to be placed in her chambers." Fishing into a small leather pouch at his hip, Seti pulled out three silver.

Just as quickly as the smile disappeared, it reappeared on the merchant's face before quickly turning to awe. "Of course, your Holiness." And he set to work, wrapping up the dress to be shipped to the pharaoh's palace. "If I am correct, you're the high priest, are you not?"

"Yes, I am," Seti said.

"I thought so. If you would please, Holiness, tell the pharaoh that the gown comes from Rekhtet's store and let him know that if they need anything else to come to me."

"I will let him know," Seti said.

Finishing up, Rekhtet collected his fee and thanked the two for their business. The two walked away from the bazaar and towards a residential block. The homes in the block were run down and the cries of children could be heard over the yelling of stressed-out parents. A stray dog darted around the corner and down an alleyway.

"Where are we?" Enheduanna asked.

"This is where my mother grew up. Father fell out of favor with his father when he took a lower-class woman as his wife. I would visit here occasionally as I was growing up. I wanted to visit the house before the Festival, if that's all right with you." The two walked up to Seti's home. A fat, tan cat mewed at him as he approached. He reached down and scratched her behind the ears for a moment before leading Enheduanna inside. The cat followed behind them.

"Oh, the cat's followed us," Enheduanna noted.

Pulling out a piece of dried fish from a bowl on the lone table in the room, Seti dropped it for the cat. "This is Bast. She's a stray who had kittens before I left for my, uh, trip to Messopotem. I've been trying to make sure she's well fed so that both she and her babies get enough to eat."

Walking further into his home, Seti sat down on a mat on the floor. Bast walked over and began rubbing herself against him, purring loudly as he scratched her behind the ears once more. Enheduanna wandered around the room, taking in its simple interior.

"How is it that you're so humble even though you're *the* high priest?" Enheduanna asked.

Looking over, Seti replied, "I'm not sure what you mean."

"Well," she began, "even though you are the cousin to your king, ruler of a very large nation, and though you hold a seat of power, you still keep this run-down home in the slums of your capital city. You even feed the stray cats, for An's sake! How are you not more like that general? Now he's a self-entitled bastard if I've ever met one."

"What a mouth my future queen has," Seti mused. Thinking about the issue further, he continued. "But all joking aside, I suppose I know that if it weren't for my uncle Rameses, may Osiris preserve his *ba* for all of *djet*, I would not be in the position I am in today."

Enheduanna tilted her head at the statement.

"You see, after my father died, my uncle took me in and raised me as his own. Apart from him reminding me that Teti was to be pharaoh, he treated me just like a son. He even helped me find my way within the priesthood and encouraged me to seek the ways of the gods. My armband," he said, motioning to the circlet of gold around his left bicep "is a symbol of my commitment. If it weren't for him, I would probably have died on the streets or ended up in one of the gangs."

Seti picked up Bast and placed her on his lap. Her purring intensified as he continued to rub her. A chorus of mewings sounded outside of his window. Looking over, Seti placed Bast down with an indignant meow and got up, leaving his home. When he re-entered, he carried four kittens of various colors in his arms. Dropping them on the floor, Seti returned to his mat and resumed his petting of Bast. Enheduanna made her way to a black kitten, the smallest of the four, and picked her up.

"Are the gangs prominent here?" she asked.

"Sadly, they're more prevalent than Teti knows. While he's managing his council, he doesn't take the time to truly meet his people and see their plight."

Enheduanna looked confused. "I don't understand. I haven't seen any problems."

"You've only been to the high-end districts. If you were to travel to the outer portions of the city, you would notice that the food shortage and lack of jobs have created something of a vacuum that sucks up any hope of security and mild prosperity." Pausing, Enheduanna noticed that he'd become quiet.

Walking over, she placed her hand on his arm. "Why do you care if there's such squalor in Re-Mara? It's not your job to monitor the happiness of its people."

"Enheduanna, if I didn't see to it, it may be overlooked. Raj'hmet is young and full of vision, but because of his age he gets pushed aside." Enheduanna looked sympathetic, but not convinced. "Teti is young. He wants to prove that he is as good as his father. This leaves him short-sighted. With all of the chaos of his council, he has no time to take in any of the land's other issues." Seti ceased petting Bast as he looked deep into Enheduanna's eyes. "It's the least I can do for him. He's my little brother."

Enheduanna got lost in Seti's eyes. Touched by his words, she leaned in and kissed him. As she pulled away, Seti locked eyes with her and pulled her back towards him, pressing his lips against hers once more.

By the time they left Seti's home, the sun hung low in the afternoon sky. Enheduanna held lightly onto Seti's hand, smiling coyly. "Thank you for a wonderful afternoon. And for the kitten," she said, pointing to the little, black kitten that lounged on his floor mat. "I don't know how I can repay you for all you've done. Not many people would've done what you have for me. And for my kinfolk," she added.

Giving her hand a squeeze, he replied, "Of course. I think it best if we head back to the palace. I have much to do in preparation for tomorrow."

Nodding in agreement, the two headed out towards the pharaoh's home. Unnoticed by the two, Meru stood in the shadows, watching their interaction. As they left, he turned and made a hurried retreat back to the palace.

***

Teti was walking with Khome through the hallway when Meru interrupted their conversation. The man was disheveled and huffing slightly, as though he had been running a great distance. Both Teti and Khome stared at the usually composed general as he caught his breath.

"General, what brings you here so urgently?" Teti asked.

"High Holiness," Meru said between puffs. His breathing steadied greatly since his arrival. "I've come to bring you some distressing news. You have been betrayed by someone close to you."

"Betrayed?" Teti cried. "By whom? How?"

Alerted by the sound of the general, Djet'h, V'yran and Djomar made their way over to the trio.

"Though it pains me to say this," Meru continued, "I must inform you that your bride has been unfaithful. I saw her compromise her virtue with none other than our most honorable high priest."

"What?" Teti asked.

Djet'h looked at Meru questioningly while the other two advisors sought to comfort their pharaoh.

"General," Khome addressed Meru. "How can you be sure of what you saw?"

"I was walking through the streets when I saw the high priest court the princess by buying her an expensive gown in the bazaar. I decided to follow them, out of sight, before confronting them because I wasn't sure if I misjudged what I saw."

Djet'h's eyes opened slightly as he took in Meru's words. "What else did you see? Buying his queen a dress is hardly a reason to accuse her of infidelity."

"I watched him take her to an abandoned house and the two of them... shared an intimate moment," Meru finished with a hint a smugness.

At that moment, one of the servants approached the group carrying a package. Bowing to the pharaoh, the older servant raised it. "Great Pharaoh," he said, "I have received a package for the Queen from a local merchant named Rekhtet. He sends his thanks for your business."

"Did you pay him?" Teti asked, hoping that he wouldn't already know the answer.

"Great Pharaoh, he said that High Priest Seti already paid for the package out of his own wages. If I may, very honorable considering that your ceremony is tomorrow."

"Thank you," Teti said. "You may place the parcel in her room." The servant left with another bow. Once the servant was out of earshot, Teti turned to his council, grief etched on his face. "What am I to do?"

"High Holiness," Djet'h said tentatively. "It is my unfortunate duty to inform you that they will need to be punished for their actions. We cannot have a queen who is a harlot and, though he is your cousin, our high priest should not be tasting the pharaoh's nectar."

Teti looked crestfallen; his eyes fell to the ground.

***

Glancing over at Meru, Djet'h glared at the general. *Damn it, Meru,* he thought. *How could you put Teti in this position? Either he acts the part of the ruler and kills his cousin, or he spares his family and breaks a law that has been around for ages.*

***

What do I do? Teti stressed, *I can't kill Seti. He's like my brother.*

Teti stayed lost within himself for several minutes. All stayed silent while he debated on the course of action. The sound of footsteps announced the arrival of Seti and Enheduanna. As the two neared, Seti noticed that all eyes were drawn to him.

Bowing to the pharaoh and motioning to Enheduanna to do the same, Seti addressed his cousin. "Good afternoon, High Holiness. I hope all is well." Noting that Teti would not meet his eyes, Seti asked, "Is there something wrong?"

Teti opened his mouth to reply when Djet'h cut in. "It appears, Seti, that we have uncovered your scandal."

Seti's eyes darted from Teti to Djet'h to Meru. "I don't understand," he said.

"You were seen-" Meru began.

"You were seen in a compromising situation with the pharaoh's bride," Djet'h finished. He shot another glare towards Meru. "As such, it is the law of Atunari that the two of you are to be executed." Seti and Enheduanna stared at Djet'h in shock. "What is your decision, High Holiness?" Djet'h asked, addressing Teti.

Everyone turned to face the young pharaoh. Djomar and Khome's eyes held a small glimmer of hope while Meru's shone with bloodlust. Teti could not bring himself to meet Seti's gaze. After a long stretch of silence, he said, "I, it appears, our law must be followed. I'm sorry, Seti, but both you and Enheduanna will be put to death tomorrow morning."

Seti gaped at Teti.

"My King," Enheduanna broke in, "please, spare Seti. If it wasn't for me trying to seduce him, he never would've been placed in this compromising situation." Seti turned to her in shock. Looking sorrowfully at him, she continued. "I had a meeting arranged with one of my countrymen and needed to get out of the palace in order to speak with them. In order to try and make that meeting, I needed to distract Seti and slip away. I wasn't able to sneak away."

Meru's eyes looked murderous as Teti looked pleased by the news. Addressing Djet'h, Teti asked, "What does our law say about this, Djet'h?"

"Well, it is unprecedented," Djet'h said slowly. "I guess this would be at your discretion then."

"I see. Then I will make my decision later. Now, all of you, go about your days and do not discuss this with anyone."

"Yes, High Holiness," they all said with a bow. Seti made his way back to his chambers, head hanging. Djet'h grabbed Enheduanna by the arm and led her back to her room. The rest dispersed to go about their regular activities.

As everyone departed, Teti turned and headed back to his room. His mind swam with the consequences that could result from his decision.

***

The sun had set long ago. Seti sat in his room, meditating, waiting to hear Teti's decision. His mind raced as he attempted to guess what was about to happen next.

"How could I betray Teti like that? I should've controlled myself."

A loud knock on the door interrupted his musings.

"Come in," Seti said.

The door opened and Teti walked in. Seti moved to bow, but Teti waved his hand, motioning for him to sit back down. "Seti, how could you? You've put me in a position that I don't want to be in."

"Teti, I am so sorry. I didn't mean for anything to happen."

"What am I supposed to do now?"

"I will accept whatever judgement you pass down," Seti said. "I know that Ma'at will lead you to the proper decision."

"And you will not hold anything against me?"

"No."

"Then I will pass down my judgement." Seti dropped his head as he waited for the verdict. "I cannot kill my own flesh and blood. I will spare your life and Enheduanna will be executed in the morning."

Seti looked up, shock on his face. "Teti, thank you. I cannot repay your kindness."

Without a word, Teti got up and walked out of the room.

IV

Morning arrived.

Seti did not get a wink of sleep that night. He could not accept the fact that Enheduanna would die. During the night, A'ana entered his room with a message from the princess apologizing for all of the trouble he found himself in. A'ana also hinted that Enheduanna truly regretted their situation and that she wished circumstances could be different.

Before he knew it, he stood next to the pharaoh and his advisors on the palace steps. The populace of Re-Mara lined the street leading up to the steps.

Djet'h raised his hands to quiet the crowd. "Citizens of Re-Mara, today I bring you sad news. Where before we were to celebrate the marriage of our great pharaoh, instead, we are to witness the execution of a temptress who blinded our holy ruler in order to achieve her nefarious gains."

The crowd cheered in approval.

"Bring out the condemned," Djet'h instructed.

Enheduanna walked in front of a crowd. Dressed in a simple, cream-colored gown she carried her head high, a look of haughty disdain etched on her visage. A deep, rumbling cheer erupted from the group as she neared Teti. Teti stood on a dais looking intently at the young woman. His eyes were filled with regret as he watched her draw near. As she got closer to the young pharaoh, the cheering got louder. Voices cried out for the death of the harlot and the destruction of her kingdom.

Teti looked over at Seti and saw the other man's eyes filled with sadness. His cousin's eyes locked onto the eyes of the princess and hers onto his. Over the din of the crowd, Teti barely heard her speak.

"Maybe we'll find happiness in the next life," a wan smile on her lips.

"I'll be waiting," came Seti's mumbled reply.

A soldier came up to the princess, sword in hand. Drawing his arms back, he prepared to strike.

"Hold!" Teti cried.

However, he was too late. The soldier's blade rammed into her stomach as Teti ordered the execution to be halted and he yanked his arm up, drawing the sword to her sternum. Enheduanna's eyes widened in pain as blood blossomed on her gown. Gasping in pain, Enheduanna's legs gave way from beneath her and she collapsed onto the ground.

Seti and Teti made their way down quickly to her body as the crowd roared.

"Call for the healer!" Teti cried.

Seti ran over to the princess' limp form and scooped her into his arms. He then bolted into the palace, where the healers worked. Teti followed behind.

The two ran down several halls until the healers met up with them.

"Quick! She needs treatment," Teti said to the healers.

Reaching out to Seti, the healers tried to grab Enheduanna's body from him. However, Seti made no attempt to hand her over. Head dropping, he turned and started to walk out of the palace. Enheduanna's lifeless form in his arms.

"Oh, Seti, cousin. I'm so sorry." Teti said.

Seti ignored his cousin's comment and continued walking. One of the healers stopped him and spoke softly to him. Reluctantly, he handed over her body to the healers to be taken for embalming before continuing out of the palace.

***

Wandering the streets while people celebrated the Opet Festival, Seti was lost within himself. Sights and sounds blurred together, lost to him. He arrived at his father's home, surprised at where his feet carried him. Entering, Seti saw Bast and her kittens. The little black one gave a mew in greeting.

"I'm sorry, she's gone," he told the kitten.

Dropping down onto his floor mat, Seti closed his eyes and cried. After several minutes, he looked up and called out to the gods.

"Why did you lie to me? I told Teti not to send Djet'h, just like you told me. Why did you lie?"

I did not lie, a voice said in his head.

"Then tell me where I did not follow the vision," Seti demanded.

A red-eyed man appeared within Seti's home. *"I did not lie,"* he repeated. *"However, I can help you find what you seek."* His eyes sparkled as he spoke.

"What? I will do anything."

"If you'd like to see her again, follow her into the afterlife and I will reunite you. I promise."

Seti paused. After thinking about it for several seconds, he nodded and got up. Walking towards his kitchen area, Seti picked up a knife and made his way back to his mat. Rubbing his hand on his golden armband, Seti murmured a prayer. He then scratched Bast and her kittens, one by one, behind the ears.

Finally, he kneeled on his mat, knife pressed against his chest. With great effort, he pushed the blade into his chest. His eyes widened in pain and his breath caught in his throat. Gasping for air, Seti heard an evil voice laughing.

The red-eyed man walked next to Seti and placed his hand on the man's back. *"Thank you, son of Re'nuhktet, for removing yourself from my way."* He then walked away, laughing. Through the windows, Seti noticed that the revelry had died down and screams could be heard in the distance.

Or was it that all sound was becoming muffled? Seti couldn't decide.

Suddenly, as Seti continued to struggle for breath, blood filling his mouth, Re'nuhktet appeared. *"Young one, Apophmet's vile tricks will not be ignored."*

Seti tried to look up at the god, but his vision was starting to fade as well. Dropping to the ground, he struggled to maintain consciousness.

"Young one, your death will not be in vain. As one who has served me faithfully, I will ensure that you find your love. However, before my work is done, I ask that you have patience as it may take several lifetimes to reconnect the two of you."

"Wh-what?" Seti managed to croak out.

"General Meru has worked a deal with Apophmet to sow chaos on his behalf. Unfortunately, Apophmet has won a small victory. With you out of the way, Meru and Djet'h can continue their conquest. Fear not, young one. Now, you may sleep until you awaken again. With luck, you will find your love sooner rather than later. I am sorry it had to end this way."

A solitary tear trickled down Seti's cheek as he absorbed what was being said to him. In his head, Apophmet's laughter could be heard again. With a final shuddering breath, Seti closed his eyes and went still.

***

Teti paced his chambers as he waited for news from Khome. Riots had broken out in the streets of Re-Mara at the news that the food supply would be lessened this year. Despite the execution earlier in the morning, the populace continued on the bloodlust into the afternoon. Gangs of the city's youth ransacked the merchant shops, stealing food and clothing to feed their people. Word had been sent to Raj'hmet to bring home the military force that held Messopotem to help quell the riots in Re-Mara.

Quick footsteps announced Khome's arrival. Bowing hastily, Khome said breathlessly, "High Holiness, we have something distressing to tell you." Behind Khome, four servants carried a litter bearing Seti's body.

Teti froze in shock. Tears began to stream from his eyes as he rushed to the litter. Khome motioned for the men to place the litter on the ground as Teti threw himself onto his cousin's body. The young man began to weep.

Khome and the servants stood silently as Teti grieved for his cousin's death.

Minutes passed before Teti straightened up. "Find Raj'hmet and bring him to me," he ordered. "I fear that I have been tricked. There's no way that this chaos is from just food shortages. Once Raj'hmet arrives, bring him and his brother to me so that we can discuss how to move forward. I will need the advice of a new high priest if I am to do the will of the gods."

Collector 09

Written by

C. Red

C. One

I tug once more on my supply cart, finally freeing it from the earth's grasp. At only eighty-nine pounds, my size often prevents me from being able to have a substantial haul like the other Collectors. My weight isn't my only disadvantage. Without my boots, I stand just shy of fifty-seven inches. I also find it difficult to see more than a few arm's lengths in front of me. I am uncertain whether this particular weakness is punishable by being banished to these wastelands instead of just scavenging them.

I am twenty-two years into gradual deterioration. Once a member of the Shanty District surpasses forty-nine years, they are to report to the burial site where you dig your final resting plot before execution. When I was a child, the deterioration ceremony was common. I haven't seen one in well over seven hundred days. The majority of our residents will not live past adolescence, and their body is taken to the wasteland to be disposed of. Illness is another common contribution. The Shanty District sees medical aid as a weakness.

Perhaps our customs are strange, but I would not choose to take my chances in the wasteland or inhabiting any of the other communities. Cannibalism, forced violation against women, and plunder do not exist in Shanty District like they do in other districts. These are all offenses punishable by death here. You are not held at a district against your wishes. At any time you are free to roam the wasteland, but I'd welcome execution before I'd venture that lifestyle. People not associated with a district are referred to as the dissolute ones, and are just as dangerous as some of the creatures found after dark.

We have strict rules that ensure everyone contributes so that our district will flourish. We are also lucky because we are able to choose our path. Males are allotted three jobs.

Collector. Also known as a scavenger. The Collector is the lowest ranking job in Shanty District despite sustaining the district with supplies.

Machinist. Or engineer. They also swap duty of running the supply shanty where you can trade your points for items such as rations and water.

Enforcer. It is the Enforcer's job to protect the Collector when scavenging. They are the highest ranking in the district, only second to Elder Ahlsom.

The jobs for females are the same with the addition of the Provisional. Otherwise known as a breeder. All the Provisionals are housed together except for Provisional 03. She belongs to Elder Ahlsom. Under no circumstances is she allowed to be touched by any of the other men. The other Provisionals birth, then raise the children as a collective until the child reaches five. For the next ten years of the child's life, it is harsh labor. At fifteen, considering you're still alive, the child is given the choice of their job and their number.

"Identification," the commanding voice repeats.

My left arm is extended briefly. The ink marking below the crook of my elbow reads SD-2026-09. Before we may enter the district, proof of residence must be established. SD for Shanty District. The next series of numbers mark your year of birth. The last series of numbers you get when you choose your job. Here in Shanty District, we do not have names. I am known only as Collector 09. Or 09. When Shanty District was first established, the number had significance to your rank. Now, once someone has their deterioration ceremony or succumbs to the wasteland their number will become available again.

Getting my supply cart inside the gate always proves challenging. I am constantly worried that I will not be allowed to continue as a Collector if I am perceived as weak. The only other job for me would be Provisional and I would take my life before I allowed that to happen. My thin arms shake and strain. I can feel eyes start to gather at my back. Please, don't let me become a spectacle. The cart loosens so abruptly that I fall to the dry earth, causing it to stir beneath me. It doesn't make sense until I see Enforcer 01 come through the gate.

The entire district is disrupted by the presence of the brute and some even retreat to their shanties.

Enforcer 01 leads by fear. Several times he has returned without Collectors. I'm certain it's because he murders them when they displease him. I have long awaited for 01 to have his deterioration ceremony. I've never seen his number, but he must be close in age. His hair and short beard are graying. That's usually a sign they have completed deterioration.

Still, I am bemused why he would help free my cart. He's made his disgust clear for the weaker members by leaving them to die in the wasteland. Perhaps it's because I do not shy my eyes from him like he expects the women here to. In fact, I find him a bit eccentric.

01 lived in this world before the coronal mass ejection and solar flares rendered all the amenities of daily life useless. Most people perished from

the harsh rays of the sun until the protective layer could rebuild several years later. Rumor has it that Elder Ahlsom and 01 lived together with a few others in a silo until it was safe to inhabit the earth.

I am not of their world. I was born into this one.

I follow behind 01 as his boots leave sizable impressions in the dirt. My eyes trail up his dark washed jeans to his broad back and shoulders. He is twenty inches taller than I am. I often wonder if it's traditional for men from the old world to have such a dominating stature. Another thing that is singular to 01 is the ink picture markings on his arms, hands, and neck. I assume they are also on his chest and back, but he is never seen without a shirt.

Finally. The supply shanty. The Enforcer always gets first pick once we arrive. Today, it's only 01 we have to wait on. Enforcer 04, the only female Enforcer, and Enforcer 02, my Enforcer, were told to stay behind to discuss things with the Elder. Being without my Enforcer makes me nervous so I am thankful the day is done.

I set my findings on the counter so they are able to determine my points. I've done this enough to know I will be able to have my pick of a few things this evening. "Deluxe repair kit and two rations."

"Inadequate points."

"The chemicals alone will be sufficient for two rations. Give me my things."

"The woman has an opinion, does she?" His hand lurches violently across the bartering counter.

I squeeze my eyes tight, preparing myself for an attack that doesn't come. As they slowly open, to my surprise, Enforcer 01 has stopped the assault.

He has the Machinist by the throat and hand. "Deluxe repair kit and two rations. Now." When 01 speaks, it is felt within every corner of this district and halts the tasks of the other members to see the commotion.

When the Machinist is let go, he nods fearfully and retrieves my supplies.

I notice the Machinist has soiled his pants.

As my rations are put on the counter, a remark slithers from his mouth followed by a bellowed laugh shared with some of the others.

Enforcer 01 puts a bullet through the Machinist's gaping mouth.

I use my shirt to rid the blood from my repair kit, keeping my eyes from Enforcer 01 until his boots leave my peripherals. Maybe the Machinist was cruel, but it shouldn't have cost him his life. Even worse, nothing will be done about 01's egregious actions that ended another life. While I have survived a run-in with 01 today, that doesn't mean in the future I will be as fortunate. There is no telling when he will take another life at his own leisure. Madman!

"09?" Enforcer 02 rests his hand on my shoulder.

It is absolutely forbidden to love another member in Shanty District. That is not our purpose in this life. To lust after the flesh of another is punishable by death. It makes us weak, and I can attest to this because there are times I cannot do my work properly because my thoughts are of 02 and not the task at hand. I can't say if love is forbidden in other districts.

Although, I know for a fact that love was once a very important part of Elder Ahlsom's life. To my knowledge, before the start of Shanty District, and before Provisionals, there were husbands and wives. Elder Ahlsom's wife fell in love with another man in the silo not once but twice. Even carrying her second lover's child. Enforcer 01 killed her and her two lovers for the betrayal when Elder Ahlsom couldn't.

"Stoic as ever," 02 smiles.

I often fear my reddening cheeks will give my feelings towards him away, but his concern at this moment makes me weak. 02 is patient, insightful, and kind.

"Good haul today." His knuckle grazes my cheek briefly.

Is it because he feels these feelings, too? Don't be foolish, 09. I am thankful to have a man like 02 as my Enforcer and not 01. "Thank... you." I slam my eyes shut in embarrassment for bumbling like an idiot and hurry to my corrugated shanty.

Before the light is lost, I start the repairs on my attire, then use the small scissors to shorten my platinum blonde hair just above my shoulders. Most of the Collector women have shaved heads, but my vanity prevents me from doing so. I run my fingers over the spot on my cheek where I can still feel 02's touch. Enforcers are allowed to take a consort if approved by Elder Ahlsom, though it has been quite some time since he has allowed it. The consort does help boost morale in his Enforcers, but who in their right mind would ever consider a life of servitude to Enforcer 01? I'm often lost in thought thinking about what it would be like to belong to 02. To not have to hide my feelings for him. A consort's job is to please the Enforcer and wait on them hand and foot, but I don't see 02 abusing that privilege. I'd be his equal. And, most importantly, never have to be in the presence of 01 again.

C. Two

"Don't make me beg, 09." Enforcer 02 is playful in his attempts to persuade me to attend tonight's gathering, but I fear making a fool of myself. "You should indulge every now and then."

I deny his request and retire to my shanty. Every fifth day we rest. Most of the members gather at the community shanty for social interaction and games from the old world. This doesn't interest me. I also know 01 will frequent the gathering which is equally unappealing. How am I to relax with him? I cannot allow myself to be in an environment with 02 where I could possibly let my guard down and my feelings for him known. It's too risky, although what I do in my spare time is just as unwise. It is forbidden to have books because it aids the delusion of love, and time is better spent contributing to the prosperity of Shanty District. I only keep one at a time to lessen my chance of being caught because I would have my eyes gouged for it and it's hard enough to see as it is. My book is buried strategically in the ground below the wooden storage I keep extra attire in. Books that are more colorful and childish in cover art tend to be easier to read. My hope is to one day be able to read the more solid covered ones with no pictures. Until then, the journey of this hungry worm will do.

When the sun rises, I realize just how dangerous it is to keep books because I don't remember falling asleep while reading it. I'm frantic to bury it before I am discovered. I've lost time I could have used to groom from the well, so I will have to gather at the gates without that option.

Enforcer 01 seems to be having a rough start to his morning as well as he fumbles to get on his harness where his guns are stored. Nor is he in a pleasant mood, but when is he ever?

I find it strange that he's come from around the side of my shanty. His quarters are on the other side of the district. It doesn't make sense for him to come this way. I've heard stories about this liquid they sometimes consume that impairs their motor functions. Maybe he didn't even make it to his quarters. Something else that concerns me is that Enforcer 01 is the only one I see. Where are 02 and 04 at? As the rusty hinges on the gates open the steel, I'm uneasy to know another day will be spent with 01.

I'm constantly on the lookout for a new book. Despite being forbidden, they are also extremely rare to find. I wonder if it's because prior to the collapse of the old world, books were becoming obsolete. Perhaps replaced by the cellular device? A device that's purpose now is to strip for parts. These are plentiful throughout our search. I have already gathered three. Being a commodity like this, they don't fetch many points. I'll be lucky by the end of this haul to have enough for a refill of my canteen.

The other Collectors and I witness Enforcer 01 beat Collector 13 to death.

"Let this be a lesson to one that desires the flesh of another."

It's a horrific lesson to watch, but I know if I don't respect the Enforcer and his decision, I will also be beaten. As 13 gasps his final breath, it is more imperative than ever that I hide my feelings for Enforcer 02 if I want to have my deterioration ceremony.

"Disgusting." 01 spits on 13.

My lips part in disbelief, not from the beating but from Enforcer 01's disregard for hydration. It shows how well the Enforcers live compared to us. I'd never be so careless to void something so precious.

"Back to work!"

Once the others scatter, I circle back around and take 13's canteen, as well as a few other items he had on his person. His cart isn't too far down the stream, so I loot what items I find worthy.

Enforcer 01 finds it amusing, even stopping to watch me.

"He won't be needing them." I don't understand why I am explaining my actions.

"Why don't you fear me as the others do?"

I don't like talking to him when he's not wearing the protective lenses over his vacant eyes. "I fear you when your actions are not justified."

"So you feel his death was justified?"

"Rules are rules. To lust after the flesh of another is forbidden."

He slides the protective lenses up his nose until they are in place. "Good girl." Enforcer 01 takes a drink from my canteen before dropping it back into my cart.

I wait for him to continue down the path before wiping the mouth of the container. It sickens me to know his lips have touched what mine will. I hope that my answer pleased him, and he's not waiting for a moment that I become vulnerable to show me why he should be feared. My head tilts in confusion when I notice something in my cart that wasn't there prior. I didn't put this in there and it wasn't taken from the Collector. Was this dropped by Enforcer 01 by mistake? Once I catch up to him, it's not as easy as just asking him a question. I find it awkward to address him about this because every way to explain it sounds ridiculous. "Enforcer 01, did you drop this in my cart?"

He barely acknowledges the item before dismissing that it doesn't belong to him.

It angers me that he acts as if I'm not even worth his time. "This is not mine."

Enforcer 01 bares his teeth, leaning over right in my face. "Then I will confiscate it. This is certain to bring a significant amount of points, wouldn't you agree?"

I don't need his charity because I don't want to be in debt to this man, and if it's not charity but some sort of test, it's not a test I wish to fail.

He kicks my cart over in a tantrum I thought was reserved for a child.

Most of my things wind up broken and unusable. I suppose it's karma for looting the other Collector's things. One thing is for sure, I will go hungry tonight.

The following day, I get my Enforcer back, although our time together is brief when I don't pay attention to my footing. I fall to what I think is my death, but I wake up in my shanty. I'm uncertain how much time has passed and hurry to gather my things and cart.

"You should be resting after the fall you took."

I don't want to displease 02 by disobeying him, but I need to eat. "I was careless."

"You are human, 09. It was a mistake."

"It will not happen again."

"All right," he smiles.

The day is unseasonably warm, which means it will take the water I've boiled twice the time to cool. Inside Shanty District you must use your points to drink. However, in the wasteland, you may consume at your own risk. I don't have much of a choice from all the foolish decisions I've made over the last few weeks. I'm famished and lightheaded from my tumble. I dig close to the shore while my water cools to see if I am able to find any worms for quick protein. I'm so thankful when I do find one that I almost cry. "Ow," I whimper when my wrist is seized by Enforcer 01.

"Have some respect for yourself." He shoves my hand back as the worm slips from my fingers and into the shallow body of water.

I hardly doubt Enforcer 01 knows what it's like to go hungry.

"Drink."

I will not drink from this man's canteen and drink my water that is still hot just to prove my point.

"Woman, you try every bit of my patience."

He has patience? That is news to me. A clear bag is set in my lap. In it, I find smoked meat strips from one of the wild animal kills. I have already let pride prevent me several times from earning points. As I take a mental inventory of my cart, I worry this might be my only consumption for the day. I muffle a thank you through my stuffed mouth.

Enforcer 01 swipes the bag. "If I wanted to watch you eat like an animal, I would have fed you like one. Try it again!"

I nod fearful and chew this next piece more than twice.

"You shouldn't be out here after the fall you had. Your Enforcer is incompetent to let you come."

All of a sudden he has reserves about who comes out into the wasteland? This is a man who constantly has to replace his Collectors because he can't keep his hands off them, yet is going to lecture me about my Enforcer? Some nerve. "It was my choice."

"You are incapable of making choices for yourself, otherwise you wouldn't be in this predicament."

I didn't realize taking this food would come with a lecture. He refuses it when I try to give it back, so I pocket it.

"Keep eating."

"My stomach is upset."

"Yes, probably from that dirty water. Another foolish decision. Drink."

I close my eyes and try not to think of him previously drinking from his canteen before giving it back. His insight angers me because he's right. How many foolish decisions have gotten me here? I am the weakest of all the Collectors. The runt. My anger gets the best of me, and I lash out at him. "I don't need you to take care of me! I have my Enforcer for that."

"Then perish in the wasteland like the others!" The bagged meat is swiped from my hands along with his canteen. He makes it a point to purposely dump my water before I'm left alone no better off than I was before.

Sometimes I think about what it would be like for 02 to take up for me. Today is not that day. I fall in line with the other Collectors as we start back to Shanty District. Enforcer 02 and Enforcer 04 also fall in line. It seems we all live in 01's shadow.

I skip my run the following day because I am too weak from exhaustion. Hopefully, I'll get some much-needed rest.

"You've never missed a run," a voice wakes me. A voice that belongs to Enforcer 01.

Here I wasn't even by his side today yet I've managed to displease him.

"Is it because you're famished or because you didn't want to be near me?"

"Both, though mostly the latter."

"09, I'm harsh on you because you are bound for much greater things than a Provisional and you are too free of a spirit to be confined within these walls as a Machinist."

Did he just... compliment me?

"I upset you?" he continues. "**Good**. Use that to your advantage. I expect you to be at the gates before everyone tomorrow, and well-rested. Eat. You will need your strength to reimburse me for the water, meat, and this here."

It smells better than anything I have ever consumed. "Thank you." I'm genuine in my gratitude because I know how rare a gesture like this is in our world. Maybe it's not fair to judge this man on the stories, but rather small things like this. Things he isn't obligated to do.

When Enforcer 01 sits beside me, he takes up most of my bedroll. "Open."

I'm speechless as ever when he feeds me the murky colored liquid. Inside the liquid, I find fresh cut vegetables. I've never been able to get my hands on some before they are taken. This is exactly what I need to gather my strength. However, I flinch when he touches my cheek.

"I would not harm you, 09. I'm checking to see if you have a fever."

"I've never seen you show compassion towards someone, yet I see glimpses of it here. Or all the days you've helped me get my cart inside Shanty District." Am I wrong about him? Could it be that I turn a blind eye towards his positive actions because that's what everyone else has always done?

"I know the stories that have polluted your judgment about me. I killed that Machinist in the supply Shanty because I didn't trust that after I left he wouldn't mean you harm."

"What about the brutal murder of Collector 13?"

"I was a witness when he tried to force himself on another one of the Collector women."

That's what he meant when he said, "Let it be a lesson to one that desires the flesh of another." Have all the people he's killed been rightfully put to death because they are going against our rules?

Enforcer 01 laughs when my face turns sour. "Not a fan of broccoli, I see."

"I don't want to come across as ungrateful, but the consistency is strange."

"When I was a child, I always heard that if you don't eat your vegetables you won't grow to be big and strong. Broccoli is still one I don't care for." He sets the other piece on the dirt.

I pull in a sharp breath before snatching it from the ground and shoving it in my mouth.

"Why would you eat something that's been on the ground?!"

"Why would you waste food by putting it on the ground?!" My teeth grit in frustration. "I am constantly hungry. Thirsty. Yet, you waste both precious resources constantly. Even as we sit here, my stench lingers throughout this shanty, but you have an aroma that I can only assume comes from bathing in water. Last week, I watched Collector 24 die because her body was depleted of it. You don't waste food because you dislike it. And you especially don't waste water."

"I didn't realize you were so passionate about the subject."

"You don't understand what it's like to go hungry. Every day I must fight to bring home the items necessary for survival because what's my other option? Provisional? I'll die before I willingly accept that life."

Enforcer 01 departs as the last words leave my lips.

I don't regret what I've said, my only regret is because this was a rare moment that I'm sure he has only allowed me to see. I just can't bite my tongue on something like this.

I was able to get enough points to pay Enforcer 01 back, which he refused despite his instructions. With my surplus in points, I fetch a small ration for myself. One that is almost inhaled at the expense of my fingers. Something rolls across the dirt. I've never seen this in a ration before. The small bottle looks to be some type of flavoring. I inhale the liquid contents as the scent makes my eyes pucker. "Tab..." The word is too advanced for me. Although the odor is strong, it's pleasant. It's overwhelming in flavor. A rare find. Something that I will savor for the more flavorless rations. I've spent too much time on the spicy liquid bottle and didn't realize the sun has almost set.

The night is something truly horrifying between the sounds and suffocating darkness. If I spent my time wisely, instead of staring at Enforcer 02, I might be able to afford a small oil lamp. Until then, I shut my eyes and think of him to calm my nerves. Maybe I should make an attempt to attend the gatherings to help speed things along. Such a fool, 09.

All right, now I truly do feel the part of a fool as I stand awkwardly by the door ready to flee the gathering.

"Why don't you socialize with the others? Isn't that why you are here?"

I highly doubt that's an invitation to join Enforcer 01 and the others. More like a demand. Why can't he just leave me alone? I'm not bothering anyone standing here.

"You should speak when you are spoken to." Enforcer 01 grunts displeased before he leaves abruptly.

My chest is so tight right now. I am thankful he's gone. My anxiety doesn't settle despite Enforcer 02's arrival. In fact, now it's worse. As I try to inch my way out, the entire attention of this room is turned towards me when Enforcer 02 shouts how pleased he is I could attend. Even more embarrassing is when I try and smile.

"You look as if you're in pain," he chuckles. "Come now. Relax."

When I am no longer the focus of the room, I find it easier to do so. What I didn't know at these gatherings is that food is served, and you don't have to use your points for them. I load the food up in the crook of my elbow as if it's my last meal, which Enforcer 02 finds hilarious.

"Slow down, you'll choke." He wipes the corner of my mouth where I let gluttony get the best of me.

I'm thankful we're interrupted because I am trembling from his touch.

Enforcer 01 has challenged 02 to a tabletop game.

I suppose I'll halt consumption to spectate. As much as I loathe every fiber of my being for thinking this, 01 cleans up nicely. He's always rather anal about his appearance, but the white dress shirt complements him well. Perhaps I should have spent some time on myself, too. Maybe 02 would be more interested in me rather than this game. A game that is confusing to me.

What seemed like innocent fun turns into a brawl when 01 accuses 02 of cheating. I don't know the rules of this game, but 02 is honest in everything he does. It seems to me that 02 is accused because 01 does not want to lose. Not that it surprises me. I'm ready for the game to be over with anyway so I can have a brief moment with 02 before the night closes.

01 breaks the stick across the tabletop he's been using to hit these large colored marbles with. His temper is intimidating alone because of his size.

What's to stop him from striking one of us with the stick? 01 seems calmer once he starts to consume the liquid that impairs motor functions. Maybe it will impair his mouth.

"09?"

Now, there is a sound that I will never grow tired of.

Enforcer 02 takes me towards the corner of the room. He says there's something he wants to ask me.

I'm certain he can hear my heart beating and even more so when he asks my opinion on becoming his consort.

"So, she can smile." His finger traces along my bottom lip. "I'll give you some time to think about it."

I don't need time. Please, take me with you. Perhaps it's for the best. If I seem too eager, it might arouse suspicion. When he tells me goodnight, I can't even bring myself to say it back. My excitement is consuming me in the best way possible.

There's still a bit of light left once I return home, so I decide to use that time to read. This book is incredible. As you flip the page, some of the pictures rise upward. My fingers run along the beautiful architecture as it brings a smile to my lips. It fades once a shadow is cast over me and my book. "Enforcer 01?" I know what this means and close my eyes so I don't have to anticipate the moment he gouges them out. At least his strength will make the assault almost instantaneous.

"Fool," he snarls.

I know. I am a fool for keeping the book. Though, it's his next choice of words that confuse me.

"I will *never* allow this for you."

Perhaps he did not see the book? I can feel it under me. Certainly, his rage doesn't come from the literature. Am I just not understanding what has displeased him? I know I do not imagine when he abruptly leaves my shanty. What won't he allow for me?

The following day, Enforcer 02 is sentenced to the burial site. Enforcer 01 accused him of tampering with his tattoo and assures everyone that he has surpassed forty-nine.

That can't be. Enforcer 02 is only ten gradual years past my deterioration, but the will of these people is easily manipulated and the deterioration ceremony begins.

Enforcer 01 watches me the entire time as if he expects me to break, then he can accuse me of feelings for 02.

I understand now why it is important not to pollute my mind with love. 02 is wrongfully put to death because I allowed myself to lust after him. Who is going to protect me now? Since I was a child, 02 has always looked after me. Now, I am on borrowed time.

I feel a great emptiness from his deterioration ceremony. It distracts my thoughts and my tasks, causing me to make careless choices that almost cause my demise. Again. I also have not brought home enough to even be considered for a ration. It takes several weeks to starve, but the longer I go without my rations, the weaker I will become. My alternatives are becoming a Provisional or being exiled. Both are just the same word for death.

C. Three

I'm waiting at the gate to scavenge on our day of rest because my days bleed together. I can feel 01 behind me as if he's taunting me. He'll get no reaction from me. We'll stand here all night. Thankfully, we don't have to. I close my eyes, taking a deep breath. If I spoke to Elder Ahlsom would it even make a difference? Would he care? It doesn't matter anyhow. My days are numbered without my protector.

"Collector 09?"

My ears perk at the calm voice. "Machinist 18," I smile. For as long as I can remember, Machinist 18 and I have always been close. He's the one who convinced me that I'd be a better Collector than Machinist.

He grips my shoulder. "I'm sorry."

I close my eyes to trap my tears. I've never told him about my feelings for Enforcer 02, but he knows. Machinist 18 is madly in love with Elder Ahlsom's Provisional. If anyone can understand about not having control over who you love, it's him.

"His death is not on you."

"But it is, 18."

"Maybe this won't bring you comfort, but 02 did not have your best interest."

How can he say that? I bite my tongue for several reasons. The most pressing one being I do not trust that 01 isn't lurking around here in the shadows.

"Come to the gathering. Clear your mind."

"And then what? After a few hours, it's right back to the guilt. Goodnight."

"Yeah," he sighs.

After a considerable amount of time contemplating it, I move my wooden storage and dig for my book. Only... it's not there! I scoop the earth from the hole faster. Where is it?!

"It has been destroyed."

I whip my head towards Enforcer 01 as my blood boils.

"You may thank me by accompanying me to the gathering. Go to the well and clean yourself. If you are to be seen by my side, you will be presentable."

"I don't want to be by your side!"

01 points to the hole my book was taken from. "You forget you don't have a choice."

I keep my eyes sunk to the floor as I putter behind 01. Being submissive like this sickens me, and he makes my displeasure clear to most of the other members. Especially to Elder Ahlsom.

"Go fetch me a drink, woman," 01 orders.

I'd rather fetch him the bottle to the back of his head. As if I'm not livid enough, 01 tells Ahlsom that I am a liability as a Collector, but then a horrible realization comes over me. 01 is manipulating Ahlsom. This is confirmed when I hear Ahlsom say that he wants 01 to be my Enforcer. Since Enforcer 02 died, I've been under the protection of 04. How is Elder Ahlsom that naive to not see what 01 is doing? My days are surely numbered with 01.

I don't speak a word to 01 as he walks me back to my shanty.

"You are better off with me than 04."

"I was better off with my Enforcer until you murdered him! He wasn't that many years past my gradual deterioration."

"He was a coward."

"You're the coward. 02 was everything you'll never be. Patient. Insightful. Kind."

"Do not mistake his kindness for anything other than your inability to accept that you are lonely."

And just like that, a switch inside me flips. It's a personal vendetta now to have the strength to stay alive. To see him have his ceremony. To watch him succumb to his wounds and collapse into his resting plot. Then, we can all live without this savage.

Even in my sleep, he disturbs my dreams, and when I awake in the morning it's because of him as my door is flung open and almost right off the hinges.

"I said you are late, though I suppose that won't matter when you belong to me."

Panic fills my face. "You can't force me as your consort!"

"You forget my position within these walls. I do whatever I desire. If you don't prove yourself out there to me today, it will be your last, 09."

Having to prove myself to this man only assures me that my future is set. He'll force me into this life until I find the courage to take my own.

I spend my time searching for books on our supply run since he's made my future known, then find it amusing when he discovers them and reprimands me for it.

"Keep trying my patience, girl. You will pay for it later."

I point at a book atop of a shelf in a decrepit home. "That one is too high. Fetch it for me."

When he starts to bare his teeth, I strike him in the face with rebar then turn to run.

As I flee the home, some of the other Collectors' screams cause me to freeze. I don't need my sight to know what the dissolutes from the wasteland force on our women in the distance, and I start to cry.

Enforcer 01 covers my eyes, bringing me closer to him.

This compassion from someone who will basically force me into this same thing makes me wonder if his words do not have validity behind them. That he'd rather see me miserable but safe in his quarters as opposed to the alternative. Not but a minute ago, did I strike him violently yet he is the one who comforts me. He cannot block out their screams, which terrify me. My tiny hands tug at his shirt as I try to bury myself deeper against him. "Make it stop."

"There," he points, taking me to higher ground.

I huddle between some rocks so I'm hidden because he says the dilapidated house isn't safe.

"I will come for you, but stay put."

"Just shoot them!"

"The noise will draw in the others." The hesitation is concerning. It seems that even a brute like 01 has limits. His palm touches my cheek in a confusing embrace. As if he knows this is the last time he'll touch me. He's gentle and caresses my skin before leaving me.

I can't bring myself to watch and I don't comprehend why. Here is someone I continuously wish to die, but now the thought frightens me.

"No," I cry when I'm discovered and pulled from the rocks.

01 wastes no time and fires up at the dissolute. He's right because the noise from the gun brings the other dissolutes in waves.

I hurry to my hiding spot, covering my ears from the screams and sounds of death until it's 01 that I hear.

There are a few painful grunts and one last breath before it's completely silent.

Has he... perished? I can't make much out of what's happening due to my impaired vision, but I do notice two dissolutes gather around him.

"Strip his flesh from him as proof to bring back to the others, then we'll raid Shanty District."

I cover my mouth in horror when they strip him of his shirt and actually start to filet the skin open on his side. Morally, I will not sit here and watch them do this. 01 died protecting me, and his death will not be made a mockery of by some skin trophy.

The dissolute Enforcer 01 shot had a gun on him. I'm not familiar with how to use this weapon, but I know the basics. Point and squeeze the trigger. Difficult for someone with the skills and sight. Impossible for someone like me who doesn't possess either. The first shot fired makes me overconfident when the man is struck in the neck and drops to the earth. Oh, this is much easier than I thought. I turn the gun to the other man as he charges towards me. Each shot fired misses him, and the gun is knocked from my hand as he tackles me. I try to reach for the gun before he does, but that is not his intention. My face is splattered with blood and the man collapses on top of me. It takes all my strength to get out from under him. I'm shaken up by the attack while looking around to see who assisted me.

Enforcer 01 lowers his gun before his arm gives and it flops beside him.

I thought he had perished? He will certainly bleed to— I'm startled by another man. It's a struggle to kill him, but their weakness is because they desire more for the flesh than their own life and he's put to death. I'm thankful that I was able to protect myself because I did not have assistance this time. This right here is the very reason why we are taught not to lust after another. It does make you weak, and the dissolute's innards I'm stepping through proves that.

My eyes well up once more, when I see how my fellow Collectors were murdered and left bare. With the demise of Enforcer 01, I am alone in the wasteland. It still doesn't deter me from trying to wake him.

I'm unsure what to do because medical aid is not taught to us. However, I think back to the times I've repaired my attire from a rip. Perhaps I could do the same with his skin? I use parts of his shirt those men cut to try and stop the bleeding. Clothing is much easier than skin. Forgiving, too. It seems like all I'm doing is poking another hole in him to bleed out of. The work is tedious and exhausting but his wounds finally stop bleeding.

I trace my fingers over the ink markings on his chest and stomach just as I thought they'd be there. They are vibrant in color and quite beautiful. Almost as if they tell their own story.

Enforcer 01 takes a painful, labored breath.

I draw my hand back, frightened, ready to explain myself for touching him without permission.

"Don't start what you can't finish."

What I can't finish? What is he talking about? He seems playful despite his injuries, but I'm still confused.

He inhales a sharp breath before springing upward when he realizes what once surrounded us. "Are you..." 01 feels for his gun, which I retrieve for him.

"Fine, though I cannot say the same for the others."

He doesn't seem too concerned with the others once he had confirmation I was safe. Enforcer 01 snarls when he examines his gun.

"Did I break it?"

"The magazine is empty."

"I don't know what that means."

"All the ammunition is depleted."

Now *that* I understand. "I apologize for wasting your ammunition."

"Don't. I failed you as your Enforcer. Put you in a position you should never have been in. On your own." His head bows. "For that... I'm sorry, 09."

The fact that he takes this attack so personal only upsets me more.

"I should have protected you."

"You about gave your life in doing it."

01 disregards me as he starts loading up useful supplies from the others.

"Please, rest. I'll do this."

He kneels beside the cart when he loses his balance, and I start my search.

I'm able to scrounge up some items before returning.

01 always finds it comical that I am very meticulous on the way I organize my cart. It's one of the few times I'm given a genuine smile. However, it fades when he takes one of the books from it. "Keeping a book in your shanty is dangerous. You need to bury them under the walls."

"You speak like you've done this before."

"Despite what you think you know about me, I am quite the avid reader. It is one of the many things I miss from the old world."

"Really?" I don't know why I ask this of him. He just admitted that he did. He's right. I am surprised. I plop down next to him to catch my breath. "What books do you like?"

"Anything I can get my hands on."

"It's still difficult for me to read. I did enjoy a few horror books, though."

"Well, you *are* straight out of a nightmare."

I laugh at his words. "What are some other things you long from your world?"

"The company of another woman. Their touch. The way they smell."

"Do you not frequent the Provisional quarters?"

"No. That is something I have always disagreed with Ahlsom on. It might look as if they have a choice, but if not a Provisional, they are exiled. What life is that?"

Those have always been my words. If I'm not a Collector, I might as well be exiled before I become property. I bring my knees up to my chest, wrapping my arms around them. Have I been wrong about the man I thought Enforcer 01 was?

"Are you cold?"

"No."

"You will be. We need to find shelter. Once the sun sets, the temperature will drop substantially and we will die without fire."

I never realized how much our shanties protect us from the elements. Not having that makes me unnerved. I don't understand why we just can't use this house to seek shelter in. I'm going to speak up so he knows. "It would be wise if..." The house collapsing drowns out my voice.

"What were you saying?"

"That it would be wise to get going," I lie, hoping he can't see through my lies like all the other times. Wait, how is he going to walk? He can barely stand and falls twice doing so. It's ripping the thread and his side is bleeding again. "Sit in my cart. I will find us a place for the evening." When he starts to refuse, I interrupt him. "If you don't let me get us to safety, you will not live to see it and I can promise you that I will certainly die if I am left alone in the wasteland. Get in the cart." That goes over better, and we begin the arduous journey.

The sun diminishes faster with every minute. We've been searching for shelter for eighty of them.

Enforcer 01 has me gather wood along the way and other objects he sees that will be of use.

My arms are exhausted. There is not much left I can give.

"09, stop."

I stand paralyzed by the horned silhouette of a creature.

01 stands up from the cart. "Come."

"What is that?" I know my sight is not reliable, but I have never seen something like this before.

"It is not of this world. I need you to do as I say. If we are detected, I will not be able to protect you in my condition without any ammunition or my machete."

His urgency scares me, so I do as he asks. We walk quite a distance before 01 can't take anymore, and leads us to a secluded rock formation. I try my best to listen to what he tells me to increase our odds of survival. 01 instructs me how to make fire from items he gathered. It takes me too many attempts, and my hands are bloody from how irritated they are.

"Look at me. You must succeed at this. If we lose the light, we will die."

"I know this!" I dislike being so overcome with emotion that I act childish, but I am doing my best. I take a deep breath, trying again. The situation is dire, and right as the wood snaps in half, I finally get my ember.

"Good girl!"

"I did it," I beam.

"Cup your hands like this and blow. Give it oxygen. Now place the bundle under the wood."

The warm heat feels incredible. Even more so that this is my fire.

Enforcer 01 also shows me how to make a trap and has me set it before the light is lost.

Now that my tasks are done, I have time to dwell on my pain. My hands ache and the skin is gone in several places from the friction.

"Let me."

I don't want to be vulnerable, but can't spare the energy arguing. I give in and open my hands to him.

Unlike what I've seen, 01 is gentle, as if he'll cause further damage. We can't spare the water, but it doesn't deter him from putting my comfort first.

My eyebrow tugs up curiously. "What is amusing you?"

"When I was a child, I was raised by my grandparents. My grandmother used to kiss my wounds to make them better."

"What is a grandmother?"

"It would be the person who birthed your Provisional."

I don't know who my birther is. It's always bothered me to a small extent because all the other members of the district know their birther. Sometimes, I just pretend it's Provisional 03 because she is the only one with hair my color and small in size like me. I bring my hands up and, despite disagreeing with Enforcer 01, press my lips to them. "I don't feel any different."

He starts to laugh. "It works when someone you care for does the gesture."

Well, that's not going to happen seeing as he's killed the only person I care for. Things have been civil. I need to harbor this resentment immediately, so I make small talk. "Your beard seems warm."

"It is an inconvenience, but my vanity keeps me from shaving it off."

"That's the same reason I do not shave my head."

"Your hair color is a rarity. Even in my world, that shade of blonde was not often achieved without a chemical."

There are so many things about his world that I don't understand. People concerned themselves with this? "How wasteful."

"It was different. We had things like that at our disposal."

"I just concern myself with when I'll get my next meal."

"That's not living. You don't deserve this life."

I don't wish to speak with him anymore on the matter. It's upsetting my stomach. "See you come morning."

Which is the longest night of my life. I don't sleep well because I'm not sure if his actions are pure. Who would even believe me if I tried to say that he forced himself on me? It disappoints me that I would think something like that of him because 01 seems to be a man of his word on that matter. Especially if he won't even frequent the Provisional quarters.

I turn over to the most wonderful smell.

"I checked your traps. Come see your kill."

It's a small creature, but it will be plentiful. I'm not sure what animal because he's skinned it away from our camp.

"It's hot," he reprimands when I try and remove a piece. "It's almost done."

"I'm hungry now, though." I fear how much longer we're together. Right now it's civil, but I don't wish for him to take my life because of some minor inconvenience that's angered him. He has put back on his protective lenses that cover his eyes. Thank, Ahlsom. Still, they fascinate me because he's the only Enforcer who has them. I hesitantly trace my finger down the metal frame. "What are these?"

"Sunglasses." He slides them from his face, flipping them around.

I shy away, startled.

"Hold still. They're prescription. In the old world, it was very common to need corrective lenses to see. I need them to see far away, that's one of the reasons I wear them."

"Does anyone know?"

"It's not punishable by death to need glasses, 09."

I step outside and scan the horizon with his corrective lenses to view the beautiful hues of the sunrise that I've never seen before and our vast lands. It is not my intention to, but I shed several tears in front of this man. I apologize for my moment of weakness and hand them over.

"Mine is to protect from the sun's rays, but you may use these for now." In his bag, he retrieves me another pair. They are gray with clear lenses rather than black ones. "Better?"

"Significantly." His acceptance of my eyes being such a hindrance is shocking. I live in fear of being excommunicated for something I cannot help. This weight lifted is relieving.

"Pack your cart. Let's return."

My new lenses make me eager to leave so I can get a glimpse of everything I've missed, though it's cut short.

"Dust storm."

I flip my cart on its side so it can take the brunt of the wind and sand.

"There," Enforcer 01 points. "The truck."

"What's a truck?"

"Move," he warns, taking my hand.

"What about my—"

"Leave it!"

The metal contraption has a side hatch that we crawl into. What I expect to be dank and suffocating turns out to be quite different. The first thing I take note of is how my seat is more comfortable than my own bedroll.

After 01 shuts his door, he presses his hand against several spots in front of us. "Close your vents to try and minimize the amount of dust that gets in.

I don't know what he means, so he does it for me. "A truck is from the old world?"

"It was one form of transportation. I used to own this black— never mind."

"I don't mind."

"Get some sleep until it passes." He leans over and I find my heart beating a little fast, though once he pushes down the knob on the hatch door he returns to his seat.

I feel foolish and disgusted with myself to have some type of reaction from him being that close.

"I am proud of your actions. No other Collector could have done as you have."

There's not much I feel from his praises, but at least I know I will not be forced into a life as his consort since I've pleased him. Still, I saved his life. A man that I have eagerly waited for his deterioration ceremony, yet I've prolonged his terror over our district. I'm nauseous from my actions and scoot farther from him. Not responding to him will surely cause one of his famous temper tantrums, but thankfully it does not come, and the night comes to a close.

Morning is cold and distant. I welcome the familiarity. Part of me worried he would take back my lenses, but he doesn't acknowledge me until we make it to Shanty District and are greeted by Elder Ahlsom. Most of the Collector females submit to the Elder and touch their lips to his cheek or shoes. I have never got on my knees, nor will I ever. As much as Elder Ahlsom takes credit for Shanty District, it's not his to take. It was Enforcer 01. The closeness the two have trouble me. I know that Elder Ahlsom has surpassed forty-nine, yet he is granted immunity. Does this mean Enforcer 01 will be given that same dispensation?

Elder Ahlsom touches my shoulder. "Good to see you've both returned."

My cheeks flush the same when 02 used to touch me, but it is not for the same reasons. He makes me uncomfortable, and his touch feels inappropriate. I also feel as if he knows this and continues to do so to assert his dominance over me. To put me in my place. Elder Ahlsom has said several times he thinks my place is within these walls. It makes me ill thinking about becoming a Provisional, or even worse, his own personal one. I become more flush when his fingers circle around the back of my nape.

"No thanks to Collector 09," Enforcer 01 snarls. "She is the entire reason for this unnecessary delay. If I had any sense, I would have left her in the wasteland for the dissolute ones to do with her as they choose." 01 spits on the ground close to my boots.

"Come now, you must be famished." Elder Ahlsom finally removes his predatory fingers from me, as he gestures his hand to the gathering shanty.

I'm so disgusted by both their actions, I don't acknowledge either and start for the well. I dip my hand down and touch the cool water to my neck. I'm so prideful, I debate breaking these lenses just to spite 01. Leave me in the wasteland?! I am the one who saved him. In fact, the only reason those dissolutes found me was that I was trying to save him. I can't even think. My mind is muddled with emotion and complete chaos. Some nerve!

I'm unable to sleep thinking about what slithered from 01's mouth. It is forbidden to enter the shanty of an Enforcer without their consent, but as long as I can speak my thoughts before I'm murdered, so be it. He will know where I stand. I will not be made a fool of.

Once darkness falls, I cautiously make my way by lighter to confront Enforcer 01. It's a slow process because the flame keeps burning my thumb.

I'm flung to the ground with such force, it disorients me. I feel along the gravel and dirt for my lighter. As I hear something snarl, my hand stills. Oh, my, Ahlsom, what is that? My shaky hand extends outward, striking the flint wheel to spark the flame. I see the creature briefly before his breath puts out the flame.

C. Four

Ahand wraps around my gaping mouth, silencing my screams before they are vocalized. As I use the lighter once more, my eyes move down to see the hand against my mouth has markings on it. Markings that belong to 01. Then those marks, and myself, are splattered with blood. The silhouette of the creature I saw in the wasteland is very much a reality and falls before us. Beheaded. I frantically try to rid the blood from my face and hands, but there is so much of it. It frightens me. Blood always has.

"This way."

I keep my head down, moving it side to side in disagreement. That's when my arm is yanked to him. "Leave me be."

"If I let you be, your body would be disposed of in the wasteland with the dissolute ones."

"Then that is my fate."

"You are a fool."

I don't understand why he'd spare my life to take it behind closed doors. Maybe it is punishment for my tongue.

It's no secret that the Enforcers are given the most lavish dwellings, but his is even more extravagant than the Elder's Provisional. I haven't seen a bed since the one that she retired to. His is entirely over the top, but there is a part of me that does wonder what it would be like not to sleep against the earth. "Why am I here?"

"Because there are some things that you should know." Enforcer 01 mimics all the times 02 would graze my cheek and lips with his thumb.

I never thought that someone would be a witness to his touch.

"Tell me why your skin doesn't flush in my presence like it did when Enforcer 02 put his hands on you."

I don't grant him a response.

"The way you lust over him like some animal in heat—"

"Not lust, love. I **loved** him." I have committed so many crimes, I've lost count. My only regret is that I will be put to death before I can see 01 perish.

"I didn't want it to come to this, but your hatred for me is corrupting the truth about the person 02 was. Don't you see, 09?"

"It's true, 09," Machinist 18 tells me when he enters Enforcer 01's quarters.

What... what is 18 doing here?

"When I told you that Enforcer 02 didn't have your best interest, this is why." 18 hands me a letter. "This was a request made by 02 to Elder Ahlsom."

I can't read it that well and fumble over most of the words.

"Allow me to read it for you." Enforcer 01 takes it from my trembling hands.

Enforcer 02 requests Collector 09 be exiled for the egregious murder of your Provisional. I discovered her hiding the weapons used to kill 03 on a run. When confronted, she confessed to the murder and asked in exchange for my silence if she could be my consort.

"Lies. This is... all lies," I weep.

"Enforcer 02 had several letters like this to frame and disgrace others so it would eventually put him in control of Shanty District."

How could I be so foolish to believe he loved me? I'm apoplectic by the truth.

Enforcer 01's hand touches my shoulder. "When I overheard 02 ask you to be his consort, I was furious. That is what I meant when I said I would never allow that. Machinist 18 caught me outside and said he needed my help. He showed me the letters. This district is just foolish enough to believe 02 surpassed forty-nine. Though, that isn't even the worst of it, 09. Multiple Enforcers are interested in you as their consort, which has piqued the Elder's interest."

"Ahlsom can force you into that life, and he will. Not a Provisional, but his Provisional," 03 adds as she comes from Enforcer 01's bathroom.

While I will never get on my knees for Elder Ahlsom, I kneel for Provisional 03, taking her soft hands in mine and kissing them. "Ma'am, I apologize for not seeing you sooner," I stammer, not knowing she had been here the entire time.

"Please, don't kneel for me."

"Why do you trouble yourself with what happens to me, Ma'am?"

"Because I am your birther."

My face pales, which speaks volumes because I don't comprise much coloring as it stands. I knew it. We have too many resemblances, though how conceited to compare her beauty to mine. She is the most beautiful woman I have ever seen.

"Your father is the one who built Shanty District. The Provisional was something incorporated by Ahlsom after your father died."

A father, I assume, would be the birther's lover? This terminology is still strange to me. "I'm bemused. Isn't Enforcer 01 the one who built this place?"

"No. I did have a hand in building this place, but it was your father who laid the groundwork. He asked that I look after you when he suspected Ahlsom had plans to murder him."

03 squeezes my hands in hers. "I have no choices, 09, but you do. I know that it seems like Enforcer 01 is harsh with you, but that is because he cannot bear the thought of you being another body to be disposed of in the wasteland. None of us can."

Enforcer 01 takes a step towards me. "Right now, you have a choice like 03 said, but that window is closing." 01 reveals where his identification marking is. Behind his ear. "And mine is, too."

This is his last year. We're going into his final month.

"You are intelligent, 09," Machinist 18 begins. "Think back to all the times you thought 02 to be your protector. What is the common denominator?"

That 01 was always a witness to it. "When I fell in the desert, were you the one to bring me home?"

"How else would I know you fell?"

Everything I have ever known has been a lie. I scoot the tears from my cheek, unable to bring myself to look at anyone because I am ashamed for not seeing all of this sooner.

Provisional 03 gives me an embrace before she leaves Enforcer 01's quarters with Machinist 18.

Even on one knee, Enforcer 01 is taller than me. "Woman, do you not see the lengths I have gone through to keep you safe? That I have always gone through. I will not sit idly by and watch you become breeding stock."

Do not mistake his kindness for anything other than your inability to accept that you are lonely.

This entire time I have mistaken Enforcer 01's actions to be Enforcer 02. How many countless times have I gone blind to 01's good deeds thinking they were 02's? "Why do you disrespect me in front of Elder Ahlsom?"

"I said what I did to Ahlsom because I wanted his hands off you. I can't describe what it does to me watching another man's hands on you. If you only knew the lust I have for you. How delusional I am to think that you are mine, and I do not like to see someone touching what belongs to me."

"But I don't belong to you!"

"I know, and it's just as maddening. The adoration I have for you is suffocating at times. I can't do my tasks, I can't even think because you consume every one of my thoughts. The only time that I feel a sense of ease is when you are by my side."

My eyes must be the size of the frames on these lenses. Everything to leave his mouth are the thoughts I keep to myself about 02. My thoughts aside, this man just admitted that he loves me.

"If I wasn't harsh with you, and you did return my adoration, I would have been killed before I could make the preparations to leave. The Collectors you have witnessed me kill, or have heard stories about their demise, it's because they have come in the way of those preparations or they were just casualties of the creatures. 09, it has never been my intention to frighten you or disrespect you. I'm... sorry," he chokes before this man loses his composure.

I thought his temper was frightening, but watching him sob over the guilt he feels is worse. "How long have you had these feelings for me?"

"I have lusted after you for the last one thousand, two hundred and seventeen agonizing days."

I am familiar with that number because that is the amount of time that I have loved 02. When 01 makes an attempt at touching his lips to mine, I shove him off me as my hand leaves a red imprint on his cheek. "Maniac!"

Watching how he's still submissive to me with his head bowed speaks volumes. For twenty-two years, I have watched Enforcer 01 reign, what I thought to be, terror over our district. Still, he's never been one to show weakness.

"I have longed for your touch and to know you reject it is an even worse feeling than you loving 02 because it shows me that, despite the efforts I have made, you would rather stay here knowing your fate than have any part of a life with me outside these walls. It also shows the aversion you have towards me. I am truly a fool to believe you'd ever return my love."

His words cause my stomach to ache. 01 really does have my best interest. Even tonight when I was facing death from the creature that had breached our walls. Don't pass this up because you are stubborn. He has admitted his wrongs, and that is all he can do.

Still, I can't. I deny 01 and return to my shanty because I need time to absorb this new information. Time, I know, that neither of us has.

C. Five

In a way, I feel the same as when 02 died because my days bleed together. I often catch 01 staring at me through my peripherals on supply runs. While Enforcer 01 has taken my news with a heavy heart, it never once stops him from keeping me safe. The brute just seems... lost.

On our day of rest, I go to the gathering to see the other Enforcers that are interested in me.

Enforcer 01 leaves abruptly when one of the others touch my shoulder.

It's quite the group of degenerates that I want no part of and flee from the shanty as fast as I can because my head is spinning. My heart leads me to Enforcer 01. I enter his shanty unannounced to find him on his chair in a daze. "Why did you leave the gathering?"

"I didn't want to witness another man's hands on you."

"What's stopping you from speaking up? You've never been one to bite your tongue." As I observe the fogged stupor on his face, it comes with realization. He didn't speak up because he wanted me to have the decision. In a world where so few decisions are my own, this one belongs to me.

His knuckles brush my cheeks as it pulls me from my thoughts. "I never meant to bombard you with all of this, 09. To make you feel like you had to come to a decision because I'm not long for this world. I just want you to know that I do love you."

As he speaks, my eyes well up from how genuine his words are.

"Do you see the trunk behind you? Those are some of the preparations that I've made. I want you to gather your things. It doesn't matter if you ever return my adoration, I just want you safe. Getting you as far away from Shanty District is the priority." His eyes trail a bit before they sink. "Perhaps, one day, you might feel something for me like you did for Enforcer 02. You shouldn't feel foolish for loving him. Know that greed can easily overtake people."

"The actions that I loved don't even belong to him. They're yours."

Enforcer 01's hand hovers close to my arm as if he's waiting for my approval to touch me. When I allow it, I'm moved against him.

This type of affection doesn't exist with our people. It's something from Enforcer 01's world. I find the gesture to be intimate and satisfying. I don't think it's a matter of one day feeling something for him. It's just trying to sort all these new emotions out. I feel his lips settle against the crook of my neck. I'm unable to get my arms all the way around him so I just squeeze as tight as I can.

He grins against my skin. "You are quite strong, but you always have been."

When he picks his head up, our eyes meet. While his are filled with doubt, mine aren't.

I know exactly what needs to be done. As I lean in to press my lips to his, I'm startled when Enforcer 01's door is kicked open and Elder Ahlsom stands in the doorway.

If he had come a few moments prior, both Enforcer 01 and myself would have been put to death.

"May I have a word with you? In my quarters."

"I'll be right behind you," Enforcer 01 says under his breath, "I just need to grab something first."

Do I even have a choice? Elder Ahlsom makes it seem as if I do, but his intentions are not pure and I find this to be true once in his quarters. My stomach turns when I see the sorrow in Provisional 03's eyes as she rises from the couch. Like my fate is sealed before I have a say in it. "You can't keep me here."

His condescending smile goes dark and he strikes me across the face.

"Ahlsom," Provisional 03 begs, wrapping me in her arms. "Stop."

"And if I don't? What are you going to do about it?"

"I will kill you if you touch that woman again," Enforcer 01 threatens.

It is a crime to threaten the Elder, but it doesn't stop 01 from taking up for me. All my existence, I have fantasized about the moment my importance is put above others, and that moment has come. "Enforcer 01 has asked me to be his consort, and I agree. I belong to him." Perhaps I've fabricated that statement, but 01's face has no opposition to my words. I award him a smile and it actually feels natural, unlike the other few times.

"Fools," Ahlsom sneers, removing his gun and firing at Enforcer 01 twice.

"No," I shrill, hurrying to 01's side. Everything happens so fast, yet it seems like an eternity until I finally reach him. "You're going to be all right," I snivel, applying pressure to the entry wound on his shoulder.

"I wouldn't count on that." Elder Ahlsom stands at Enforcer 01's feet and fires several rounds into his chest. "Dispose of him in the wasteland," he orders some of the other Enforcers who have entered his quarters from the commotion. He hooks my arm, yanking me from the floor.

I sob, reaching for the man I loved as they drag his lifeless body from the room. "Monster," I scream, pounding my small fists against Ahlsom's chest. This time, when I'm struck, I black out.

When I regain consciousness, Provisional 03 is dabbing my cheek with a soft rag to clean the blood. The right eye on my protective lenses has been shattered from where Ahlsom struck me. My eye is almost swollen shut and my cries don't help ease the pain. Several blood vessels have burst in the white of my eye. It is nauseating to look at and I turn away from the bathroom mirror.

What should have been a beautiful moment between 01 and me has been taken, just like he has. I'm so numb from the loss of 01, and now the overwhelming guilt starts. It's suffocating. "I never told him how I felt."

"Baby, he knew."

"I should have never gone back to my shanty that night 01 admitted he had feelings for me. 01 is gone and soon I will become an old man's propagator," I sob. As 03 comforts me, I halt my tears because I know I am stronger than this. Anyone to pique Enforcer 01's interest would have to be. It's why he dedicated his life to me, and I'm not going to repay him by weeping. I'm going to stick to my convictions all right. "Stay back," I warn 03. My voice fills the entire bathroom when I call for Ahlsom.

"What are you doing!? Keep your voice down. You'll only anger him further."

Good. This is what I should have done the day he put those predatory fingers on me. I pick up the aluminum waste receptacle and hurl it towards the mirror. It shatters into several pieces that I sift through.

Elder Ahlsom barrels through the door. "What is the meaning of this?"

"I would take my life before assuming your Provisional." I press the glass to my wrist as he charges towards me to stop the assault. When he reaches for the glass, my false attempt to harm myself and lure him in has succeeded. I draw back the glass and stab the piece into his throat. I'm not strong or tall enough to lodge it deep, but I have plenty of glass and shiv him in the stomach repeatedly with more. "I will never belong to you!"

Elder Ahlsom staggers backward before I find myself staring down the barrel of his gun.

So be it, and I accept my fate. At least, in death, I will be with 01. I draw my eyes closed just as the gun is fired, but I feel no pain. When my eyes reopen, I'm still in the bathroom. Ahlsom is belly down on the floor as his blood fills the cracks in the tile.

My eyes shift upward to see my protector lowering his gun.

I blink in disbelief because I cannot explain Enforcer 01 standing before me.

01's white button down might as well be red. The corner of his lip tugs up weakly before he falls to the floor.

What kind of cruel fate is this? Losing him once all to lose him again?

As I approach him to be at his side, he's tugging open some of his shirt. I help him unbutton the rest, only to find another piece of clothing under the shirt.

I'm joined by Provisional 03. "Of course! 01 knew Ahlsom's intentions when he threatened him. That it wouldn't come without bloodshed." 03 touches 01's neck. "09, he is wearing a bulletproof vest. Help me get him from his other shirt so we can loosen the vest."

I don't comprehend what she's told me even after his shirt is stripped. Only when the straps come off this vest, do I realize this attire has halted the ammunition. All except two. The one in his shoulder, and one by his ribs. He has several bruises already surfacing from the force of the ammunition hitting the vest.

Provisional 03 instructs me to bring her several things so she can begin extracting what has pierced his skin.

Seeing him in agony as she removes shards of metal frightens me, and it's not even the blood this time. I can't do anything for his pain but squeeze his hand and wipe his brow with a cool rag. Tears fall against Enforcer 01. "What if he was shot in the face?"

Enforcer 01 grits his teeth. "Fifty-fifty."

"I am not amused!"

"There. That's the last fragment. He has a long recovery. The impact from the bullets has broken his ribs, not to mention the gaping hole from it." 03 works diligently, but 01's eyes are heavy.

Enforcer 01 moves my hand up, turning it over. He presses his lips to one of the lacerations from the broken glass.

It only works when someone you care for does the gesture.

It is quite the comfort, indeed. I admit my adoration for him, though he never hears it. "Enforcer 01?" I shake him several times, but he is not responding.

"Baby, move aside."

I didn't know this about Provisional 03, but she was training to become a doctor prior to the collapse and she is still very knowledgeable in that field. The knowledge that stabilizes 01 for now. Several members help take him back to his bed, where I wait patiently.

I'm losing hope that 01 is going to pull through and I know that is not fair to him. Maybe I'm just trying to prepare myself for the worst. Right now, all I have is uncertainty.

I often spend my mornings weeping as I ready myself. Enforcer 01 is still unconscious and it's been several days. Provisional 03 assures me he will make a full recovery and this is just his body's way of dealing with the trauma so it can heal. I don't know what to believe anymore.

C. Six

I dip my bucket into the well for water to groom Enforcer 01 with. The looks that the other members give me only make me hurry with my task. Some fear me, as one of the stories claim that I stabbed Elder Ahlsom to death. Though that does have some validity, his death is not all mine to take.

Most members are just eager to hear word about Enforcer 01's demise. "You should be ashamed of yourself the way you lust for that murderer!"

"Not lust. Love. I *love* him," I correct her.

The woman spits at me before continuing on her way.

No matter how hard Provisional 03 has tried to turn Shanty District into a place where we can live out our days, the people are quickly turning against her. I worry leaving Enforcer 01 alone at night, because several people have already made an attempt on his life. I have been doing my best to protect him, even pulling his gun on a few of our people though, luckily, the gun was enough intimidation.

Enforcer 04 gave up her life two days ago in an attempt to save his. Before her final breath, she admitted that she was in love with him. Perhaps she saw what took me years to.

I drop the bucket and clean my face before returning to 01's quarters. The water masks my tears, but what does that even matter? It's not like—

"Enforcer 01?" His bed is vacant, so I hurry to his bathroom. The nerve. His incessant need to be clean and waste water has delayed our reunion. My eyes shy from his flesh when he steps closer. "My apologies, I didn't know." I hurry from the bathroom, mortified despite him calling after me. I can feel my shame surface on my cheeks.

"09."

Please let him have pants on. I squeeze my eyes shut just in case. "I didn't know you were awake."

His fingers trail my jawline. "09, look at me."

I peer one eye open, feeling a sense of relief that his dark washed jeans are on. "You should be resting."

"Have a seat." Enforcer 01 kneels in front of me, scooping my hands up. I see his eyes fill with even more guilt because my wounds have healed. "I've left you alone for too long."

"You were injured."

"It is not an excuse."

"Chastise yourself for things beyond your control, but know this, 01. I've never felt stronger. I'm no longer the runt. I didn't need saving because we have saved each other when the other wasn't able."

His lips eagerly claim mine as if he couldn't stand another moment without the embrace.

It's foreign to me. I try to mimic his movements so I'm not so inept. Emotion gets the best of me, yet it intensifies the gesture of affection. One that, when I pull away, leaves me feeling weightless. "I need to be honest with you, and myself, by admitting my unremitting adoration for you. I have always been in love with 02 because of his actions, but I find those actions are yours. How could I not love you? I regret that I judged you based on the man from the stories, and not who you really are."

"I have waited for those words, but I am not deserving of them."

"Then earn it. Do what you think you must, but I love you, 01." I softly touch my lips to his, though nothing 01 does is ever gently returned, and I lose myself under this man.

That evening, his lips to my neck moving up to my ear wake me. How can something forbidden feel so good?

He stops briefly, tugging something out from under him with a grunt. My shoe dangles off his finger. 01 snickers about his findings.

"What is so amusing?"

"Your shoe. In my world, they were hi-top skateboarding shoes for men. Well, this is actually considered a children's size."

They are all that fit me other than my boots. It's difficult to find ones in my size without much wear and tear. Perhaps he requires me to wear shoes that are more feminine. "Do they displease you?"

"No, 09. I have your adoration. Nothing you do will ever displease me."

I touch my fingertips to the coarse graying hair along his jawline and all the way up until I reach his ear before I touch my lips to his.

"09," Machinist 18 calls, though he turns the shade of red that I was yesterday. "I'm sorry, I didn't know, but this is urgent. You and Enforcer 01 are not safe here. As we speak, they are gathering outside."

Enforcer 01 is quick to react.

I wasn't frightened until I notice that 01 isn't preparing to fight, he's preparing to run.

"There's no time to pack," Machinist 18 informs us. "I will hold them off as long as I'm able."

I am barely dressed before my hand is seized by Enforcer 01 and he leads me to a small hatch. His front door is broken down and we both barely escape his quarters before Shanty District opens fire on us. I worry that Enforcer 01 is going to be shot again, and everything will be in vain.

"Hide."

"No, the last time I did that you almost perished!" His gun firing scares me.

"Through there then, 09."

He could have given me a gun, but each time another member is shot I understand why he didn't. It takes an extreme toll on you to murder another person. It's a burden he never wishes me to have again, and I am grateful for it.

Shanty District becomes the last of our concerns once we are ambushed by several of the creatures. While intimidating, the creatures are easily distracted when we are joined by the rest of Shanty District. It becomes a way out for Enforcer 01 and me.

"Let them destroy each other. Come." He extends his hand as I take it.

I'm skeptical of the creature's origin. Most everyone has their own theory as to how they came about, some a little more imaginative than others. I know it's something that we'll inevitably come across without the protection of Shanty District.

Anyone who meant me harm, Enforcer 01 disposed of in the wasteland. A place that we now call our home.

Much to our surprise, Machinist 18 joined us, along with Provisional 03. Now the two are free to love each other openly.

Even though we are a small group, all of our different skills help aid our survival. Not only had Provisional 03 saved Enforcer 01 back at Shanty District, but she was able to barter several items in exchange for her knowledge of medical aid.

Machinist 18 built us a suitable dwelling near an isolated stream.

We stuck with what we knew. I scavenged and Enforcer 01 kept me safe while doing it. "Before the earth collapsed, what was your name?"

01 leans over, touching his lips to my ear.

I coil my hand around one of his fingers, satisfied with his response.

"But that is for you to know, and only for you to use when you are under me."

He'll get no argument on my end.

The road ahead is uncertain, but I don't question whether it's dangerous because I no longer live in fear. Enforcer 01 will protect me, just as he always has.

DIRK DARINGMORE
and the Vanishing Archaeologist

Written by

Nicholas Walls

There were many strange and wondrous things in the galaxy. Amidst all the Inter-Galactic Republic's thousand worlds, some phenomenon remained as yet beyond the reach and understanding of the interstellar society.

Dirk Daringmore hated the mysteries for that. "Insolent mysteries, defying the Republic's scientists. Well, where the lab boys fail, Dirk Daringmore will prevail!"

"Who are you talking to?"

Dirk turned from where he'd been heroically posing, leg propped on a rock and looking into the distance, perturbed at the interruption. They recently had, after all, searched for just the right spot for almost fifteen minutes before finding it. It took real effort to ensure a properly dramatic posture.

Dirk glared at his traveling companion, a tall youth with the uneven tan lines of one accustomed to the outdoors. Dressed in loose tan fatigues, quite in contrast to Dirk Daringmore's crisp Republic issued blue and red uniform, he was as dotted as Daringmore with the orange dust so common to these dry lands. The lad stood next to two Oruques, four-legged shaggy mounts that lived in the dry region.

Still, no need to upset the natives, Dirk told himself. *They don't know any better*. "Don't trouble yourself, Hakim! A young local lad like you need not worry about such things. I only need you to focus on guiding us through this dusty land to find the lost Doctor Irvingston!" Dirk pronounced the last as if it were a quest for the lost colony of Camelot itself.

The tall youth frowned. "For the last time, Mr. Daringmore, my name is Aarobi and I'm a student, not some uncultured tour guide. I'm only helping you find Doctor Irvingston because the University asked me to."

Dirk chuckled quietly. *What silliness these locals concoct.* "Of course, Sanjay. Now lead on."

Biting his tongue, Aarobi turned their shaggy mounts and led them deeper into the Stormy Quarters.

***

The Stormy Quarters were a patch of dry, rocky land on the planet of M'Qual. A land fraught with myths and rumor, a land of mystery and subject to much debate, much like the Bermuda Triangle of Old Earth. The rocky valleys and peaks earned their name due to the frequent electromagnetic disturbances, jolts of blue lightning arcing between orange tinted stone pillars. The region played havoc with radios, compasses and other electronic device caught in its pull. Modern science had yet to explain the strange phenomenon. As such, the University of M'Qual established a permanent facility to further the advancement of knowledge and provide a basecamp for students and faculty to explore the lightning haunted Quarters.

All of which Aarobi excitedly explained to his gaudily dressed, and now profusely sweating, traveling companion. Being a pragmatic minded military man, Dirk asked the obvious question.

"Yes, yes, very fascinating. Why don't they simply bombard it from orbit like civilized folk?"

Aarobi looked horrified at the prospect. "It's an important scientific find! I've been up and down these valleys for years and still haven't mapped all of its twists and turns, much less unraveled the mysteries of its catastrophic effect on advanced technology."

Dirk tugged at his collar, struggling to deal with the heat that treacherously assaulted the officer. "Exactly."

"Exactly...what? I don't follow."

"This place is a nest of recidivism and rebellion. It destroys Republic property, offers countless hiding places for enemy agents, and refuses to allow good old Republic science to investigate it properly. If it had nothing to hide, it wouldn't resist our exploration."

Aarobi gaped in stupefied wonder for a moment, desperately trying to follow Dirk's self-evident logic, before turning away and riding in silence. Dirk nodded to himself, satisfied. With a bit of work, he would instill proper Republic values in this backwards provincial!

***

Despite the day's determined attempts to undermine his dignity, Dirk Daringmore proved as resilient to heat stroke as common sense. Furthermore, the decorated veteran's favorite method to beat the heat involved allowing hot air to escape him by endlessly regaling his captive audience with tales of his heroism.

Which sounded suspiciously like larceny, assault, arson, and worse besides to the untrained ear.

"...and then I kicked the little bugger out an airlock. Hah! You should have seen his fuzzy face. He was practically begging me not to flush him out into space. Probably should have thought of that before he tried stowing away aboard my ship!"

"But didn't he only stowaway because your fleet bombarded his homeworld, destroying his home and everything he loved?"

"Yes, but I fail to see what that has to do with anything. That's no excuse for invading my ship! Really, when you think about it, it's a home invasion. A ship is a man's home away from home! I had a right to stand my ground."

"You said he was only four feet tall and unarmed."

"Quite. That certainly made my job easier. The fuzzy monster should have come prepared. It's alright. A provincial lad like you wouldn't understand."

Aarobi's incredulous and inventive strings of curses were cut off by a sudden crash as a lightning storm race through the canyons, streams of dancing energy roaring just overhead. Both looked up, squinting at the bright lights, mesmerized by the intricate play of the crackling forces. Blue actinic light raced along orange rock and their shadows were thrown against stone walls in a dizzying kaleidoscope.

For a time, both sat silently, watching nature's play before shaking themselves out of the hypnotized stupor. One, such as the aspiring scientist Aarobi, might presume that Daringmore would see the value and beauty in the Stormy Quarters. The first uttered word of Dirk bolstered that belief.

"Incredible."

Then the captain continued in indignant tones and dashed the college student's hopes.

"Incredible that this place would add 'mind control' and 'attempted assassination of a Republic officer' to its list of crimes!"

"What in the name of the Uncounted Nebula are you talking about?"

Dirk turned to his poor, slow-witted companion, shocked at the boy's thickness. "You witnessed it first hand, Hakim. That lightning nearly came down right on top of me and when, in its ineptitude, it couldn't reach me, it tried to entrance me with its dancing lights." The recently demoted-for-criminal-acts-against-sapient-species-and-their-livestock officer scoffed. "They underestimated the iron will of Dirk Daringmore."

"But it's a storm, it happens naturally."

"Does it, Narobi? Does it? Doesn't it strike you as odd that the lightning occurred just as we happened through?"

Aarobi's befuddled look caused Dirk to worry that the lightning had entranced the youth. Dirk's hand inched toward his blaster. It wouldn't be the first comrade Dirk had put down, it wouldn't be the last. Regrettable, true, but heroes like Dirk made the hard choices.

For his part, Aarobi plowed onward, oblivious to the homicidal plotting of his companion. "When the electrical storms occur frequently enough to give the Stormy Quarters its namesake, no, I really don't consider it odd."

Dirk sighed, bitterly disappointed in his companion. "Oh, Sanjay, I don't know what they teach you at universities these days."

Aarobi muttered some local benediction under his breath, one which Dirk recognized from his encounters at the spaceport.

"Hap'N'Quith Rom to you as well." Dirk said the insult with a broad smile on his face.

"What?"

"While I acknowledge your local customs are backwards and quaint, Dirk Daringmore certainly takes the time to learn about the natives, at least after my last mandatory cultural sensitivity course."

"Well. That's...good." Aarobi smiled broadly. That someone had taught Dirk to say "Look at me, I'm a jackass" in M'Qualli framed the whole expedition in a new light.

***

Dirk looked warily at the striated rock walls as they pressed deeper into enemy territory. Or at least Dirk treated it as such. He took some solace that the young student seemed just as interested in their surroundings, though Dirk feared it might not have been out of good wholesome paranoia. Dirk would hate to be slain because the boy cared too much about studying rocks and not enough about killing the enemies of his country.

"Stay sharp, Hajib. They have eyes everywhere."

The scholar's sigh was both deep and heartfelt, likely stemming from an inability to bear such strenuous combat missions. "I don't suppose you have any clue as to who this mysterious 'they' are?"

"Does it matter? The enemies of the Republic are numerous. The Golgathans, the Sleen Effrontery, errant tax accountants!"

Dirk initially mistook the grinding noise to be rocks scraping against one another. It took the Republic officer several turns to check for expected ambush to realize the noise came from his companion rather than the canyon walls. Specifically, his mouth. *Goodness*, thought Dirk, *he'll wear out his teeth doing that.*

"Allowing that is the case, shouldn't we be focused on locating traces of Doctor Irvingston? That is why we're out here after all."

Dirk's scornful laugh bounced through the canyon walls. "Vigilance never tires, my boy. Never lower your guard, even for an instant. It's what 'they' want!"

The grinding intensified. "And Doctor Irvingston?"

"Humph. Yes. Quite. Let's find him, too. Probably kidnapped or in cahoots with the enemy. Possibly BOTH. Yes, we will have to be extra vigilant."

Dirk politely chose to ignore the quiet whimpered mutterings of his young guide, who leaned over his mount with head in hands. *A pity the boy could be unmanned so easily. Perhaps a mercy killing is in order. It seems only fair. Can't have him jeopardize the mission at a critical moment.* Dirk's hand wandered back to his firearm. Deciding to give the lad one more chance, Dirk held off on his pre-emptive euthanasia.

They continued on in this fashion, winding deeper and deeper into the echoing, brightly colored rocks. Storms came and went, entire galaxies of sparks bloomed and died above their heads. Sadly, the beauty was lost on both sojourners. Dirk continued his one-sided tirade, hoping to keep the scout distracted from the burdens of the journey and instill wholesome virtues in him at the same time. Multi-tasking was one of Dirk's skills.

Any halfhearted objections by his companion were swiftly quashed, bowled over by the Republic officer's endless verbal harangues. Aarobi grew listless and haggard, bludgeoned by the flood of platitudes and insane invectives against man, woman, and beast. Not that Dirk noticed his companion's moods. Determination, particularly of the blind variety, was one of Dirk's virtues.

Some miles of winding trotting under this endless monologue and Aarobi let out a blood curdling yell, lashed his mount into a gallop, and bolted into the canyons.

"That's the spirit, Sanjay! Finally, some enthusiasm. Charrgggeee!"

Dirk followed suit, convinced his guide was getting into the swing of things. The two wound through the caverns at break neck speeds, taking turns without a clue where they were going. Some might have said they were utterly lost. Dirk preferred to call it scouting in force.

The chase ended abruptly with Aarobi pulling his mount to a halt in a dead end. Dirk, being less familiar with the beasts, went flying when his came to an abrupt stop.

To the surprise of many, including the mounts, the sweaty blue and red comet hit the wall, not with a splat, but a sighing glide as the seemingly solid slab fell open without a hint of resistance.

After a moment of gape mouthed awe, wavering between shock, relief, and muted disappointment, Aarobi approached the newfound hole in the striped orange wall.

"Mr. Daringmore, are you all right?"

"Hahaha! Dirk Daringmore is not easily disposed of! Good instincts, Sanjay. I knew you were the scout for the job. Always rely on the natives' primitive instincts, that's my advice." The thunderous confirmation of Daringmore's continued health elicited a complicated relief and bitter regret in the college student.

Dirk chose to take the mumbled inconsequentialities of his young ward as affirmation of Daringmore's wisdom. The officer looked around the unexpected alcove with a practiced eye, blaster drawn. A network of tunnels yawned outward, only the sunlight from his impromptu opening and tiny torches dotting the area created tiny circles of light.

This was enough for Dirk to consider it confirmation of an enemy presence.

"Ah ha! We've snuck into their stronghold from an unexpected quarter. Quickly, private, move out. Now is the time to strike."

Aarobi stood rooted outside, holding the reigns of the ugly beasts that bore them to the tunnels. "Mr. Daringmore, I'm not a member of the Republic military. I'm a student, a scientist."

"Dire times call for dire measures, son. You've just been conscripted. Welcome to the Republic Armed Forces."

"I'm pretty sure that's illegal..."

Any further protests were cut short by the humming barrel of Daringmore's blaster leveled at his chest. "Desertion is punishable by summary execution, Jahrobi. Now get in here and take point."

Without further argument, the khaki and cobalt duo marched into the unknown, albeit one more enthusiastically than the other.

***

"Fascinating" was not a word Dirk would use for the labyrinth of tunnels they found themselves wandering but it seemed to be his scouts favorite description of the situation they were in. By the fifteenth time they'd stop to examine some new bit of dusty rock or other, Dirk decided discipline had to be reasserted.

At gunpoint and via pistol whipping.

"Ow! Why did you do that?" The khaki-clad collegiate looked up in shock and hurt, earning a second whipping to put some steel in the lad's spine.

"Pay attention, private! We aren't here to look at some privative cave dweller's carvings. We are here to look for enemy action."

"Mr. Daringmore...I mean sir..." A threatened third smack from Dirk's gun ensured proper protocol was enforced. "This IS evidence of, ah, enemy action. These carvings are incredibly ancient, possibly thousands of years old."

Dirk gasped, aghast. "The enemy has been here that long?"

"No, not what I meant. These carvings indicate an advanced society right here in the Stormy Quarter, one which predates our oldest records. A whole lost civilization dwelling amidst this desolate land. And we had no idea...."

Dirk sniffed. "We can discuss your lax vigilance later."

"...Except for Dr. Irvingston, of course. It was his pet project. We all thought he was mad."

"Confound it! This proves it. Collusion with the enemy, right under our noses."

Aarobi nodded absently, engrossed in the stone carvings. "So many of his notes make sense now." A delicate finger stabbed at a series of spirals and swirls, surrounded by and interlaced by jagged lines. "Here, you can see where it started, the motif of the storms. They repeat over and over until here, it comes to represent a cycle of it. A perfect repeated cycle. Almost as if they could harness the storms. If they could tap the Stormy Quarters' electrical tempests, why, that would be virtually limitless power. All within a pre-fusion society!"

"Which means they must have a superweapon hidden away to unleash at the hapless Republic. Come Sanjay, time is of the essence."

Daringmore yanked the academic to his feet by the collar frog marched them through the torch lit gloom, one hand at Aarobi's neck while the other kept his pistol firmly lodged in the student's back for encouragement.

***

"That is a big hole."

Aarobi's astute observation referred to the abyssal pit the two intrepid explorers found themselves standing in front of, a small wood and rope bridge stretching across its pitch black depths. Only the flicker of torches on the other side proved there was an end to the chasm.

"You first, chum."

"Me? Why? Aren't you the brave hero, as you've told me so many times?"

"Indeed I am and good for you for paying attention. Some of my heroism might rub off on you yet. No, you are going first because I, being bigger and more strapping, might snap the bridge."

Aarobi looked at his companion with an arched eyebrow. "Really?"

"Of course. That and I have the blaster." Dirk wiggled the raygun for emphasis.

Argument settled, Aarobi moved cautiously onto the worn rope bridge, gingerly stepping on the wooden planks. The whole thing creaked and groaned, swaying ominously.

"Are you sure this is safe?"

"No. But we men of action laugh in the face of danger."

Dirk, seeing his young ward needed further encouragement, stepped up behind him, aged wood groaning ominously. The barrel of Dirk's blaster in the back worked wonders as well. The Republic officer trusted its motivating potential.

Gulping audibly, Aarobi continued onward, hands white-knuckled on the coarse rope hand rails. Step by faltering step the pair marched out to the other side.

"See, my boy? Nothing to worry about." Dirk gave Aarobi a comradely slap on the back. Alas for the reedy academic, the blow sent him sprawling to the wooden planks. The tension proved too much for the venerable bridge and the rope began to fray.

Keen senses alert for danger, Dirk acted as an officer and gentleman should. "Every man for himself!" Stomping over his fallen comrade, Daringmore dashed for solid ground. Daringmore's boots hit bare rock just as the bridge gave way, dropping Arrobi into the sygian depth and the tattered wooden remains slammed against the rock wall with a dusty thump.

"Poor lad. Your sacrifice won't be forgotten...Hakim? Sanjay? Bah. No matter. Dirk Daringmore will persevere in your name...whatever it is."

Taking a moment to smooth his hair and dust off his boots, Dirk marched jauntily onward.

***

Dirk entered the vile heart of darkness under cover of nightfall. Well, it counted as nightfall in the tunnels since there was no sun. The evils Dirk witnessed there left no doubt as to the righteousness of his goals. Carved stone ziggurats dotted a cavern large enough to house a Republic battle cruiser. Torches lit clean thoroughfares and everywhere, brightly clad pallid folks walked and talked quietly with one another, smiles and handshakes abounded. Lightning danced among high towers, new sparks racing from the stone above to glowing orbs and into homes, light radiating from devices within.

Such peaceful nonchalance only highlighted the arrogance and decadence of the enemy.

"Think you're safe from Republic justice, fiends? Think again!"

Dirk's monologue echoed from the stone outcropping he crouched upon, to the befuddled looks of many of the local inhabitants. They pointed and gasped at the strange pompodoured figure looming above them.

"Well, since infiltration has failed....ATTACK!"

The crowd scattered as the screaming Dirk Daringmore leapt off his stone outcropping, gun blasting away. Dirk rampaged through town to the babbling protests of the inhabitants, indiscriminately annihilating all foes of the Republic he saw, such as several lampposts, more than a few garbage cans, and a handful of darkly vined shrubbery.

"Plants without sunlight? Surely an atrocity!"

"Young man, what exactly do you think you are doing?"

The voice, cultured, outraged, and speaking crisp Galactic Common, brought Dirk up short in his horticultural genocide. He turned to see a short, frumpy looking fellow with a winter white handlebar mustache as bright as his skin was dark, wearing the same khaki dress as Dirk's now deceased scout.

"Dr. Irvingston, I presume?"

"Indeed, I am! Who are you and why in the name of all creation are you blasting away down here? You are interrupting a very important first contact scenario."

"First contact?"

"Indeed! These are the fabled U'quithi people of legend, the "Stormbound" in Galactic Common. You see, the name denotes a fascinating interconnectedness between…"

"Are you certain they aren't enemies of the Republic?" Dirk's finger twitched, half convinced that the good doctor had gone native.

"Quite certain!"

Their stimulating intellectual exchange was interrupted by the cries of the cave-dwelling populace. A group of them slowly walked forward, calling to Dr. Irvingston. As they got closer, Daringmore could see his fallen comrade being carried on a stretcher.

"Sanjay! You survived!"

"It's Aarobi, you jackass, and no thanks to you!"

"Poppycock. Freak accident. Nothing more could have been done."

"You trampled me!"

"In my haste to get us both to safety, of course. I did everything I could."

At this point, Irvingston finished conversing with the pallid pall-bearers and leaned forwards to glance at the stretched bound youth, squinting as he adjusted his glasses. "Aarobi? The second-year student or Masshi's?"

Aarobi looked pathetically happy to see another familiar face. "Dr Irvingston! You're alive! This place...all your theories...it's all real!"

"Yes, my boy. A lifetime of study, all leading to this. It is a dream come true. Don't worry, we will have you out of here in a jiffy."

"Umm...professor...I'm afraid the bridge leading out is gone."

"Besides." Interjected Dirk Daringmore, hero of the Intergalactic Republic. "With such a delicate first contact, having such a renowned figure as myself at hand will be sure to aid diplomatic relations. It's a good thing I was here, my young ward, else we never would have had such a momentous opportunity. Ahh, I truly am amazing. Hero, Man of Science, Diplomat."

Daringmore stared off into the distance, grinning from ear to ear and already imagining the camera opportunities, even as his travelling companion fainted dead away in horror.

The Lady and the Hunter

Written by

T. M. Lowe

The itching and tickling is going to send me into madness at this rate, but I have to wait just a little bit longer. It's the one big downside of fishing. There are several upsides and I choose to focus on those instead: the nice haul of goods, treasure, and meat the village will provide Aideen and me in exchange for us helping them gather a larger amount of fish, crabs, and oysters than they ever could have in the past in those tiny, little dingy boats of theirs.

Another upside to this fishing deal is spending time with Aideen, doing something we both enjoy together. It's funny to think about, this cranky old dragon and a runaway princess. Had someone told me such a friendship would form, I'd have laughed them out of my cave and chased them with a gout of flame for the presumptuous insult. Now? I enjoy her company. I am happy she chose to stay.

Rather ironic that we're now fishing for the very same village that tried to sacrifice her to me so that I would stop eating their livestock. Heh. I guess life is funny like that sometimes. Not that it was easy at first. Aideen had to talk to their leader for a long time. Many times. And much of the village still hides when we come to fish for them, but a few more poke their heads out of their huts each visit in, I assume, curiosity.

My favorite upside is the salt water, though. It was especially helpful to soak in it right after my injury. The prince's lance tore my right shoulder up something fierce and Aideen did what she could to mend it, but it hasn't been quite right since. I have a bit of a limp now and can't fly for as long as I used to, which is why it's nice we can fish together. We so loved our flights together – and still do; it's simply a little different now. A little harder. Vexing, but it is what it is.

The sea has helped keep infection from rotting my shoulder and now all my skin has sealed back over the wound. It's left quite a nasty scar, which is fine. Builds character. Makes me look like a survivor- tough and mean, you don't want to pick a fight with me! But it will always be vulnerable because once a dragon loses scale, well... Those don't grow back.

Ack! Confound it, this *really* is maddening. I am good at fishing because the creatures are drawn to me whenever I swim out here. They like to pick and clean between my scales. When I feel enough have gathered around me, I signal to Aideen to pull up the cinches and the nets floating around me, trapping the fish inside. But, until then, I have to endure the tickling of their tiny mouths against my skin. I want so badly to shiver and swat them away. I hate being touched by others; but if I move, it will scare the fish away from the nets and we'll have to start all over again.

So, I remain perfectly still. My body bobs with the small waves, my wings stretched out to help me float and soak up the lovely warmth of the sun. I look around with only my eyes, keeping my head and neck motionless. The sunlight sparkles on the water like diamonds spread out across the ocean. It's really quite beautiful. I could sit and watch it all day, I believe. If I wasn't so attached to my old cave, with my treasure and Aideen's wall paintings, I might consider finding a nice cave down here along the shoreline.

Ah, there we are! An entire school of fish has found me and gone into a cleaning frenzy against my scales. In one fluid, slow motion, I raise my head to look straight up at the sky, pointing my snout at the sun. Aideen yanks on the cords and I can feel the nets close up against my sides. The fish panic, trying to swim away and bouncing the nets against me, but it's fruitless. They are ours now.

I kick and paddle my legs, bringing us towards the white, sandy beach. My right shoulder twinges a little, but the warm water helps to soothe it.

A small crowd of villagers has gathered today and they cheer as I haul in our bounty. They babble in that strange human tongue of theirs, but I can recognize a few odd words here and there, thanks to Aideen teaching me. Her name and mine are said a few times in the conversation as the workers detach the nets from me and take them away.

One of the small men... no, wait, what is the word? Humanling? Like a hatchling not full grown to a dragon, but what is the human equivalent? Child! That's it. A child approaches me with wide eyes.

"Pestifar?" he says, an upward inflection indicating that he has a question for me.

I look down at him and bow my head once.

"... you... crab?" he asks.

I only catch the words I know in his sentence, but it's enough for me to understand. He saw the fish, but wants to know if I brought any crab. Not yet, little one. Aideen and I fish first. Diving for the crab cages disturbs the water so much that we quickly learned to catch the fish before doing anything else. The crab can wait.

"Crab come soon," I croak out, enunciating each word as carefully as I can. It's hard. My tongue and lips do not move in the same way as the humans, so their language is challenging to me.

I lower myself to the ground and Aideen slides off my back, removing the rest of the ropes and trappings so that I am free of all burdens. She smiles up at me and pats my forearm with her gloved hand. I bobble my shoulders and give her a little warbling trill in return. She laughs softly, then turns and walks toward the village proper.

I return to the sea, wading out into the deeper water. There are rock formations that rise up and stick out of the inlet in various places along the coastline, and I use these as markers for remembering where the crab traps are laid. I take a deep breath, close my nostrils, and dive. When I open my eyes, my inner eyelids slide into place. It makes things a little murky to see, but keeps the salt water out.

Near the bases of the towering rocks, clumps of oysters like to form. I visit them first, grabbing onto a cluster with my scaled talon and breaking it off in a large chunk. I spin around and locate the crab traps. A piece of rope is tied to the top of each one, making it easier for me to grab them as I swim past. Holding the oyster batch in my right talon and the crab trap ropes in my left, I beat my wings and hind legs.

I surface and take a fresh breath. Heh. That's always fun, diving around and flying underwater. I grab the ropes with my teeth to free up one of my talons and swim back to shore. The villagers titter with excitement again and rush up to take the rewards of my ocean harvesting. The child who had asked me about the crab earlier claps his hands together, cheering. I snort a draconic chuckle at that.

The men and women begin sorting through the traps. I look up and sweep my eyes around the village, trying to locate Aideen. I don't see her. Which I don't like, but I also don't panic. This village has been good to us and I trust the humans in it.

Huh, that feels odd to think for a moment. A dragon trusting humans? Strange world, but there it is. I suppose the reverse is true as well, though. The villagers probably think it odd to trust a dragon. Especially one who still thinks their livestock is tasty.

"Pestifar!"

The man's voice pulls my attention back down to my feet. He holds up a crab to me. It looks like the largest one from the haul. This pleases me. I give him a toothy grin and accept the offering, lowering my head towards him and opening my mouth. He's a bit hesitant - smart of him, you should never be entirely comfortable with putting your hands in a dragon's mouth - but lays the crab on my tongue. When his limbs are clear of me, I bite down with a satisfying crunch, enjoying the taste of the sweet meat inside the shell.

I swallow and open my eyes again, and I spot Aideen near the village's stables. I did not recognize her at first, but her long, red hair - the same bright shade as my scales - gives her away in an instant. She has chosen to change her garments while I was diving, dressed now in riding leathers and a green top rather than her old, well-worn green dress.

She beckons me over. I oblige.

There are a few horses milling around inside the fence line, but they whicker nervously and push to the far end of the stables when I approach. A man steps out from the nearby building and walks up to my lady. He holds a saddle, but the harnesses are much longer and look far more intricate and complicated. Aideen and the villager exchange words, then she motions for me to crouch down.

Ah. I see where this is going now. A replacement for the simple rope-and-blanket saddle she had fashioned for me back when we first began flying together.

There is a blanket still involved, I spy from the corner of my eye, but it is better-shaped for the saddle she places upon it. This actually feels a bit less awkward, though being saddled at all will never feel quite natural, I suspect. The straps are also padded and *that* feels like a wonderful change from those chafing ropes.

Aideen finishes tightening all the belts and loops and harnesses. Pfffft, glad she can make sense of all that leatherwork. It looks a mess to me, but at least I'm not the one having to put it on myself. She points up, asking me to stand. Odd. Doesn't she want to give the new saddle a sit? How is she going to do that if I'm not crouched down for her to climb up my side?

I do as she wills and stand to my full height. The lady gives me an appraising look. Then, she catches me off-guard by jumping up and grabbing something on the left-side strap. It gives her enough of a hold that she pulls up and hooks a foot into another strap, then shimmies into place in the saddle.

Huh. That's a pretty neat trick. And I won't argue with not having to always crouch and rise, especially now that my right shoulder likes to scold me for doing that too often for its new liking.

Aideen pats my left shoulder and points towards the center of the village. I follow her lead and walk us over. The leader of the village meets us there, and he and Aideen speak to each other. Several large crates are brought forth and opened for inspection. I see a few containing what certainly smells like wrapped meats and others containing those jars of food she likes. The remaining crates look to hold various goods, clothing, paints, books, and the like.

A glint of gold catches my eye and I cock my head to gain a better viewing angle. Ah, yes, some coins and jewelry to add to my hoard and... oh, what's this? I reach down and grab the oddly-shaped object between the claws of my thumb and forefinger, lifting it up. A golden chalice with silver engraving, studded with precious stones. A happy trill escapes me and I hear a few of the humans chuckle.

I bobble my shoulders in excitement and carefully place the cup back into its crate. That will make a fine addition to my treasure hoard. Very fine.

The villagers seal the wooden boxes back up and place them into fishing nets. Then, they motion me forward and I place myself between the two lines of netted crates. I crouch as low to the ground as I can. Ropes are thrown across my back and the crates are then secured to the ropes. When I stand back up, I shift my weight on my legs, testing the waters. The crates are evenly distributed, and I nod in satisfaction.

Aideen waves a farewell to the gathered crowd and I start our journey home. It would be faster to fly, but between the earlier efforts of diving and swimming plus the extra weight I am carrying, I feel too tired to make the effort. And I don't want to aggravate my shoulder any more than I have to today, all things considered. Walking is fine, if not quite as exhilarating.

Right at the turn where the forest path begins to climb up the mountain, I hear a scream and then a roar. A dragon roar. A female dragon roar.

"It hurts! Get it off, get it off, get it off!"

Aideen gasps and I bound off in the direction of the yells.

There is a quiet, tranquil pond nearby. It attracts a lot of deer and a lot of bear, which means it also attracts a lot of hunters. I generally avoid it since I know the area, but if a dragon isn't a local, I can see how it might look like an inviting place to grab a drink and a quick nap.

I crash through the brush and into the clearing of the pond. As I suspected, someone got caught. The green-scaled female thrashes about in rage and panic. Her left front talon is caught in a bear trap that appears anchored admirably well into the ground. She should be able to rip free of it eventually, but that will likely mean losing some fingers or possibly the whole talon itself.

"Keep away from me!" she shrieks. "Get back! I'll kill you! You did this to me!"

Wait, what? She can't possibly be addressing me, can she? I just got here.

The green shifts directions and spews fire at the ground to her right.

Oh, I see now. A human male in black clothing, sporting a bow and quiver of arrows on his back. He has his hands held out in front of him, trying to placate the female dragon.

Heh. Good luck with that, son.

"I WILL END YOU!"

More flames, and the hunter shows an impressive degree of athleticism by rolling out of the way.

"… … … help you!" he shouts at her.

I only catch some of that, and I'm sure she understands none at all.

So, she's caught in a trap that may or may not have been originally set by that hunter. And the hunter may be genuinely trying to help her out of the goodness of his human heart or he is more likely lying so he can get closer for the kill.

Yeah, no. No good will come of this. We should go.

I turn to take us back on the path home to our cave when Aideen slaps my shoulder. I swivel my head around and growl at her.

"No," I intone. "No good." This is dangerous and none of our business to get wrapped up in.

My lady pins me with a withering glare nearly equal to my own.

"Help," she says, pointing back to the chaos.

Um, no. Seriously. This is *not* happening. Aideen can point and babble at me all she wants to, but I am my own dragon and can make my own decisions. If she thinks for a moment that she's in command of me, she's got another think coming. And we are not getting involved in whatever *that* is back there.

Green cries out again, her voice now filled with pain more than panic or rage. "Go away, go away! It hurts, someone help me... my child... what will become of my child?"

The desperate, haunting call of a fearful mother. It is not just her own life tangled up in this trap, it would seem.

I close my eyes and sigh. Deeply. Loudly. Helplessly. Aideen does not understand what the dragon is crying. The hunter probably doesn't either. But I do.

I am my own dragon, and I can make my own decisions.

I turn back around and return to the pond. Green is still fighting the trap to free herself. The hunter is still trying to approach, but she kicks out at him and keeps him at bay.

"Hello, Green," I call out to her amiably, "we're here to help."

"Stay back!" she shouts. "Stay away from me, Red."

She's in a state of panic and lashing out at everything, but she cannot escape this situation on her own. I have to get her to see that.

"Green," I continue, "I want to help you out of that trap. I want to help you and your child."

That gets her attention. She stares at me, not with a single ounce of trust in her eyes, but at least she appears to be listening now.

"But in order to help you," I reason, "I need you to remain still. And I need you to focus on me instead of the humans."

"There's more than one?" she asks in alarm and then freezes as she notices Aideen on my back. "You're in league with them! You've been enslaved! Ensorcelled!"

I really can't get mad at her. I would have thought the same thing of a saddled dragon consorting with humans, back before Aideen befriended me.

"I am not, but I know you won't believe me," I answer. "However, you are trapped and your child is doomed unless you let us help you. There is no other choice here, no other option. You know this."

She snorts at me, nostrils flaring. She is frustrated, I'm sure. The green dragon looks from me to the hunter to Aideen to me again with wild eyes.

"Help you," my lady calls out to Green.

The dragon glares at her as if she would eat the woman if my body wasn't in the way.

"It's pointless, she can't understand you..." I start to explain to Aideen. Then I stop and realize that she isn't going to understand me either because I was speaking to her in the dragon tongue. What a headache to try and go back and forth between my language with Green and the limited vocabulary I have of Aideen's people.

"You understand that human?" Green asks, accusation and disgust in her voice. "You speak with her?" She flinches, probably with a new wave of pain in her talon.

"I know a few words, yes," I answer. "And she wants to help you, not hurt you. Look. She helped mend a wound on me." I point to my scarred shoulder. "A human's lance. Aideen, my lady, slew the knight who did it and healed my hurt. She can heal you, too. But you have to let us first."

Green looks conflicted. Water gathers in her eyes and her breathing becomes labored. "I don't know," she mumbles, maybe to me, maybe only to herself. "I don't know. Humans do not help dragons. Humans only hurt us, kill us."

"Some, yes," I agree. "Not all. Not Aideen. Maybe not him either." I point to the hunter, who stands watching but does and says nothing. I briefly wonder what this must look like to him, two dragons grumbling and growling to each other.

The female dragon moans and whimpers, pulling at the bear trap. "Okay," she whispers, bowing her head and shivering.

"Aideen, help," I tell my lady, automatically crouching to the ground to let her off me before remembering the new saddle lets her do that on her own.

She swings down and approaches Green. The hunter walks up beside her and the two exchange human words. I watch Green, ready at a moment's notice to tackle her if she shows any sign of aggression towards my lady. That's when I notice what she meant by her child. I had thought, perhaps, she had a young hatchling hidden in a den somewhere. But she is not that far along yet in the course of nature. Her belly is heavy with an egg. She still needs to lay and hatch it.

Aideen and the hunter kneel down on either side of the dragon's talon. They each grab a side of the trap and carefully pull back. When the pressure releases, Green yanks her talon out and the humans let it close shut again. Green whimpers, holding her trembling talon low for Aideen to see.

It's bad. Really bad. The trap had bit deep and two of the dragon's digits are barely attached. Her thrashing around hadn't helped at all, I am sure.

Aideen looks up at me, frowning deeply. "Cave," she says, then points to each of us in turn. "All go cave."

It's my turn to frown. Green will have trouble walking, and I don't understand why the hunter has to come with us at all. But I started this, so there is no turning back now.

I back up from the group, crouch low so that the supply crates on either side of me touch the ground, and wriggle forward again to slip loose from the ropes. That is added weight I don't need right now.

At Aideen's confused expression, I point to the crates and say, "Come back soon."

She nods, and I return to her side, lowering myself down again. My lady climbs aboard, then offers her hand down to the hunter. He looks at us with wide, frightened eyes and shakes his head. Aideen says something to him. Looking reluctant, he grasps her hand and she helps him up behind her on the saddle.

"Come, Green, let me help you," I offer, slipping around to her left side.

She looks at me, uncertainty in her eyes. "Where are we going?"

"To my cave," I reply. "Aideen has her healing tools there and you will be safe. Your child will be safe."

"Why are you doing this?" she asks suspiciously.

And it's a valid question. We dragons are generally loners by nature, only coming together to continue the species and then parting ways once again. A female dragon would typically find a den to herself and hatch her child alone. And once that hatchling grew large enough, it would go out and make a life of its own as well.

Somewhere along the way, when I got mixed up with Aideen, I had lost my natural taste for solitude. But that wasn't going to be an easy answer for a fearful dragon to hear.

"I don't know," I finally answer, "but are you really going to reject the help right now?"

She shakes her head and wraps her left arm around my shoulders, holding her wounded talon lamely in the air and leaning her weight against my right shoulder. I bite back the grunt of pain. Of all sides, my right is not the best to be supporting two dragons, but it can't be helped at the moment.

It's a slow, hobbling road we walk, but we finally reach my cave entrance at the top of the mountain. I help Green to the uncluttered side of the cave and she lies down. Aideen climbs down and the hunter follows in her footsteps. The lady runs to the corner of the cave where she keeps her garments and retrieves a kit I recognize – it's the one she uses to mend old clothing and repair tears.

Oh, this will be tricky. Sewing clothing is one thing. Sewing a strange dragon will be entirely another.

I sit on my haunches in front of Green and rest what I hope is a comforting talon on her right shoulder. "This will hurt," I warn her as

Aideen kneels next to the dragon's ravaged talon, "but it's the only way to heal this much damage."

To her credit, Green handles herself well as my lady works. She closes her eyes and whimpers at points, but makes no move to harm the humans. The hunter hovers nearby, assisting Aideen when she babbles to him. When it's over, the lady wraps the dragon's talon tightly in fresh cloth, both covering the wounds and immobilizing the digits from moving while they heal.

Aideen puts away her kit and the hunter continues to hover around as if unsure what to do with himself. I glance at the cave entrance and see that it's nearly dark outside now. We're all here for the night, at least.

Green sighs. "If it's all the same to you," she says, exhaustion in her voice, "I'd like to sleep now."

I nod.

"And..." she continues hesitantly, "thank you, I suppose."

"You're welcome," I respond, "I suppose."

Green chortles.

I smile.

Over in the corner, Aideen and the hunter are babbling very quickly. Sometimes intensely, with raised voices. He seems to say many things to her, and my lady responds in ways that make me very uncomfortable. At some things he says, she looks very troubled. As if receiving bad news or worrying tidings, but I know not what they are. And that bothers me. At other things, she smiles and gives him this... this bright, glowing sort of look. Almost the kind of look she gives me at times, such as when I bobble my shoulders and trill at her. I do not like sharing her look with him like that, but this is probably not my place or business either.

Still, it irks me.

Harumph. I'm tired, too. A bit hungry as well, but that can't be helped with no fresh catches and the supply crates left at the pond, so I go without. My right shoulder complains to me of the day's exertions, but I ignore it. I follow Green's idea and curl up in the opposite corner from everyone. Normally, my lady would join me, laying a blanket between us and settling up against my side. Instead, I spy her in the back of our cave, a small candle lit for light, still speaking with this hunter fellow. I frown and close my eyes. Harumph.

I do not know how much time passes, but I am brought out of my sleep by the sound of talking. As the fog in my mind lifts a little, I realize it is Green mumbling in her sleep. I can't make out any of the words. She isn't saying anything loud enough to actually be addressing anyone here. She's just... sleep-talking, apparently.

Great. Of course. Because that's exactly what we need.

I close my eyes again and try to ignore her.

I wake up once more when I hear moaning. This is too much, simply too much now! I might as well go sleep outside at this rate.

When my initial grumpiness at being rudely awoken again subsides, I recognize the pained voice as belonging to Green. I slither over to her in the dark, using the small bit of moonlight shining into the cave as a guide. She is no longer talking in her sleep. She is wide awake.

"Is it your wound?" I ask quietly, trying not to wake the humans.

She shakes her head. "It's time. I need a nest."

Oh. Wonderful. I'll go fetch one right away.

She grunts in pain, tensing up and curling in on herself. I feel completely helpless and honestly have no idea what to do. I've never seen an egg laid and have no clue what is involved.

"Aideen, help!" I call, then promptly feel stupid. My lady isn't going to have any more of an idea what a pregnant female dragon needs than I do, and I can't even try to explain the situation to her. I have no human words for "egg" or "nest".

But bless her, she comes running over with a candle to try and help anyway. Because I asked. She looks at the shivering Green, then at me with large, worried eyes. Silently asking me for guidance that I cannot give.

I sigh heavily, then try to think of a way to mime this to her. I pat my stomach, then hold my forelegs out as if showing it growing. I point to Green's stomach. She moans again, more loudly. Aideen's eyebrows draw together tensely, though I am not sure if it is from confusion at my clunky act or concern for Green.

"Dragon," I say to Aideen, pointing to Green's stomach again, then holding my talons barely apart. "Small. Come soon." Ah! There it is! "Small dragon come soon. Help." I say fully together, pointing to Green's swollen belly.

Aideen's eyes suddenly light up with an expression I easily recognize – it's her look of understanding, of solving a riddle. She rushes off to her corner of the cave where she stores her own hoard. In a few moments, she comes back with her arms full of blankets and clothing. She sets them down beside the female dragon and arranges them together, interlocking and weaving the materials until they form a sort of circle with an indentation in the middle. Huh. Perhaps she *does* know how to make a nest, assuming that's what she's created.

My lady taps Green's foreleg and points to the makeshift nest. The dragon cocks her head for a moment, then leans forward and pokes the blankets and clothing with her snout. She smiles, and rewards Aideen with a happy trill.

She then looks at me. "Your human is smarter than I would have thought."

"That she is," I answer with a nod. "That she is."

Green grimaces, then slowly pulls herself to her feet. "I suppose now is as good a time as any to lay it."

Aideen hovers nearby, probably waiting to see if she can be of any more assistance. Good. Because I want nothing to do with any of this.

I walk outside and sit on the ledge that overlooks the valley below. The stars are shining brightly tonight, and I gaze up at them to drink in the still calmness of the night. I can almost pretend that everything is normal and right with the world, save for the occasional grunts and groans emanating from my cave. Until my silent revelry is interrupted by the hunter walking out to join me. Oh, great. Bonding time? Just what I wanted. I certainly didn't come outside and leave everyone else in my cave because I wanted to be *alone* or anything.

I end my sigh with a grunt as I watch him from the corner of my eye. He looks up at me and clears his throat.

"Pestifar?"

I turn my head and look down at him. "Yes."

"You ... ... speak?"

"Small. Speak small."

He nods, smiling and chuckling to himself. That better have been a surprised laugh and not a mocking one.

"Cylen," he says, holding a hand to his chest and patting it. He points to me. "Pestifar." Then points back to himself "Cylen."

"Cylen," I acknowledge, nodding my head once.

"Yes!" he exclaims, smiling and laughing again. Then, he holds his hand out and up towards me.

I really don't like this guy. He is far too friendly far too quickly, and he is not Aideen. And she smiles at him too quickly as well. I like none of this nonsense.

The hunter's smile falters a bit when I leave his hand dumbly hanging in the air. After a moment, he awkwardly lowers it back to his side. He looks away, then back at me again. "Aideen loves you," he says. Then, he repeats it again, slowly, pointing to the cave then crossing his heart and pointing to me as he enunciates each word.

Yes, fine. I understood you the first time. I swear if he keeps talking to me in this manner, I am going to pick him up and squeeze until his spine makes a satisfying snap.

"I love Aideen," I reply. "I no love you."

The hunter's smile falls completely at that and it pleases me immensely. He babbles for a bit, but I can't make a lick of sense out of it, so I simply shake my head.

He frowns and babbles a few more things. "Aideen ... ... danger."

"What?" I shout more than ask, bristling.

But from what he says, I cannot understand anything other than there is some type of danger to Aideen. I do not know from where or when or from whom.

"You?" I ask, growling, impatient. "You danger Aideen?"

"No, no, no," he says. "I no danger Aideen."

Right words, but he says them too quickly. His face is red and he looks nervous. He is hiding something.

"You protect Aideen?" he asks. But he really doesn't ask. He says it without an inflection at the end, more like a statement.

"Yes."

"Good," he replies. "Soon, you protect Aideen. Soon."

That is incredibly cryptic and I do not like it. But we seem to be at a language barrier limit, so I likely won't get any further clarification than to be on my guard in the near future. A strange thing for him to know and impart. A messenger of some sort, perhaps, sent to seek out Aideen and warn her? I wonder again at who this hunter is, who just so happened to be near a trapped and injured dragon and offering help when she was trying to roast him alive. Does he have some ulterior motive here?

"Pestifar?"

I am given no further time to ponder it when Aideen calls for me from the cave entrance. I turn to look, and she beckons me to return. I do so, leaving the hunter to his thoughts.

Inside, Green looks exhausted, but has the largest smile on her face. She has curled herself around the nest of human trappings, which now has a large, green egg nestled inside the middle space. My lady excitedly points to the egg and babbles. Then, she announces, "Tikadon!"

Come again?

She repeats the word while carefully stroking the top of the egg.

Green lets out a few stunted chirps, chuckling. "Your human likes to name things, it seems," she explains. "She has apparently decided my child shall be called Tikadon."

"Sounds about right," I quip. "One of the very first things she did in this cave was determine I should have a name. So, Pestifar it is."

She snorted. "Not bad, I guess. She calls me Renji now, so that must be mine. Feels odd, you know? Dragons don't have names."

"Some of us do now, clearly," I answer. "Pfffft, maybe we're the special ones, haha!"

"Special or cursed?" Renji replies, chirping again. "We're human-touched now. Not sure how to feel about that."

"I've chosen to embrace it," I counter, enjoying the banter. And, frankly, enjoying the absence of pained noises. "It became clear early on that I was stuck with her, so it was either fight it or live with it."

Renji nods. Then, her look of exhaustion begins to claim the smile on her face.

"You should rest," I offer, which gives me an easy pass to try and sleep again as well.

She answers with a warbling trill and settles her head down on the stone floor. I bow my head to Aideen and curl back up in my corner to attempt sleep once again. Perhaps the third try will succeed this time.

I wake to sunlight filtering into our cave. The others appear to still be asleep, so I take the opportunity to slip out and attend to my needs. When I return, Renji has not yet stirred, but the humans have. I motion them to follow me back outside so as not to wake the sleeping mother.

I point to Aideen. "I fetch crates. You come? Cylen stays, protects?"

She looks thoughtful for a moment, then shakes her head. "I stay, protect. Cylen go."

Well, then. I hadn't quite expected *that* response. I blink at her a few times, not at all pleased with her decision. She and I always fly together. I do not like the idea of someone else in the saddle, especially someone I fail to trust. And I do not like the thought of leaving her alone in my cave again. Yes, there is another dragon present, but she is wounded and has newly laid an egg. She is vulnerable right now.

Regardless, Aideen saddles me up, the hunter grabs some rope and his weapon, and we take off. The crates are not too far away, down at the bottom of the mountain. But I am famished, so I opt to find us food first. Flying low, I sweep over the forest until it thins out into meadowland. This flushes out a herd of deer and the hunter is actually an impressive shot. He manages to down two doe while we're in flight before I even have a chance to breathe fire.

We land and I rip into one of the deer. While I eat, he secures the second doe to the back of the saddle to bring home to the ladies. I tear off a haunch from my deer, bake it in some quick dragon fire, and hand it to Cylen. He looks confused for a moment, but then thanks me.

After our shared meal, I fly us over to the pond where we met yesterday. Thankfully, the crates are still there and seemingly unmolested by thieves or poachers. Cylen assists me with getting them securely strapped on either side, and I walk us back up the mountain path at a steady pace.

When we get close to my cave, I slow down. Something doesn't smell right. I approach cautiously.

"Leave!" I hear Renji shout. "Or I will end you where you stand!"

"But, sweetheart," a male voice croons, "that egg in there... I'm sorry, but it smells weak. It may not survive. You should let me help take care of that for you. Maybe give you a nicer, stronger egg instead."

That voice. I recognize it. And a rage fills me like never before. My vision goes red and I storm over the remaining distance.

"Blue!" I yell. "I warned you once to leave and never return, or I would not ask kindly again."

The invading male turns suddenly, looking startled to see me, and immediately backpedals. "Red!" he calls out, as if in greeting. "My old friend! I didn't think you still lived here..."

"I do, and you've made your last mistake."

Something within Blue's eyes shifts. When I'd confronted him before, he had been craven and cowardly, begging and scuttling away. I do not know if the passage of time has changed him or if he realizes his life depends on his actions now, but he lunges at me instead of fleeing.

An arrow unexpectedly imbeds itself in Blue's left eye. He screeches.

Renji pounces on his hindquarters, sinking the claws of her right talon into Blue's flesh while keeping her bandaged left one held protectively against her chest. She bites into the base of his tail. He cries out and turns to defend himself.

From the corner of my eye, I spot Aideen leaping up to the saddle strap. It makes me wild inside to remain still when I need to leap into battle, but I've an idea of what she intends to do. And as I suspected, I feel the weight of the crates and deer carcass fall away as she uses her trusty dagger to cut the ropes binding them to me. She and Cylen dismount and retreat to the cave entrance, the hunter sending a few more arrows in Blue's direction.

I am unleashed! As Blue reaches back to swipe at Renji, I tackle him and we both go rolling across the ground, a tangle of limbs. I keep my wings pulled as tightly against my sides as possible to avoid injury to them. Blue snaps at my head, but I avoid him and kick his belly with a hind leg. He grunts and pulls us into a roll again, flapping his wings to try and pull free of me.

Bad decision.

Renji roars and tears through the membrane of his right wing. Blue bellows in fury and pain. He spins to fend her off and that's when I tackle him from behind. I shove him down into the stone of the mountain ledge and sink my teeth into the back of his neck.

Blue howls and thrashes, doing everything he can to try and slither free. I push against him with my full weight. From the corner of my eye, I spot Renji doing the same, pinning his hind legs down and keeping them from kicking out at me. I crush my jaw in as hard as I can until there is an audible crack. A few moments pass and Blue stops struggling.

I remain still a little longer, catching my breath. Renji tentatively backs away from Blue's body.

"Are you okay, Pestifar?" she asks.

I draw in one more long breath, close my eyes, and let it out. "I think so."

Then, I decide that I want this idiot's body out of my sight once and for all. I roll Blue to the very edge of my mountain perch and shove him off. His carcass disappears in the distant trees below with a satisfying thump. Let the wolves and wild dogs have that creep.

Life goes by in a sometimes awkward, sometimes pleasant blur after Blue's end. I am no longer quite as nervous about leaving Aideen or the others unattended in my cave now that the skulker is gone. Cylen and I go hunting for fresh game. Aideen and I go fishing for our regular trading runs with the seaside village. Renji's left talon heals and she watches over her egg.

Today, however, the current pattern changes. When Aideen and I leave our cave, there is the acrid smell of smoke blowing inland from the coastline. It makes me uneasy. When we come within sight of the fishing village, my fear is realized: it's on fire.

People are running in panicked circles, some fleeing into the nearby forest, others desperately fighting to put out the flames. Interspersed between the huts, working to light more thatched roofs on fire, are men dressed all in black. Wait, I recognize that outfit. I think. I swoop low and scoop one of the bastards up in my right talon. He screams and wriggles around, trying to escape.

Yup. He's wearing the *exact* same outfit that Cylen does.

I squeeze the man until his screams cease, then give him the escape from my grasp that he so desperately desired by tossing his remains into the woods.

I'm furious. That so-called "hunter" is back in my cave, possibly endangering Renji and her egg. But the village needs help and I'm here now, so I push Cylen to the back of my mind for the moment and focus on the task at hand.

With a mighty roar, I make my presence absolutely known for any who may have already missed my arrival. A few of the villagers look up at me and actually cheer and wave, as if I am their savior in this moment. I puff my chest out with pride, smiling. And then I dive in low and grab two more of the attackers. I squeeze the life out of them as well, then turn towards the sea.

After I dump their bodies for the fish and crab to enjoy, I land on the beach. Without a word, Aideen jumps off my saddle and breaks her fall by rolling into it on the sand. She unsheathes her dagger and runs towards the middle of the village.

"Aideen!" I call after her, not wanting her gone from my sight. Remembering Cylen's words about her being in danger. But she ignores me, bent on whatever her current mission may be.

I grumble and grab one of the small fishing boats, pulling it into deeper water and forcing it down. Once the boat is filled with seawater, I awkwardly drag it up the shoreline. It's a slower haul than I would like - it is too heavy for me to try and lift, not that I could walk on only my hind legs anyway - so I have to grasp the front with my right talon and sort of crab-walk sideways, pulling the combined weight with my stronger and non-cranky left foreleg and hind legs.

Finally, I arrive at one of the burning huts. I grasp either end of the boat with each front talon and heft it up and over like a giant bucket of water, dousing the flames. I smile when I see my plan work, then frown at the thought of repeating the trip. My right shoulder is already yelling at me.

I repeat this five more times until all of the fires in the village have been put out between my efforts and the villagers'. I'm exhausted and panting, and then I spot my lady talking with the village leader. I slowly amble over. As I walk, villagers approach me and pet my flanks. I hear a few say "thank you". I grin at them and let out a warbling trill. I hurt, but I did well today.

Aideen finishes her conversation and looks over at me. Her face is serious and grave. She climbs up the saddle straps and pats my shoulder. "Home," she orders.

Yes, ma'am. I'm thinking the same thing. My shoulder is screaming at me, I'm tired all the way down to my bones, but I cannot wait a moment longer to confront Cylen.

When we arrive back at my cave and the lady hops down, I immediately rush in. Renji is curled up with her egg and Cylen is reading a book. He looks up and smiles. I wipe it off his face when I pick him up and hold him inches from my teeth. He exclaims and babbles.

"You," I growl. "You danger Aideen!"

"No," he counters. "No danger."

"Pestifar," Aideen shouts. "No!"

"You danger," I repeat, grabbing his black clothing between the claws of my thumb and forefinger and tugging at it for emphasis.

Cylen goes silent.

I roar.

"STOP!" Aideen shouts, then punches my elbow to get my attention.

I look down at her, still enraged. She glares back at me and we're in a stand-off again.

"Maybe you should listen to her," Renji offers, her voice gentle and capitulating. "She is your friend, yes? Has she led you astray before?"

It pains me not to end him right here and now, but the green scale has a point. Aideen is my friend and she also seems to care for this hunter to some degree, so his death would likely upset her a great deal. He has also had ample opportunity to attack us and hasn't yet.

I set him down. He scurries back a few steps.

"Thank you, Pestifar," Aideen says, then converses with Cylen.

I grumble to myself. I hate not understanding what's being said when it seems so important now.

Renji tugs my attention away. "Dare I ask what happened out there to bring this on?"

I tell her about the attack on the village and the matching clothing that led me on the offensive upon our return.

"Pestifar, come," Aideen calls as I finish my tale.

I turn around and see that she has pulled out the carved stone figurines from a game we sometimes play. They represent various human ranks in their society, with certain moves and powers. I see she has left the wooden board in the storage crate, however.

Aideen sets the figures down and begins arranging them, but not in the way that a game would normally start. I wonder at this. And then I realize she may be using the figurines as a way to try and explain what's going on in a way that bypasses our language barrier.

When she finishes, I study the layout for a moment. The Grey Queen and the Grey Castle are set next to each other. In front of them are Grey Soldiers and Grey Assassins. The lady has left a goodly distance between them and the other side, where several Red Soldiers are huddled together in a small group. Behind them stand the Red Queen, the Red Knight, and a Grey Assassin.

"Aideen," she says, pointing to the Red Queen.

I nod.

"You," she continues, pointing towards the Red Knight.

Fairly ironic, but, okay, I follow.

She picks up the Grey Assassin who stands next to us. "Cylen."

I growl again. I knew it! But why hasn't he attacked and why does Aideen seem to like him?

Aideen takes the Grey figurine and replaces him with a Red Assassin.

Hmmmph. She's saying that Cylen *was* an assassin against us, originally, but... changed places? Defected? Curious.

She picks up a few of the Grey Assassins and places them around the group of Red Soldiers. "Village."

Today's attack. I nod my understanding so far.

She then points to the large space she left in the middle. "Sea."

Ah, so whoever this enemy is, they are across the sea from us. Yet, apparently still able to send enemies here to harass us. But why? To what purpose? The late Blue's words from before come back to me unbidden: *"Princesses are nothing but trouble for dragons."* It rankles me that cretin might possibly have been right.

Aideen takes a deep breath, then grabs a few of the Grey Assassins and the Grey Soldiers. She sets them around our carved representatives. She shows me and Cylen knocking them down. But then she brings more. We defeat them again, and yet even more still come.

This will not stop, apparently. Not unless something is done.

Next, my lady grabs Cylen and my Red Knight, along with her Red Queen, and travels them across the sea to surround the Grey Queen and the

Grey Castle. My figure knocks down the castle, while she and Cylen's figures knock down the Grey Queen.

Who is this queen, I wonder, who wants Aideen dead? Surely not her own mother, but you never quite know with humans. Perhaps the mother of that prince Aideen slew when she saved my life? Or maybe it's not even a queen at all, but some other powerful enemy she's using the Grey Queen to represent.

Regardless, it's a lot of ill omens to swallow. My lady is being attacked and will continue to be attacked unless we cross the sea and end her assailant. I presume she learned this from the turncoat assassin, which also bothers me. What if this is simply an elaborate trap he's laid to bring Aideen and me straight into the den of his former liege?

"Pestifar," says Aideen. "I go. Cylen go." She points at their two figurines by the fallen Grey Queen. "You go?"

Upwards inflection at the end. A question. Cute that she actually thinks I have a choice in this matter. As if I would just let her go off into danger without me there to protect her.

And yet... I look over at Renji and the egg that will eventually hatch into Tikadon. Would they be safe alone? Wait, what am I thinking? Mother dragons and their offspring are usually alone anyway. It's me and this odd, unnatural friendship that has made things so turned around in my head now.

But it would mean leaving my old cave behind. My treasure hoard. Aideen's wall paintings. I despise the thought of parting with these. But I suppose we would return here when it's all over. I hope. If we're still alive.

And if Renji hasn't taken my cave over and decided it's hers now, like a proper dragon would and should.

I sigh.

"I go," I finally answer, though the words feel like dried ashes on my tongue.

Aideen smiles up at me, but for the first time, it does not fill me with confidence or joy.

A cracking sound grabs my attention and I turn to see Renji's egg wobbling in its nest. Aideen rushes over and falls to her knees, watching intently. Cylen and I amble closer for a better look, but keep a bit further back so as not to crowd the others.

Little Tikadon fights. And pecks. And pushes. And slowly, but surely, he – I can instantly tell he's a he by his scent as soon as he has his first breakthrough – fights and claws his way out of his eggshell prison and into the world. The young dragon blinks, and blinks again, then peeps at us. Aideen practically glows looking down at him. And as his mother reaches a talon out to pull him close and start cleaning the egg residue off him, Tikadon looks me right in the eyes.

I smile at him, giving a warbling trill and a bobble of my shoulders.

He smiles back and squeaks.

Heh. Heh heh.

A sobering thought hits me then. The assassins will not stop coming, I know. And possibly, after that, soldiers. I can fight them off if I stay here, but only in certain numbers and for so long. Eventually, they will succeed in torching the seaside village down. And now, in this cave, there are more than Aideen and myself at risk. Renji and Tikadon are in the warpath simply by being here, if I remain inactive.

It could be a final flight for me. But if I stay, it may eventually mean no first flight for him... after a remaining life of non-stop conflict for me. No, it must end. I must see to it.

I sit back on my haunches and watch as Aideen picks up Tikadon and cradles him after his first bath, Renji looking on happily. It's an image I try to burn and etch into my memory as well as I can. Something to carry with me through the battle ahead. My reason for fighting. My reason for *winning*.

The Splendid S.E.D.8 and the Aloof Android

Written by

C. Red

C. One

"Inmate 33217R, step out of your cell and to the right."

I'm momentarily blinded as I comply and wait for my next set of orders. I've been confined to this dank holding cell for two thousand, five hundred and forty-two days, in addition to the ones that have escaped me.

My instructions are vague, at best. Escort an android across a wasteland planet to the rendezvous point within a set time frame. Once the android is safe on its ship, I will be pardoned for the crimes I've committed.

"Just in case you get any cute ideas, human."

Frigid metal locks around my wrist. It's some type of detonation device that activates once I'm in the presence of the android. If I distance myself more than fifty feet, it will discharge. I feel little, if anything, about my assignment. I'm uncertain which one is worse. Either I can wait to die a slow death in here, or be sent to an early one on some distant planet. My only opposition towards leaving, is that it's candied kiwi day. Figures.

I jiggle the airlock hatch as a grunt escapes me. This capsule hardly meets the minimum requirements for flight. My mission could very well be over before it even starts. I dislike space travel immensely. It's the landing and the taking off, because heights frighten me. When I'm given intravenous sedation before takeoff, I start to wish I would had asked more questions.

Most planets only take a few hours of travel. Where exactly are they sending me?

My eyes lazily open after arrival. I heave a breath a little more dramatic than I should. Earth. No wonder they didn't brief me. A planet that is truly unique. Of all the endless scenarios like nuclear fire, disease, or invasion of a more intelligent species that would devastate a planet, this civilization destroyed itself with greed and corruption. I didn't realize Earth was even habitable again. From my birth, only the most heinous stories come from Earth.

"Inmate 33217R?"

When I acknowledge the stranger, I'm taken to a small outpost, but it doesn't come without criticism.

"They sent *you* to protect the device?"

Perhaps it's because I'm lanky or small in stature. Maybe because I'm a woman. Whatever the reason, he is unwise to judge me based on my appearance. My lack of empathy and my efficiency in weapons make me dangerous. I've killed countless species for a variety of reasons, some even as insignificant as the hydration bladder on their back.

"He's been held up in the livestock pen."

He? Since when did we start humanizing scrap metal?

I've seen everything you can possibly imagine at forty-four years of age, but I have never seen anything like this.

The twenty-one-inch android snickers as it extends an articulated arm and uses its end effectors, or what would be the fingers, to pet the animal.

This is absurd. I'm not a babysitter. "There's been a mistake."

"No mistake. This is the device."

The only emotion I seem to possess is disdain and that's made clear when the android rolls its way over to me on its oval-shaped heavy-duty caterpillar tracks.

"Greetings!"

My attention is turned to a device all right—the one on my wrist, which is activated now that the android is in range. At least the explosion will be instantaneous because I am not suitable for this assignment.

When I'm approximately fifty feet out, I tap the device, perplexed as to why it hasn't detonated.

"Greetings," the android repeats.

I find this **thing** as unnerving as its sickly pewter-colored patina. The top portion from the waist up of the android definitely embodies more human-like traits. Especially its wandering, curious eyes. The markings on the android's side read S.E.D.8.

"It stands for Scientific Exploration Device."

"I didn't inquire."

"What's your name?"

"We won't be together long enough for it to matter." At least, that's my hope.

C. Two

I brush the spot on my black coarse jacket where the thing has attempted to get my attention with those disturbing effectors.

"Do you want to see my findings from this planet so far?"

"No."

"You are quite unpleasant."

"Listen to my words, S.E.D.8. It's important that we gather supplies now and barter at any supply post we can. Once word of our travel spreads, so will the danger. People seeking to use you for their benefit will stop at nothing—" Why am I explaining my actions to scrap metal? "What do you have of importance that we could trade?"

"Now she wants to see my findings. I offered, you said no." The android extends one effector up at me.

Very well, I don't require its help. "Wait, where are you going? You must stay within fifty feet of me. Stop!"

"We don't become winded. You will. I suggest you apologize or this will be a very short journey."

Apologize? I'm not apologizing. I didn't do anything. Surely it wouldn't attempt to— "That's too far!" The device on my wrist starts to flash in warning as I release the items I'm holding and take off in the direction of

S.E.D.8. "You almost destroyed me!" I push the android over when it attempts to continue forth.

Its mouth panel drops wide open as its eyes shift side to side. "Put me upright!"

"Next time, know who you're threatening." I tug on the droid until it's back on both tracks. The metal on it becomes so hot, I scald my hands. I find out this is actually some type of defense mechanism these machines have.

It seems pleased with itself. "You might think that you don't need me, but you do. We need each other."

"I don't need anyone."

"If you're always this unpleasant, I imagine that people don't want to be around you."

"I'm fine alone. I prefer it."

"I feel sorry for you."

"You don't feel anything."

"Neither do you." The android turns so it doesn't have to face me.

Fine by me. Now, I can get back to work.

The one beneficial thing about having S.E.D.8 as a companion is that it won't need to consume. I've never been one for large meals, so I can focus my priorities on ammunition. All the weapons at the outpost are overpriced, which means that we are a long way from another one. This is typical of Earth. Gouging prices for their own personal gain.

"See anything you like?"

Some of these weapons don't even have all the components. If I were alone, I'd slit the merchant's throat and take what I want. I'm sure if I did, the device would have something to say on the matter as it leaked coolant in an emotional protest. "Fill it," I order the man, putting my side satchel on the counter.

"I'm being harassed." S.E.D.8 tugs on my jacket when I continue to ignore it.

"Stop that. Stay by my side." We haven't been together but a short while and it's already grabbing the wrong attention.

"There they are again." It rolls closer, almost crushing my foot.

Before I can even take my gun from its holster, I focus in on the attackers. "Those are children. They're harmless."

"I barely escaped with my life."

"Quiet, I'm counting." Between the merchant's incessant babbling, S.E.D.8, and the busy sounds of Earth, I am exhausted and the sun is still quite powerful so I know it's not time to sleep for several more hours. "Where are we on this map?" I slide it across the counter for the merchant. It takes numerous attempts to find someone capable of reading the map and pointing me in the correct direction. It becomes pointless to begin the journey today. "We'll need to stay here for the night."

"I dislike the people here."

It seems this thing and I have at least one thing in common. "Follow me. Always within my sight."

A quarter of a mile outside of town is where we hold up for the night. I build a fire low enough to the earth so it doesn't draw attention, which the android refers to as paranoia. So be it.

"Earth is still difficult for me to understand because I do not have many files on it. That was our purpose here when I was left behind."

"Surely there are other planets in comparison."

"Nothing in my travels. What planet were you sent from?"

"Calypso 57L." Calypso 57L is as miserable as they come. Solely used as a planet to house prisoners but otherwise uninhabitable. The average temperature is just above freezing all year round, due to the minimum access that the planet has to the sun. It only houses three Homo sapiens. Well, two now that I am no longer a resident. Earth is the only planet that I've been to where the human race is common.

"Did you work as a prison guard?"

"No, I was a prisoner." When it asks me why, I knew I should never have opened my mouth. Not because I'm not accepting of my crimes, but because I loathe small talk. "I've hurt a lot of species in order to survive."

"Will you be pardoned once I am home?"

"That's the idea." If this device on my wrist doesn't self-destruct after my mission, though it would hardly surprise me.

"If it detonates at fifty feet, what's to stop it from exploding once I'm far enough on my ship?"

"I don't have an answer for that."

"Sounds like you should have asked more questions."

I use what's left of the sunlight to find the most efficient way to the rendezvous point. The temperature falls dramatically the final few moments we have the sun.

"Why do you wear an atilla?"

"What?"

"Your banned atilla military jacket."

Why does my attire even matter? "I like it."

"How old are you?"

"Forty-four. Enough with the questions. I need to plot out our journey." Though it's pointless because I'm out of time. "Wake me if anything enters our camp." I know this thing won't require sleep, but its glowing irises creep me out. "Will you shut your eyes?"

"They are."

My attempt to cover its head doesn't go over well, so I roll over.

"How long will your melatonin secretion process last?"

"Six to eight hours."

"How long is one hour?"

"S.E.D.8, enough!" It's at that moment I realize the irony of its name.

I'm sluggish the following day for numerous reasons. Though the most pressing one is staring back at me. "What? Speak."

"I'd like a soda, please."

"You can't have soda. How do you even know what that is?" Of course, soda is common throughout most planets so it's something the android would have encountered before. Now, if only I could get this thing up to speed on everything else.

"I'm programmed to—"

I rub my brow annoyed. "Yes, I'm aware. I wish I didn't."

S.E.D.8 fishes a few tokens from my pocket. "I'd like the soda now, please."

"I'll retrieve you that soda all right and pour it over your circuits."

"You're saying hurtful things."

"You're an android. You don't feel anything."

"I am more human than you will ever hope to be."

"Your insult is ineffective."

"Is that so? Your increased heartbeat tells me otherwise."

Fifty feet isn't that much of a distance, but it will have to do at this moment because I don't want to be around it. I'm plenty human. Just because I choose to void my emotion doesn't make me the android. It doesn't even know me. I have my reasons for the way I am. I don't have to justify myself. Especially to some tin turkey.

C. Three

It's almost been thirty days since the journey started, yet I feel as lost as when I started. There's not much time left. The counter on S.E.D. 8 is getting closer to 0. "You can come out now," I inform the android before rummaging through the corpses of the marauders I've murdered. Of all the things they've acquired in their travels, food isn't one. We'll need to locate an outpost soon, but the towns are becoming just as dangerous as the rest of this wasteland.

My nose becomes my guide over my map. There's a small market with vendors cooking up all sorts of things.

"Eighteen tokens."

"That's ridiculous." Though, it's really not. Meat of this quality is rare. "I'll give you ten." I feel a tug on my jacket. "Not now," I dismiss S.E.D.8. "Do we have a deal?" As I reach for the meat on the stick, I almost lose my hand when the vendor's knife stabs into the counter. "All I have are twelve tokens, and I need two to bargain for fresh water."

"Not my problem. Perhaps you'd like some crackers instead." He brings his fist down hard on the sleeved saltines.

As I observe the market, I notice that most of the others are packing up their shops for the night. Water is more the priority, so I trade my two tokens for several canteens. When I return to the meat vendor, he's lowered his price to ten.

"Will you tell me now?" S.E.D.8 points at the small cloth material. "What is this?"

I completely forgot about the android and its numerous attempts to get my attention. "It's an old world thing. People with powers and heroes wore them."

"I don't believe you have any idea what you're talking about."

What was that thing called? I know I've stumbled across it in books. "A cape thing."

"A cape thing. I want it. Purchase it for me."

"Purchase it for you?" My sigh is heard across the counter when the vendor asks what it's going to be. "How much for the cape?"

"It's not for sale."

"Aww, oh, no," I condescendingly tell S.E.D.8. "I'll take the meat stick."

The merchant glances over my tokens. "All right, I'll make you a deal for the cape. Ten tokens, and I'll throw in the crackers."

S.E.D.8 seems almost childish in hopes that I'll get this cape for it.

I stare at the meat, the cape, the saltines, and then S.E.D.8 before giving the delicious meat back and taking the crushed packaged saltines instead.

The android's effectors move greedily together. "I believe you're getting soft in your old age."

"I must be."

"I'd like you to hang it off my shoulder, please."

"I'd like to hang you off something."

"You're saying hurtful things."

"What do you even want with this stupid thing anyhow?"

"Because I'm like you now."

Like me? I touch my hand to my left shoulder, forgetting my cloak that hangs off the back of it. "Mine is to protect me from the dust storms." The last planet I sought refuge on was FeO, otherwise known as the red dust planet. Getting caught in a dust storm is deadly, though I'd welcome FeO over Earth. In fact, I'd welcome Calypso 57L over Earth.

S.E.D.8 snickers boyishly and turns in circles as the cape floats or whatever it's doing.

"Not that far out. You'll end up—"

"Help! I'm being consumed!"

"—falling in the pond..." Despite S.E.D.8's small size, this thing weighs entirely way too much. "The pond is dangerous because of all your components. Stay away from it."

"Thank you for my cape thing."

"Oh." I've never been thanked before. It feels... nice. "It's just called a cape. Let's find a spot for the evening."

"I dislike the night because I don't want to be alone."

"We're fine." You see, this is what happens when I'm not cautious because we were ambushed just outside of the market. The marauders I'd killed earlier ended up being part of a much larger group. I haven't endured all this for it to end here, and make each of my shots count when I'm not able to use my knife.

There was a brief time when I thoroughly enjoyed taking other people's lives, because there was something to gain from it. Now, I feel apathetic. Maybe I really am getting soft in my old age. Which really isn't all that old. I only feel the sluggish effects of age. Effects that almost cost me my life, and S.E.D.8 to be taken. My eyes are heavy from the fight as I sink to my knees. "S.E—"

C. Four

I'm disoriented when I wake up until I see the glow from S.E.D.8's eyes. I should be dead from the lack of fire alone, but S.E.D.8 has kept me warm with the defense mechanism it has. "Thank you. I would have perished if it hadn't have been for some type of warmth."

"As I told you in the beginning, we need each other."

I notice that the cape I purchased is around me for even more warmth. Another first. No one has ever cared about my well-being enough to see that I'm comfortable as I sleep. I inform the android I require another hour of sleep before we start the day. Which, after fifteen minutes, I regret even trying. "Are you... singing?"

"Humming."

"Humming?"

"Humming. A low, steady continuous sound."

"I'm sorry I asked."

"Do you dislike everything? Is it your purpose in life to respond with derision?"

I don't know why I feel vulnerable, but I tell S.E.D.8 the story about how I used to listen to an older musical artist from Earth. That I wasn't always filled with discontent. "...and he had this dance called the moonwalk."

"Impossible to walk on the moon. No gravity."

"I comprehend that, but when he—"

"Illogical."

I show S.E.D.8 how to do the dance, but it is not amused. "Whatever. Here's your cape. We're leaving."

"You seem butthurt that I'm not interested."

"Where did you learn that word?"

"In the market last night."

"Tch. Come on." Maybe I am... *butthurt*... but I'm not about to tell it that. I try to deshell these impassive boundaries I've created, and look what happens? I'm dismissed. I don't even know why I care or why I'm getting emotional about this. It's a good thing today's journey will be strenuous. Something to keep my mind occupied.

The sun on this planet is miserable when it reaches its highest point. Considering where I have spent the last few years, that speaks volumes. In the later hours of the day, it's blinding as it faces us. I'd welcome a dust storm right about now. "Why have you stopped?"

"Is this another pond?"

"Hardly. Maybe at one time." I've read about this place. It's called the Salton Sea. I have to reprimand S.E.D.8 when it thinks it's playing in the sand. "Those are bones from the decomposed fish you're wading through. They're going to get lodged into your caterpillar tracks."

"I know what I'm doing." Like clockwork, the cries begin. "I've made a terrible mistake!"

My annoyance couldn't be any more known. It takes several hours to repair its tracks, which means we'll need to make camp here. However, I rather enjoy it here. In all my travels, I've never seen a place like this before. The population is scarce, but it doesn't stop the residents from being welcoming. Considering all the protest we've been met with, it's refreshing.

"What is this?"

"Don't your files tell you that?"

"Why would I ask if I knew?"

"It's a slide." When it just stares back at me, I shrug my shoulders. "You know... fun." I hoist it up, thankful it's not too far from the ground because S.E.D.8 is the heaviest thing I have ever lifted. When it won't move down the slide, I give it a friendly nudge.

It falls flat on its face. "I dislike slides."

That's enough adventure for one day. "Let's turn in for the night."

"Wait. There is something I wanted to show you. I've perfected the moonwalk."

"Of course you have. You have no legs."

"The definition of a leg is—"

"Please don't recite the dictionary to me again. I know the definition of a leg."

"Don't you want to see the dance?"

"No." Why should I give this thing my time when it was so dismissive of me earlier? When it keeps on implying things about my character, I let emotion take over in some childish fit. "You want to know what's eating me? Here I have all this potential as a soldier, but it's wasted on a can opener!"

"That is offensive!"

"You don't have feelings! How many times have I told you that? At this point, I can guarantee that you weren't left here on accident by your kind. It was to get a break from your incessant chatter. If I could do things over again, I never would have come to this miserable planet. I can only hope that you'll be distracted by something of insignificance long enough so that I can run the fifty feet necessary to end myself because it's a better alternative than having to spend one more second with you." It was the most I have ever said, and every word caused the android to slouch further into submission until silence falls.

It rolls forward, extending its arm towards me.

I thought for sure it was going to murder me where I stand, but I stare at my now bare wrist.

S.E.D.8 clicks the device around some of its wires. "You're free to go." It spins around before rolling away from me.

I rub the parts of my skin where the metal has left bloody impressions. "Wait. How will you protect yourself?"

"It's no longer your concern. Farewell."

That day, I learn a new emotion. Guilt. It consumes every part of me, though I mostly feel it in my stomach. "S.E.D.8." It continues down the path. I know that this thing is stubborn, but this goes beyond that. Have I been wrong? Is it plausible to believe that androids can feel emotion? I barely comprehend it, yet S.E.D.8 has a perfect grasp on it. *He* is more human than I will ever hope to be.

"Please," I beg, winded. I never beg. I've been following him for almost three miles. He's already almost caused his demise several times, but even rescuing him awards me no salvation. "My name is Riddle," I shout in a desperate attempt to salvage what I've ruined.

There's a gleam of hope when S.E.D.8 stops, then turns to face me. "That's odd considering you don't have a humorous bone in your human makeup."

It's something I have always thought, too, and the main reason I don't share my name with anyone. I don't wish to be the brunt of the jokes that follow. "Yes, I am fully aware of the irony. May I... travel with you now?"

"I want compensation."

Maybe I'm arrogant to think that my name alone was the compensation, but I wait for him to speak. "Well?"

"Don't rush me."

After a substantial amount of time, he tells me that he will inform me later. All this agony and I'm no better off than I was. "We'll need to make camp here." We don't have the time to get into town before it's completely dark. It's fine by me. The sea is beautiful in its final seconds before the sun sets.

"We're surrounded by a bone beach of death, and it stinks."

"You don't have a sense of smell and you're only saying that because you heard someone else say that it stinks." Thankfully, I won't need to worry about fire because of the humid temperatures. In my bag, I find something to settle my stomach. Well, that was my intention.

"What are you consuming?"

"Debatable. The bag says potato chips." The grease and salt content alone makes them practically inedible. I never thought I'd long for the mushroom and coconut pudding they served to us in the brig.

"I'd like some, please."

"How many times must I reiterate that you can't have food?"

The hatch drops open as he eagerly waits for me to feed him.

Fine. I agreed to be more pleasant. I've been given this second chance. Here goes nothing. "Satisfied?"

"I have no way to taste it. I just know you have to do everything I say because of the events from earlier." He gives a chortle at his own words.

Give me a break. "Goodnight," I tell him.

C. Five

"Riddle, are you all right? Your melatonin secretion process never takes this long."

I'm not asleep. In fact, I've been awake for several hours staring into the distance. I feel at home at the Salton Sea.

S.E.D.8 is finally going home today, and I have plans to return here and live out the rest of my days once he's safely on the ship. "We should get going. We're not far."

He hasn't said a single word for the last few hours.

"You're not wanting to return, are you?"

"I don't have any feelings on it."

"That's the only thing you don't have feelings on, then." When I'm not granted a response, my mind starts to wander. "What would happen if you didn't return and the counter goes to 0?"

"This planet will be destroyed to protect the sensitive information in my files." S.E.D.8 shows me the counter on one of his inside panels. "Time is of the essence." We have less than an hour to get him to the rendezvous point.

Not that I have any objections to the demise of Earth, but even I believe that to be harsh. "There's something that I want to tell you, S.E.D.8." It doesn't come easy because I've never felt a connection with anything before.

"I want you to know that I—" My arm is grazed by a bullet, followed by another one that strikes me in my shoulder blade. I grit my teeth, applying pressure to my arm. "This way." I'm frantic to get S.E.D.8 to safety before I take concern over myself. Out here, in the desert, there are several places to seek refuge, but that refuge doesn't help when you don't know where the danger is. I have known since I accepted this mission that I might have to give my life up to keep him safe, but we're too close for me to fail now.

"Riddle, I know what I want."

"Now is not the time!" I get my rifle so I can use my scope to see where the bullets are coming from.

"I don't want you to perish."

"I'm not going to perish. Keep your—" This time when I'm shot, it knocks me to the earth. I'm disoriented and start to hear voices surround us.

When one of the men grab S.E.D.8, the skin comes right off his hands.

"I told you not to touch it!" A chain that is built into a vehicle locks around S.E.D.8.

"What about her?"

"Leave her. Get in the truck."

"Excuse me," S.E.D.8 begins, "I don't belong to you. Get this restraint off me! No, that's my cape!" He reaches for it on the ground, but the truck jerks him away from it.

I don't care about the well-being of this planet. By those men taking S.E.D.8, it ensures the demise of it. My concern is for my friend as he screams terrified when he's dragged behind the truck. I know what it's like to have metal slung around you. Then, you're at the mercy of something else taking you to a place you don't want to be.

I use all of my strength to push myself up into a slump against one of the rocks. Shooting any part of the truck, or the driver, might cause further agony to S.E.D.8 if it were to flip. The odds of hitting the chain become scarcer the longer I wait.

"Riddle! Help!"

*They sent **you** to protect the device?*

My carelessness will not cause S.E.D.8 his demise. I hover my finger over the trigger and take my shot. The bullet pierces the metal chain as the truck goes one way and S.E.D.8 goes the other. I release the breath I've been holding in relief.

When I help remove the chain from S.E.D.8, the weight concerns me. A simple task like this shouldn't be so exhausting. I know my time on this planet isn't long. "Come on," I grunt, fitting him with his cape. "We need to hurry."

My words are hypocritical because I am the one slowing us down. If we're ambushed again, I don't know if I can even be of use. The strain from holding my own gun is overwhelming.

"Riddle, rest."

"No. We must keep going." The timer is entering its final few minutes.

"But—"

"S.E.D.8, no! You are the only thing in my life that I can look back on and say that I did it for the good of something other than myself. If the timer depletes entirely you die, too. I knew the risk when I accepted this mission. I have accepted that I will certainly perish, but I cannot allow that to happen to you."

"I don't feel pain. We just... cease to exist when our time comes."

"Please, come on."

S.E.D.8 extends his arm up and clings to my pants. It's his way of helping to keep my balance.

If anything, it's more of a hindrance, but the simple gesture is kind. Especially knowing that I won't be alone in these last moments.

I can barely lift my legs and that's even if I'm going in the right direction because the blood loss is taking its toll. Luckily, S.E.D.8 keeps us on course. Just... a few more feet. After losing my balance several times, this is as far as my body will allow me to continue. I take in another painful breath once we finally make it to our destination. "What does your... timer..."

"The countdown has finalized."

It makes me feel better knowing that I can leave this world and his kind will come for him. A moment that I don't have to wait long on as the ship descends to Earth. I double over, then collapse.

"Riddle? Your core temperature is too low." S.E.D.8 covers me with his cape.

The pain is excruciating. Blood is coming up faster than I can swallow it, causing me to choke. I extend my finger towards the ship. "Go home, S.E.D.8."

"You saved me."

"That is my job."

"It hasn't been your job since I removed the device."

"Maybe I am just getting soft in my old age."

"Your heartbeat is faint." His eyes shift worried as his mouth panel quivers. "Riddle, if you don't die, I promise I won't be annoying."

My shaky fingers curl around his effectors. "I never should have made you feel that way." I regret so many things. Not taking the time to learn more from him is my biggest one. My time spent with him is what I want to leave this world remembering. How he constantly found himself in trouble by his curious nature.

I know what I'm doing... I've made a terrible mistake!

His sassy words bring a smile to my lips. "S.E.D.8, thank you for teaching me what it means to be human. For making this last month actually worth living." The first thing to seize up is my motor skills, followed by my hearing. All this time wasted being miserable and hurting people when I could have protected them. My eyes become heavy as darkness swallows me up before they even close. I'm terrified what waits for me on the other side from the egregious crimes I've committed.

C. Six

Despite my belief that I would suffer by my actions, I'm comfortable. Though, I find the bright lights that I'm seeing to be obnoxious. Then this beeping noise starts as the frequency increases. The light ceases instantly, followed by a rusty creak. As my complete sight returns, I appear to be in some type of infirmary. My instinct is to protect S.E.D.8, but I realize that's no longer my purpose in this life.

The doctor's boisterous laugh fills the room. "We weren't sure if you were going to pull through."

I don't find it all that comical. "Where am I?"

"Mecca."

I'm just as lost as before I knew my location and repeat my question. The doctor tells me that I'm not far from where the rendezvous point was. "Did he make it home?" Wait. That doctor said we. Who else would care if I made it?

"Hurray!"

Oh, no, why?! What is S.E.D.8 doing here? "Why aren't you on your ship a million miles away from me?"

"Good news! The data collected with you from Earth was given to my kind. I have outlived my usefulness, so they left me here with you. We're going to be together for a long time. Isn't that great?"

"There are hardly words..."

"Well, you've never been much for words anyhow."

"You couldn't let me die a war hero in peace?"

"No, and just because you have the cape doesn't make you a hero."

"It's a cloak."

"Where will we go now?"

All right, so, maybe I was excited, another new emotion for me, to see S.E.D.8. I just won't tell him that. I'm sluggish to move and shuffle across the infirmary once I'm able. Nothing is broken, and I have all of my fingers and limbs. "Where exactly do you suggest we go?"

"Anywhere! We're free to explore."

Almost free. It takes me a full week to recover, and even when I'm released I'm easily exhausted. After numerous days and thirty miles later, we finally see the sign that says '*Welcome to Bombay Beach*' by the Salton Sea. This will be our new home.

"Do you want me to scout ahead?"

The very thing I once protected now protects me. "No. We're safe here."

When a small bird flies over us, S.E.D.8 opens up fire on it, pulverizing the bird instantly. "Heh. Sorry, I didn't want to take any chances."

I cough out feathers, swatting them from my face. "You had a gun mount this entire time?!"

"Yes."

"I want you to know, at this point, I'd welcome fifty years of manual labor than another ten minutes with you."

"You're saying hurtful things."

I shake my head and continue down one of the streets as we look for a dwelling. He would have a gun mount on him. I can act as annoyed as I want, but the corner of my lip is curled in amusement. I've been given a second chance and I won't waste it being angry.

The heat is sweltering here, but it doesn't deter me. Most of the residents didn't even pack their belongings when it was vacated so we won't need to scavenge much. Graffitied on a piece of furniture reads:

May you find whatever you seek.

I'm certain I've never sought after anything, but what I've found is purpose. Prior, my purpose has always been simple. Survival. Now, I have so much more. Companionship. Fulfillment. Peace. "I think this small trailer will be sufficient." There's a market down the way, and a diner. "Don't you find this agreeable?" Where did he go now? "S.E.D.8?"

"Look, Riddle, the earth is bubbling."

Bubbling? "Wait, stop!"

"I know what I'm doing."

"That's volcanic mud. You're going to—" I cup my palm to my nose as my eyes well up from the stench.

He is covered from head to track from the thick goop. "I've made a terrible mistake!"

Sounds of Happiness

Written by

K.N. Nguyen

D*ON! DON! DON!*

The rhythmic beat of drums reverberated in the crisp afternoon air. Kylie paused as she listened to the music change from a powerful crescendo to a pulsating beat.

"Mom, listen! Can we go check it out?" Kylie exclaimed.

Loretta smiled down at her little girl and nodded. "We can watch for a little bit. Not too long, though. We still need to get Daddy's birthday present."

"Thanks, Mommy!" Kylie cried as she tore off towards the sound of the drums.

Weaving her way through the mass of bodies, Kylie soon found the source of her interest and wiggled her way a little closer. Being a petite eight-year-old, that wasn't too difficult a feat. In front of her a group of seven performers, mainly women, pounded on their drums. *Kiahs* and other shouts of encouragement could be heard interspersed throughout the song. Kylie stood mesmerized. As the song ended, she joined in with the crowd's applause.

A second song started and time stopped. Images of cherry blossom petals swirling in the wind flashed through her mind. She could almost feel a gentle breeze stirring her hair and rustling her dress. Halfway through the song, a hand gently squeezed her shoulder. The cherry blossom petals disappeared as she spun around and saw her mother.

"We need to go, Kylie."

"But Mom!" she protested.

"I'm sorry, but we still have a lot to do today."

With a small sigh, Kylie turned from the performers and walked towards the mall with her mom. After a few quiet minutes, Kylie looked up at her mom and asked, "Can I do that someday?"

"Of course you can, baby girl. You can do anything you want."

Kylie beamed as she and her mother entered the mall. The drums could still be heard faintly in the distance. Her braids bounced from side to side as she bobbed in time with the music.

***

Ten Years Later - Late August

"Kylie, it's time to go," her mother's voice called out.

"Coming!"

Kylie ran down the stairs, grabbing her book bag as she flew out the door. In the car, her parents and little brother waited. Taking a deep breath, Kylie smiled and jumped into the car.

"I can't believe my baby girl is about to go to college," Loretta exclaimed. "Don't you go getting any ideas," she said, pointing to Kylie's little brother, Marcus. "I'm not losing two babies so soon."

"Aw, Mom," Marcus said, "don't go treating me like a kid."

"That's right, dear," their father, Vernon, chided. "If we treat them like kids, they may never grow up. Wouldn't it be great to have our son living with us until he's thirty? That's the sign of a true babe magnet, right? Man with a curfew?" He said with a wink.

"Hey, hey, let's not get carried away," Marcus said. "I never said I'm living here forever. That's not cool. Who wants to be the guy with the curfew?"

Kylie and her parents laughed.

With a sigh, Kylie looked out the car window as her house disappeared from sight. Trees blurred past as the car merged onto the freeway towards her new campus. Kylie hummed to herself, a quick little beat playing in her mind as she imagined what her future as a college student would be like.

Half an hour later, the car pulled up to the sprawling grounds of Featherbrooke University. The worn, red brick buildings and towering pines greeted the family. As they clambered out of the car, Kylie tried to take in as much as she could. Seasoned students leisurely walked around the campus while others, most likely incoming freshmen like her, nervously gawked, sticking close to either their friends or family.

A squeal broke her from her reverie. "Kylie!"

Kylie turned to see a curly-haired brunette waving at her and start to run over. "Ash, I can't believe you're here!" Kylie exclaimed. "I thought for sure you went to Stoneridge."

"We decided that this was cheaper since I wouldn't need to pay for student housing when books and tuition cost an arm and a leg by themselves. Besides, who wouldn't want a chance to be part of the big FU?"

The two shared a giggle at the unfortunate school nickname.

"What are you majoring in?" Kylie asked. The two girls linked arms and walked slowly to the bookstore where their families stood talking.

"I'm thinking maybe history. I did well on the advanced placement test and I figure I can use this as an excuse to tell my parents that I'm also going for a degree in anthropology. Featherbrooke's archaeology department has a great reputation. While looking up what I'd need for my degree here, I found a great internship online where I can actually get experience doing a dig in the Midwest. It starts next summer, and from what I've heard, they've found some interesting bones there," Ashley said with a grin. "Dinos are life, you know."

"Oh, you're such a nerd," Kylie laughed.

"Says the bio major," Ashley quipped.

"Too bad this is as close as you'll get to a paleontology degree," Kylie teased.

Ashley stuck her tongue out at her friend.

"If you two are good and ready, we have enough time before orientation to go and grab some lunch before we get your books," Loretta said.

"Yes," the two said in unison.

Another bout of giggles erupted from the pair, causing Marcus to roll his eyes. "You two are so dumb."

Kylie couldn't help but notice that he snuck a glance at Ashley as she started laughing again. A slight smile played at the corner of his lips.

"Good luck," Kylie said softly as she walked by her brother, a large smile on her face.

Glancing behind her, she watched as color rushed to his face as he attempted to look unconcerned by the comment.

***

The seven made their way to the student union's food court. Despite it being summer, a considerable number of students milled about in line, waiting to order or pick up their meal.

"I'll grab a couple of tables while you guys order," Vernon said. Quickly scanning the options, he turned to his wife and said, "I'll take a burrito."

Kylie and Ashley quickly made their way to the Chinese restaurant while their mothers and Marcus went to order some Mexican food.

Nudging Kylie, Ashley whispered, "Everyone's so tall. I thought they stopped growing after they turned eighteen."

"It might just be you," she teased. "You haven't grown since freshmen year."

"Hey, hey! I don't see you getting any taller."

"Ladies," a deep voice interjected. "Trust me, you don't want to be much taller. Otherwise, guys will find it difficult to approach you. Most don't want a girl who's too tall. Threatens their masculinity or something."

Kylie and Ashley turned and looked at the speaker. A tall guy, maybe in his early twenties with a slim frame, stood behind them in line. Winking at the two, he turned his gaze back to the menu as the two blushed furiously.

Mercifully, the cashier called the pair up to order. After paying and picking up their food, they made a beeline to their parents' table. The others had already started eating by the time they placed down their trays.

As one, the two took out their phones and began texting one another, their fingers moving at lightning speed.

What was that about?

                    I don't know

He's kinda cute ;)

                 Lol yeah. Think he's
                       single? :P

I hope so…

                            XD

"Girls," Vernon's voice cut through the frenzied texting. "Phones away. Orientation starts in fifteen minutes."

"Really?" Ashley gasped.

"Really," her dad replied.

As young college freshmen are wont to do, the two wolfed down their meal with all the grace of a pack of lions tearing apart a zebra carcass.

"Chew, girls," Loretta reminded them.

Once lunch was completed, the two families split off to attend their respective orientations. After a half hour of discussing class options and the available resources for study assistance, Kylie and her family made their way back to the bookstore. Picking out the books for her first semester, Kylie felt her phone vibrate as she walked down an aisle.

Guess who I just saw…

Confused, Kylie replied:

> Who?

Lunch Boy. Turns out he's part of some Japanese drumming group on campus. I ran into him as we left orientation.

A flush of excitement filled her chest. Fingers racing, Kylie responded:

> Are you serious? Did you say anything to him?

No :(

But he did wink at me and told me to tell my cute friend hi

Her breath caught in her chest. A faint squeal broke from her lips before she realized that she made the noise out loud. Looking around the aisle frantically, she breathed a sigh of relief that no one had heard that embarrassing sound.

Returning to her phone, Kylie replied:

```
        Let's talk later. I need to
          finish getting my books.
           Sorry for the bad luck,
                             Ash.
```

No worries. Later.

Smiling to herself, Kylie continued down the aisle in search of her next textbook.

***

With a sigh, Kylie plopped down on her bed. The soft comforter engulfed her sore body.

"What an exhausting day," she mused. "Coach T. really wants to win this year."

Reflecting on the grueling soccer practice she had, she tried to remember all of the moves they went over in preparation for Saturday's game against Wayview.

"Don't be surprised if they try and play dirty," Coach T said at the end of practice before the girls went home. "We have the skill, and as long as we play smart we'll be fine."

Sitting up to shuck off her socks and shin guards, Lunch Boy came to her mind, unbidden. His wavy hair and bright smile made her heart melt a little.

It's been a while since I've had a crush. This could be a good year after all.

Smiling to herself, she recalled a conversation with Ashley from earlier that day after orientation was over.

"Kylie," her excited voice squealed, "he's so perfect for you." All disappointment at not being the object of his interest left her as she spoke with her best friend. "Didn't you say that you like those drums?"

"Well, yeah..."

"Then he's perfect for you! It's a sign."

"I don't know, Ash. I don't want to get my hopes up by reading too much into this."

"Girl, when a hottie like that asks someone to tell their friend 'hi', that's usually a sign that he's interested. Throw on the fact that he's into music like you, hello? Match made in heaven."

Giggling, Kylie agreed.

"Hey, Kylie, I gotta go. Let's ki ki soon."

"Ki ki indeed," she muttered. "There's nothing to talk about right now."

Rolling over on her bed, Kylie let out a dramatic sigh and laid down. *Well, tomorrow is the big day. I'm finally a college student. Between labs and practice... give me the strength to tackle these sixteen units and lead our team to the district cup.*

As she slowly drifted off to sleep, she thought she could hear the steady, gentle beating of drums.

***

Early September

Staring at the minute hand inching ever closer to the ten, Kylie couldn't wait for her class to end. Though it had only been a week, Kylie's philosophy professor was so boring that he made Ben Stein seem like Jim Carey. The second hand seemed to beat with an infuriatingly slow staccato, emphasizing the dry, monotonous voice of the professor.

It's only the first week... will it get any better than this?

Mercifully, the minute hand reached the ten and Kylie sprung from her desk towards the door. Weaving her way through the sea of bodies, Kylie found herself at the student union.

I'll kill an hour here 'til Ash gets out. Maybe a round of In the Groove at the arcade will wake me up.

Decision made, Kylie trekked over to the arcade in the student union. On the way, she passed one of the ballrooms and noticed a crowd forming. Interest piqued, Kylie stopped and looked around the room. Five students in brightly colored jackets stood in front of large drums with cow-hide heads. Near them stood a tall guy with wavy hair.

He looks familiar...

Suddenly, the wavy-haired student struck a smaller drum with two drumsticks and the others joined in. The melodic twinning of the larger drums and the smaller one brought images of fireworks to Kylie's eyes. Almost unconsciously, Kylie found herself walking into the room towards the performance.

Lunch Boy? She thought as she looked at the small drum player.

With a flourish, the taiko players ended the show with a resounding *DON.*

Kylie stood staring at a brilliant full moon, alone in the room. The light illuminated only a small area in front of her, but not enough for her to make out her surroundings. Looking around, Kylie struggled to figure out where she was. A sudden outbreak of applause caught her attention and she found herself standing in the warmly lit ballroom, surrounded by students.

What? How?

"Thank you, everyone, for coming to our show," a petite Asian girl with her hair in a ponytail said over the cheer from the students. "If anyone is interested in joining our club, please see me or Heath." She motioned to wavy-haired Lunch Boy. "My name is Stacy. Thank you!"

As one, the group of six bowed to the crowd and thanked the students. "*Dōmo arigatōgozaimashita.*"

With a wave, the group began packing up their drums.

Pushing aside her confusion, Kylie wove her way through the students exiting the ballroom and towards the group. Her desire to learn more about the group drove her impulsive behavior. Three other girls worked with Stacy to pack away the larger drums while Heath and another boy worked on hefting the covered drums onto a dolly to drag back to their practice room.

"Excuse me," Kylie addressed the group tentatively.

Stopping her work and spinning around, Stacy faced Kylie with a smile. "Hi! How can we help you?"

"I saw your performance and was hoping to get some information on when you practice. I'm interested in joining."

"Oh, excellent! We practice every Tuesday and Thursday in room one nineteen Skylar Hall. We start at seven and end around nine."

"Oh, awesome. I think I can make that."

"It would be great if you come," Heath interjected with a smile. "We're always looking for new members to carry on the group and would love it if you could come. I know I would be very happy if you joined," he said with a wink.

Kylie blushed furiously.

"Don't let Heath's dashing good looks sway you," a heavyset girl said with a smile. "We've already told him that this is not the Heath Show featuring Taiko GoGo. However, he seems to think that he can seduce women to join our group."

"Oh, I uh..." Kylie said, somewhat dejected.

"It's okay," Stacy said quickly. "Erica's his sister. She likes to give him a hard time since some girls have joined for a little while, most likely because he plays with us. They don't really last that long though." She shook her head in disappointment. "It's a shame, really. We could use more members."

A few other girls walked over to talk nervously with Heath. Kylie watched as he smiled at them and told the girls about the upcoming practice. The girls didn't seem to be interested and walked away waving shyly to him. Kylie thought she heard one girl mumble to the other something about "getting his phone number".

"We really would like it if you could join us. We're losing Caleb and Alisha in December and would love to get some new people to replace them." Stacy's voice carried a hint of desperation.

"Okay, I'll see you guys tonight," Kylie said with a smile.

"Great," Stacy replied.

Kylie turned to leave, her braids spinning behind her when she heard Heath bid her good-bye. Looking over her shoulder, she unconsciously gave him a coy smile and continued out of the ballroom and towards the arcade.

***

"You actually talked to him?" Ashley squealed. "What's his name? What did he say? Dish the T, girl!"

Taking a bite of her lunch, Kylie replied, "His name is Heath and he asked me to join their club."

"And?"

"I said yes, obviously."

Ashley leaned back in her oversized chair and hugged her binder to her chest. "I can't believe that you get the first guy in college! Imagine what Emi would say if she heard that shy Ky snagged a hottie in her first week of college."

"I wouldn't say that I snagged him," Kylie said with a sarcastic eye roll. "More like found out that we have something in common."

The girls shared a squeal and went back to their lunch.

"So," Kylie broached, "would you be interested in joining with me?"

"Oh, no. I'm not into drumming like you are. I have no sense of rhythm."

"I'm sure it'll be no biggie."

"It's okay. I'm fine with not participating. Anywho, how's your week going?" Ashley took a sip of her smoothie.

"Eh, all right, I suppose," Kylie continued while opening a bag of chips. "Biological Basics is a lot like AP Bio from high school and English is, well, English, but help me if my philosophy professor is so dry. I shouldn't have listened to my orientation guide on taking his class. I barely could stay awake, and we spent the majority of class discussing the syllabus. What about you?

"My calculus professor seems interesting, but I can't really tell about the others yet. Nothing really stands out."

"Lucky you," Kylie mused. "Maybe my luck will turn around with that class."

"At least it should be an easy semester."

"True." Glancing at her phone, Kylie almost dropped her bag of chips. "Gotta go! I have class in ten."

"See ya!"

***

After an exhausting afternoon of labs, Kylie made her way to Skylar Hall. Walking down the corridor, the sound of drums increased in volume as she looked for room one nineteen. *Do I even have time to do something like this? Soccer, labs, now taiko?* Hand hovering over the doorknob, she considered turning back and going home. *No, I need this right now. Not for Heath, but I need something for me. I haven't done anything for myself in a while, and I'll need it once soccer is over.* Waiting until the drumming died down, Kylie tried to quietly enter the room without interrupting the practice.

"Hey!" Stacy called. "So glad you could make it. Find a drum and try your best to follow us."

A chorus of "*ohayō gozaimasu*" filled the room.

Kylie found a drum and stood behind it silently.

"Here, you'll need these," Heath said, handing her a pair of thick drumsticks.

"What are these?" she asked.

"Bachi. Whether it's plural or singular, it's just bachi."

Kylie tested the weight of the bachi in her hands as the group debated on what to practice next.

"So, just a quick tutorial. Whenever we do a quarter note, we call them *dons*. They can be either very big," he said, bringing his arm up above his head, fully extended, "or not as full. Eighth notes are called *dokos*. You do two hits usually and your arms don't go as high." He demonstrated the *doko*. "There are also *karas* and *tsukus*. The former are strikes to the rim of the drum, called the fuchi, while the latter are small, soft hits." Heath demonstrated the last two types of notes.

After trying her hand at the notes, Kylie nodded.

"Does this all make sense?" Heath asked.

"Clear as mud," she joked.

"Good. Just try and follow as best you can. It'll take time, but I'm sure you'll pick it up."

"Okay everybody," Stacy said, "I think the first order of business is to introduce ourselves to Kylie and then we can move on to our set for the end-of-semester show. I'm Stacy." Pointing to everyone else in the room, Stacy continued, "You already know Heath. Next to him is Caleb. Then we have Erica." She waved and smiled. "Alisha." A curly-haired red-head smiled. "And finally, we have Kiyumi." A short girl with glasses waved enthusiastically.

"We always greet each other with '*ohayō gozaimasu*' when we enter the room. It means 'good morning' and no matter what time of day it is, we always greet each other with it. We say '*oyasuminasai*' when we leave. It means 'good evening'." Stacy continued. "Now I see that Heath has been working with you on some of the basics. Let's practice Senkai Sakura."

"The big drums here are called chu," Heath explained. "That's what the majority of us play. The shime, these small ones here with ropes around the edges, are used to maintain the backbeat. Grab a chu and get comfortable with playing on it."

For the remainder of the evening, Kylie worked her way clumsily through the song. At the end of the practice, she was feeling accomplished. Though she messed up, the club was encouraging and she thought that she was picking up the material fairly quickly.

***

Late October

The weeks flew by and Kylie continued to grow as a taiko player.

"Dude, I'm so nervous," Kylie said to Ashley one day at lunch. "The semester is halfway over and Gunderson's big midterm is coming up. He's only giving two exams, this and the final. UGH..." Kylie buried her head in her hands.

"You're gonna be fine," Ashley replied. "From what your mom says, you're putting hours into studying for botany. Have faith in yourself. I believe in you."

Ashley squeezed Kylie's arm in reassurance, causing Kylie to look up and smile.

"Thanks, Ash. I'm just such a wreck right now. Everyone else has had at least one exam. I have no idea what's on this one and there's no practice exam online."

"Ladies," Heath said, sidling over to the two. "Mind if I join you for a moment?"

"Sure," Ashley said with a flirtatious smile.

"Kylie, Stacy wanted me to let you know that the end-of-semester show is on the first Wednesday in December. Since we have a little over a month to practice, she wanted to add an extra hour to the Tuesdays and Thursdays. Is that okay? Normally, she just unilaterally makes the decision, but since you're new, she wanted to make sure you can make it. I told her that you should be given a spot in the front."

"Yeah, I can make that... Wait. What? The front? Me?"

"Don't be mad, but I thought it'd be a great way for you to show off what you've learned."

Kylie groaned into her hands.

"She'd love to do it," Ashley said. "You may not know it, but Kylie thrives on challenges."

"Perfect, I'll let Stacy know." Rising from the table, Heath made his way out of the student union with a wave of a hand.

Ashley took a sip from her drink before nudging Kylie. "This is your time to shine. You've always wanted to solo during drumline. This can't be much different."

"I know. It's just so nerve-wracking because I had two years of drumline. I've only been doing taiko for two months."

"You'll be fine. You're a natural. Plus, you know percussion and have great timing."

"You're right." A wide smile spread across Kylie's face. "This is my chance."

"Well, then, with that settled, I'm going to head out. Reiner's lab is in fifteen."

"See ya."

Ashley got up and headed to the doors. Kylie reached into the potato chip bag to grab a chip. Chewing on the morsel slowly, she got up and made her way out of the union and towards the library.

Another half hour of fungi life cycles can't hurt anyone...

***

Kylie's phone vibrated in her pocket after class.

A missed call from Emi.

Kylie called her friend back. "Hey, Emi, what's up?"

"Are we still on for the movie tonight? Jo-Jo can grab the tickets for us since she's getting out of class early and we can just pay her back."

"Ah, shit! I totally forgot we were seeing a movie tonight. I can't make it, I have practice and then I need to study for a midterm tomorrow. I'm so sorry."

"Again?" Emi cried out in exasperation. "Dammit, Kylie, this is the fifth time you flaked on us. Do you just not want to hang with us anymore?"

"No! That's not it at all. I just… I'm so busy and I can't keep my schedule straight. I'm so sorry. I'll make it up to you guys."

"No, Kylie. That's okay. I didn't think this would happen to us, but maybe we need to go our separate ways. I mean, Jo-Jo's only going off to school hundreds of miles away in December. I'm sure we'll all be able to see each other often." Her voice dripped with sarcasm. "You do you. We're going to spend time with her before she leaves – because we're friends."

The line suddenly cut off before Kylie could say anything else. Staring down at her screen, Kylie felt a tear roll down her cheek. "I'm sorry, guys…"

Kylie slowly made her way towards parking structure five. She kept replaying the call in her head.

I can't believe I've flaked five times. I don't even remember doing it…

A chaotic rhythm played in her mind as she neared her car. It seemed to mirror the myriad of emotions that she was feeling at the moment. Kylie struggled to ignore the distracting beats as she walked.

"Hey, Ky!" Ashley called out.

Turning around, Kylie quickly attempted to wipe her tears with her sleeve, but Ashley saw.

"What's wrong, sweetie?" Ashley hurried over and draped her arm around Kylie's shoulders.

"I forgot we were meeting up with Emi and the girls tonight," Kylie replied, sniffling.

"Oh... it's okay. We all know how you get when you get busy. We can all hang out another day." Ashley rubbed Kylie's shoulders, trying to comfort her friend.

"No," Kylie said, suddenly resolute. "I'm gonna go after taiko. I'll leave a bit early and I should make it. Can you ask Jo-Jo to get me a ticket?"

Ashley stared at Kylie, unsure of what to do. After a pause, she nodded. "Hey, Ky, maybe you should skip practice tonight if you're going out. You don't want to wear yourself thin."

"Thanks, but I have everything under control."

Reaching her car, Kylie grabbed her gym bag from the trunk and made her way to the gym for taiko practice.

***

Kylie attempted to sneak into her room around midnight. As she walked down the hallway, she prayed that the creaky floorboard would not betray her and wake her parents. Luck was not on her side, however, as she lightly stepped on the wooden floor and hit the sweet spot. With a loud groan, the floor announced her presence, waking her parents.

"Kylie, baby, is that you?" her mom asked groggily. "What are you doing up? You know you have a test tomorrow." Rubbing her eyes, Loretta stared at her daughter, still dressed in her school clothes. "You're not just getting home now, are you?" she asked sharply.

Kylie nodded meekly.

"Good Lord, Kylie! Where were you? This has to stop. You can't keep doing all these extracurriculars. Your grades will suffer."

"No, Mom! I promise I'll keep my grades up. I've got almost straight A's this semester so far," Kylie pleaded. "We're so close to the Cup. It's my last year."

"Then you need to stop the drumming," she said sternly.

"Mom," Kylie begged, drawing out her name. "Drumming helps keep the stress away and is something I want to continue when soccer's over. Please don't do this to me."

"Go to bed, we'll talk about this later," her mother instructed.

"I promise I will do well," Kylie said as she made her way into her room.

Kylie waited until her mother turned off the bedroom light before she switched on her lamp and threw a light rag over it to dim the light before cracking open her chemistry book and studying. *I can't give them a reason to take away anything.* Poring over the books and her notes for several hours, Kylie eventually succumbed to her exhaustion on top of her notebook, the faint beat of drums lulling her to sleep.

She awoke the next morning to a puddle of drool on her notes, luckily not ruining any important information. Scrambling, Kylie got dressed and grabbed a quick bite to eat before racing to school. Once she reached her class, she sat down and waited for the teacher to pass out the exam. Her eyes felt heavy and she yawned.

Three minutes...

Slowly, the class filled up with students desperately trying to cram several weeks' worth of knowledge in the last few minutes. All too soon, the instructor said the dreaded words, "Books and study materials away. It's time to start."

Kylie found herself facing a thick test packet and only an hour to complete it. As she worked her way through the exam, she felt her eyelids droop. Resting her head on her hand for a moment, she closed her eyes.

She could hear the deep, resonating beat of drums coming at her from all directions. Looking around, she saw darkness. The only source of light was a brilliantly full moon. A gentle breeze pushed several branches into the light of the moon, the leaves dancing almost in time with the beating of the drums. Kylie slowly walked forward, trying to see more of her surroundings. The rhythm began to crescendo in a frenzied hurry as she made her way through the darkness.

A gentle shake of her shoulder jolted Kylie awake.

"It's time to turn in your exam," her teacher told her.

"Wha-" Kylie slurred.

"The exam is over. Please hand it in."

Kylie stared at her exam, barely touched, and handed it over with a depressed sigh. With great effort, she climbed out of her chair and made her way to the door.

"Kylie," her instructor called after her. "I've noticed that you have been looking a bit worn. Is everything all right?"

"Oh, yes," she replied.

"That's good to hear."

Kylie left, but before she got more than a dozen feet from the classroom she turned back and stuck her head into the room. "Is there a way to possibly make up this exam?"

Her teacher shook her head, causing a pit to form in Kylie's stomach. "There will be some opportunities in lab, however, for you to earn some extra credit. You may want to look into those options."

"Thank you very much."

"You'll also want to consider getting a good night's sleep before the next exam. A second exam like this one," he waved the partially completed packet at her, "and you will have to repeat the course."

"Understood."

***

Late November

With a deafening *DON*, the members of Taiko GoGo finished the last song of the evening. Sweat dripping slightly off her brow, Kylie put down her bachi and grabbed her water bottle. "Man, I never thought a song would wear me out that much. And I thought Coach T. worked us out."

"When is your District Cup again?" Caleb asked.

"The semi-finals are next Saturday and Sunday. If we do well, the finals are the weekend after that."

"Have you guys been to the Cup before?" Heath asked. "It's for your recreational team, right?"

"Yeah. Last year we got second place. This is the last year for half of the team, including me, so we're hoping to make it all the way this year." Kylie took a wistful sip from her water bottle. "I'd really love to win."

"Hey, Kylie," Stacy said, "maybe you should skip the next couple of practices. I don't want you to burn out, especially since exams are coming up again."

"Huh?"

"Well, I know you've been putting a lot of effort into the club, and trust me, it really shows," Stacy said with a smile, "but we want to make sure that you're not going to burn out too quickly."

"Last year we had these siblings, Mary and Francis, who were really gung-ho about the club, but after three months they stopped because their grades started to suffer," Heath said.

"Oh, don't worry, I have everything under control," Kylie reassured the group.

The group drank from their water bottles and then began putting away the drums. Alisha and Erica giggled as they discussed how cute they thought their child development laboratory instructor was.

"His hair is so great," Erica exclaimed.

"But his smile," Alisha countered. "Not to mention, his body…"

"That's my big sister," Heath mused. "Talking about how she loves her teacher."

"He's a student teacher, Heath," she replied, flushing.

Her response resulted in a hearty laugh from everyone. Even Erica joined in, face still a bright shade of red.

Why can't practice be longer? Kylie thought as she wiped a tear away from the corner of her eye.

Heath made an uncanny impression of his sister's lovestruck eyes, eliciting another round of laughter from the group. Kylie's stomach hurt from all of the entertainment and she wiped another tear forming in her eye from the mirth.

***

The crisp morning air caused gooseflesh to prickle her skin. Her braids were tied up in a high ponytail and the sleeves of her soccer jersey were wrapped up like a tank top, contrasting her dark skin against the green fabric.

"All right, girls," Coach Thompson encouraged, "this is it. We are one game away from the District Cup. We've made it a long way these last few years, but you've put in so much extra work this year and it's paid off."

"Heatherglen is a tough team, though," Assistant Coach Scott continued. "Remember how they made us work during the season. Don't stoop to their levels, either," he warned. "If they try something dirty, just keep it cool. We'll show them who's the better team by the way we play."

The girls nodded their heads silently.

"Kylie, Courtney," Coach Thompson said, "you two will be our captains. If you win the coin toss, we want this side. The sun is still rising and we don't want it in our eyes for the first half."

"Got it," Courtney answered.

"You can do it," Coach Scott beamed.

The girls and their coaches placed their hands in the center of the circle and gave a mighty cheer before heading out to get their gear inspected by the referees.

A sharp blast from the referee's whistle signaled the start of the game. Players clad in red and green jockeyed to maintain possession of the ball. Kylie and her team played like a well-oiled machine. Almost as one, the defense coordinated with the offense, keeping the ball from touching the net. Unfortunately, the other team did the same. Despite the snide comments and occasional elbow being thrown, they also managed to keep Kylie and her teammates from scoring.

With the first half winding down, the score remained zero to zero. Sweat beaded on Kylie's brow as she waited at the half line. Her fellow striker stood a little closer to the action, hoping for a loose ball lobbed her way through the halfbacks or defense.

"You're gonna lose."

Kylie turned around to look at the sweeper standing by her.

"You're gonna lose," she repeated, smiling. Her eyes held no joy.

Turning away from her, Kylie focused on the game. The ball landed dangerously close to the eighteen, the large box surrounding the goalposts. Cheers and screams mixed together. A red jersey broke from the pack and made her way towards the goal. The keeper ran out to meet the opposing forward.

The two came together in a sickening crunch. Both players went down and the shriek of the whistle could be heard as all players took a knee.

"Bitch's out of the game," the sweeper said loud enough for only Kylie to hear.

Struggling to ignore her, Kylie watched as Coach Thompson ran onto the field. The keeper, Beth, wasn't getting up. Hobbling off of the field with her coach was the striker. A smear of blood covered her right knee.

Coach Thompson yelled for someone to grab a towel as he lifted Beth into his arms. Girls in green gasped as Beth's bloody face was quickly covered by Scott's shirt.

That explains the knee...

People on both sides clapped as the girls left the field. As a new red striker entered the field, Josefina took her spot as keeper. Kylie struggled to remain focused as she heard some of the Heatherglen girls laugh and joke about the collision.

"Ky," Yvette, her fellow striker, said as she jogged up to Kylie. "Ky, we need to play smart. Hao said that they've been playing dirty all game. One of their girls ground their heel into her foot on a throw-in. Just a heads up."

"Thanks, Vette."

The sound of the whistle signaled the start of play once more. Josefina kicked the ball close to the top of their half of the field. Kylie and Yvette took off, Kylie towards the ball and Yvette keeping pace with a defender. The sweeper went to challenge Kylie. Only a few feet separated the two from the ball. With a burst of speed, Kylie beat the sweeper to the ball and faked her out, taking the open field on the left and making her way towards the goal.

A curse escaped the sweeper's mouth as the momentum moved the players towards the Heatherglen side of the field. Wind whipped through Kylie's hair as she neared the goal. Yvette positioned herself in a way to keep the closest defender from Kylie. Eyeing an open spot in the goal, Kylie drew her foot back to kick just as the whistle sounded, ending the first half.

"Dammit," she cried as the ball arced beautifully into the upper right corner of the net.

Yvette and another of Kylie's teammates could be heard swearing as well. Both teams walked off the field for their fifteen-minute break before the second half. Kylie and the others made their way to their coach. Beth was standing off to the side, an icepack pressed against her mouth. Kylie gave her a hug as she exited the field.

"That was a nice shot," Beth said in a feeble attempt to comfort her friend. "You'll get another one."

"I know. Did she get your nose?"

"No." Removing the icepack, Kylie saw the split lip. A bump also could be seen under her bangs. "Didn't lose any teeth though."

"I'm glad."

"Girls," Coach Thompson called.

The team gathered together to discuss the second half.

"Things are getting dirty, but we've kept possession the majority of the half. Keep doing what you're doing and we will have it. Don't fall for their tactics. They're just trying to get a reaction." Turning to Kylie and Yvette, he addressed them and a halfback. "Jun, I want you to hang back a bit with Yvette and Kylie. Their center defender is fast. I want you to shadow her."

"Got it," Jun replied.

The shriek of the whistle came all too soon and the teams took the field. Both Heatherglen and Featherbrooke stood tense, waiting for the kick-off. At the signal from the referee, the second half began. The game moved at a breakneck pace as an early pick allowed Featherbrooke to take possession of the ball, leaving Heatherglen scrambling.

Fifteen minutes into the half and Kylie found herself in a familiar situation. The ball was on her half, Yvette was a few yards ahead while the sweeper hugged the line. Jun could be seen fighting for the ball. Suddenly, Jun broke free and kicked the ball far upfield. Yvette got to the ball first and Kylie broke away towards the goal. Cries from the sidelines muffled in her ears as she kept pace with Yvette.

"Cross!" Kylie yelled as the sweeper closed on Yvette.

A strong kick sent the ball in Kylie's direction. Trapping the ball, Kylie took a quick moment and fired the ball into the net. Girls screamed as the whistle announced the goal. Yvette and Jun grabbed her in a giant hug. Curses from Heatherglen could be heard.

Setting up for the kick-off, Kylie couldn't help but let a small smile escape. The half continued with Heatherglen attempting to keep possession. A shot on goal was deflected by Josefina. Diving onto the ball, she stopped it and then punted it across the field. Kylie got to the ball first and broke away towards the goal once more.

"Kylie!" Jun called.

Kylie looked towards Jun just as the sweeper slide tackled her, not even touching the ball. Down she went. A whistle and a yellow card appeared in short succession. Kylie took the kick and launched the ball towards the goal, angry at the blatantly illegal move. Yvette took possession of the ball in the eighteen-yard box and was immediately tackled by the keeper. The keeper quickly regained her feet and punted the ball towards her striker. Featherbrooke, slow to react, watched as one of the Heatherglen strikers scored a goal.

With the second half winding down and the score one to one, Kylie's team started to lose their groove as Heatherglen began playing even dirtier. A handful of yellow cards flashed before the whistle blew, signaling the end of the half. Only one thing remained to determine the champion: a shoot-out. Three girls from each team were chosen. If there was another tie, then another three would be chosen.

Jun went first and scored a goal.

A familiar rhythm played softly in the otherwise silent air.

The first red jersey came up to the line. Goal.

The music grew louder.

Yvette went second. Blocked.

The music grew louder still, the tempo of the beats picking up as the tension increased.

Second red. The shot went wide.

Silence.

Her feet were lead as Kylie made her way to the ball. *I can end it now.* Staring at the goal, Kylie pictured where she wanted the ball to go. She backed up a number of steps and then ran to kick the ball.

A sudden image of a pale-faced woman flashed in her mind as she connected with the ball.

The ball arced towards the left upper corner of the goal.

Blocked.

Kylie couldn't believe it.

Third red.

A hush fell upon the field.

She ran up to the ball and kicked.

Josefina dived for the ball.

Goal.

Screams erupted from the Heatherglen side as silence engulfed Featherbrooke. Kylie and her teammates worked half-heartedly to console each other at the loss. Heatherglen girls were never the humblest of players and these girls were no exception.

Upon receipt of her second-place trophy, Kylie shared teary-eyed hugs and pictures with her team. *And so ends my soccer career...*

***

Early December

Pages lay scattered around her on the laughable excuse for a table as though a tornado passed by. Open textbooks copiously marked by yellow highlighter sat buried under binders, notebooks, and loose pages. The buzz of chatter in the student union drowned out her focus. Chewing on the end of her mechanical pencil, Kylie pored through her notes on cellular respiration.

The drums beat dully in the corner of her mind as she forced herself to treat music like the union noise. It was almost a constant in her life now. Unless she forced herself to focus, it would pound in her mind, pulsating like a second heart within her. Unlike the beginning of the year, however, the music no longer held a frantic tempo. As though in relation to her own skill level, the beats slowly were smoothing out and almost held a soothing quality at times.

Glycolysis, Krebs, ETC... Gotta remember how much ATP is made and what the byproducts are...

A tap on the shoulder caused her to jump and the rhythmic beating to stop.

"I'm sorry, Kylie," Ashley apologized. "I've been trying to get your attention for a while, but you were so out of it. I come with a peace offering," she said sheepishly as she held up a smoothie.

Without a word, Kylie nodded and moved some of her chaos so her friend could sit down.

Ashley placed the extra smoothie close to Kylie and quietly took a sip. Several minutes passed as Kylie worked and Ashley sat in silence. "Kylie," she broached, "you're wasting away."

"Huh?"

"All you do is study and practice taiko. I thought things would quiet down a bit for you once soccer was over, but you seem to be putting more energy into the two. Look at you, you've lost like ten pounds since the Cup. We're supposed to be gaining weight," she finished with a weak attempt at a joke.

Running her hand through her braids, Kylie let out a heavy sigh. Grabbing her smoothie, she took several big gulps. "Thanks for the concern, Ash, but I got this. I just need to make sure that I ace this semester. I've been doing some research and if I want to stand a chance at getting into veterinary school, I need to have an amazing GPA and a ton of internship hours."

Ashley stared at her friend, concern evident in her eyes.

"I'm planning on applying for an internship at Dr. Banner's clinic this summer while you're on your dig. You're still doing that, right?"

"Yeah. But all this stress isn't good for you. Remember when you passed out last year during finals because you pushed yourself too hard?"

Waving her hand, Kylie dismissed the statement. "Taiko is actually very relaxing for me. I know that it doesn't seem like it, but thanks to the club, I've found an outlet for myself. I just need to keep practicing to get as good as everyone else."

"Kylie, you're great. I mean, you may not have all their technical skills, but you learn the songs quickly and can keep up with them. That's really good for someone who just started."

A second sigh escaped from Kylie's lips. "Ash, I need to get back to studying. I have an exam at three."

"I understand," she replied softly. Turning to leave, Ashley went to leave the union.

"I'm free Friday if you want to hang out. I miss you..."

"I'll see you Friday," Ashley said, voice cracking slightly.

***

Mid-December

"All right, everyone," Stacy called out to the group. "The show starts in half an hour. Since we've already set up for the first song, let's go over the rest of the setlist. Caleb, Kiyumi, you'll take the solos for Senkai Sakura. Heath is on shime. I'll take solo for Jump Pop. Kylie and Erica will do solos for Matsuri. Heath, you get the last solo with Kiyumi on Hotaru."

Kylie nodded nervously as the others talked nonchalantly. Motioning with her bachi, she tried to remember her solo.

"Don't worry about it too much," Stacy said. "If you make a mistake, no one will know. Just focus on doing your best and you'll be fine."

"Whatever you do, don't stop," Kiyumi joined in. "Honestly, it's no big deal as long as you keep going. Like Stace said, no one will know. You got this." She clapped Kylie on the shoulder for emphasis, a warm smile on her face.

"Thanks," Kylie mumbled. "I'm just a wreck. I always talked about getting a solo in high school, but now that I've got one, I can't believe it. I feel like I shouldn't be given one."

"We wouldn't give you one if we didn't think you could handle it," Kiyumi replied. "You've done so well in practice. Let's just do our best."

"Yes."

In what felt like no time, Kylie found herself in the back row behind a chu. Stacy's voice was muffled in her ears as she explained the first song, Senkai Sakura, or Swirling Cherry Blossoms. As she explained the meaning behind the song to the audience, Kylie nervously wiped her hands on her black leggings.

A loud *TEN TEN TEN* rang out, signaling the start of the song. Kylie barely had time to bring up her right arm before the rest of the ensemble began.

The song passed in a blur of *don*s and *doko*s. Kylie barely had time to think about what she was playing before the song ended. In what felt like minutes, they were already at Matsuri, a song of celebration. Kylie positioned her chu up front with Erica. Taking her spot behind the drum, she took a deep breath and attempted to smile.

TEN TEKKE TEN TEKKE TEKKE TEN TEN!

The shime started off with a quick beat and before she was ready the song started. Kylie's arms flew in wide circles as she played *don*s and *ka*s. In a matter of moments, Erica was finishing up her solo and Kylie would be beginning hers. The cue came and Kylie began her solo.

Her bachi played out a familiar pattern on the drum, but something was wrong. She couldn't feel the essence of the song. Her mind would not show her the song.

Images of frantic people came to her as she played her solo. The people moved hectically around, sometimes bumping into each other in their confusion. Students and teachers looked puzzled, trying to figure out what the source of the feeling of wrongness was. Kylie watched in surprise as her song affected the audience in such a manner.

Oh, God...

A sudden, misplaced *ka* rang through the room, causing the people to disappear. With an effort, Kylie finished her solo and moved on to the cue to signal the rest of the group to join in. Six other drums accompanied Kylie's and the song was completed to a round of applause from the audience.

The remainder of the set passed in a blur. Kylie couldn't even remember what she played. She clapped numbly with everyone in the room, congratulating Caleb and Alisha on their upcoming graduation and wishing them the best as they left the group and moved on to future endeavors.

As she packed up the drums, she heard Ashley calling her name.

"Ky, girl, what's wrong? Are you okay?"

"Yeah," she replied with a sigh. "I think I got in my head. I couldn't feel the song."

"Oh... I'm sorry. If it's any help, I thought you did a great job."

"Thanks, Ash."

"Of course."

"Man, I can't believe I messed up like that. I totally choked."

"You did a great job; especially for your first time." Ashley smiled at Kylie. "Everyone was talking about how good you were for only having practiced for four months. No one I heard had a bad word to say."

"Really?"

"Really," Heath cut in. "Kylie, you truly did a good job. The *ka* was off, but the majority of the song was fine. The audience feeds off of your emotions, so only if you show anything will they know if you messed up."

"Damn... I'm overthinking this," Kylie murmured. A small tear welled in the corner of her eye as she smiled in frustration.

"Girl, you got this," Ashley tried to reassure her.

Opening her mouth to respond, Heath interjected, "By our show in May, you'll be more comfortable. I promise that you'll be able to do another solo if you continue with us. I believe in you." Heath flashed a smile and pulled her into a hug.

Kylie couldn't respond. All that came out was a strangled half-sob. She was surrounded by darkness, a brilliant full moon illuminating her against her failure.

***

Mid-March

"Kylie, baby, are we ever going to see you again?" Loretta stood in her daughter's doorframe while Kylie lay on her bed doing homework.

"I'm sorry, Mom. Things are just so crazy with midterms and taiko. Stacy is letting me put in extra time to practice for the concert in May. It's only two months away, and after December's show I really need to get my act together."

"Just don't wear yourself out, baby. You've been moving non-stop since September. March is almost over. No one can keep this pace up forever."

Scratching her head with her pencil, Kylie thought for a moment. Her mother's figure left the doorframe to retreat downstairs.

"Mom, wait!"

"What is it?"

"Can we go to the mall today?"

Smiling, her mom nodded. "Let me go get Dad."

In what felt like no time, Kylie and her parents strolled leisurely around the mall. With a sigh of contentment, Kylie felt grateful for the break from her busy schedule.

It seems like forever since I've just done nothing. This is nice.

"Kylie, baby," her father interrupted her thought. "Your mama and I will be heading over to the food court for some ice cream. Would you like some?"

"Yes! Cookies and cream, please."

"All right, we'll see you in fifteen or so."

Waving to their daughter, the two made their way to the ice cream shop. Kylie continued on her way, taking in the stores. As she walked, a store with stuffed animals and notebooks with cute animal images on the front caught her eye. Making her way into the store, her eyes were bombarded with bright colors and merchandise with adorable animals and cartoon characters emblazoned on them.

"Wow," she breathed softly.

Weaving her way throughout the large store, Kylie had to exercise great self-control to not walk out with an armful of cuteness and considerably lighter wallet. The musky scent of incense tickled her nose. Turning to the source of the smell, Kylie noticed a small section in the back corner of the store with Japanese trinkets. Heading over to the corner, a soft, melodic sound greeted her ears.

The lilting notes of a *koto* combined with soft drumming could be heard; a stand with compact discs displayed next to a small CD player. The combination of incense and music calmed her soul and left her feeling more relaxed than she had felt in months.

Fingering the little statues on the shelves, Kylie was hit with a sudden vision.

A young woman in flowing robes and long black hair walked over a bridge on a moonlit night. The stars twinkled in the sky. Looking around, Kylie found herself standing only a few feet from the woman. A gentle breeze played with her hair. She looked vaguely familiar.

The woman stood at the side of the bridge and stared at the lake ahead of her. A soft sigh escaped her lips. Tentatively, Kylie made her way towards the woman. The light from the moon was so bright that she could see a solitary tear roll down the woman's cheek. A deep pain suddenly filled her heart. It was not a sharp pain, but a heavy one, like the one she felt when her dog passed on two years earlier.

There are no drums... weird...

"Excuse me," she began, "are you okay?"

"Oh!" the woman exclaimed, rubbing the tear off of her cheek. "Yes, I am. Thank you."

Kylie stood near the woman awkwardly, unsure of what to do now.

"What are you doing here?" the woman asked.

"I... I don't know. I was out with my parents and suddenly I ended up here."

"What are you looking for?"

"What?"

"You don't know what you're doing, but maybe you know why you're here. Only those on a journey come here." The woman's soothing voice relaxed Kylie.

"I'm not on a journey. I went to the mall."

"Mall?" the woman asked.

"It's a place where people can go and buy things," Kylie explained.

"Is this not part of your journey? You wouldn't have visited me if you weren't looking for something," the woman insisted.

"I... I..." Kylie trailed off as she thought about what was going on. After several minutes of thought, she said, "I wanted to get away from my life. It's just so busy with school and taiko, I'm feeling overwhelmed."

"Oh?" She did not speak any further, instead prompting Kylie to continue.

"I know my parents will love me regardless, but I feel like I need to push myself constantly to make sure I get A's. Between that and practice, I haven't had time to enjoy college. It's always move, move, move. I just wanted to take a break from being me for a little, I suppose."

Kylie was greeted with a long pause. The moon neared its peak in the dark sky. Afraid she'd babbled too much, Kylie started to take a small step backward.

"How do you feel right now?" the woman asked.

"I feel at peace," she replied.

"It feels nice, doesn't it?"

Kylie nodded in agreement.

"Do you feel like you've found your answer?"

"To what question?" Kylie asked.

"To the one you came here with."

The glow of the moon got brighter and brighter until Kylie had to shield her eyes with her arm.

"Wait!" Kylie cried.

"Excuse me?" a teenaged boy replied.

"What?" Kylie spun around, looking at the Japanese statues and compact discs on display. "I... what?"

"Are you okay?" the youth asked. He backed away slightly, a look of concern on his face.

"I'm sorry," Kylie mumbled. Thinking quickly, she asked, "Is the song that's playing now on the disc?"

"Yeah. Would you like to buy the CD?"

"Yes, please."

Walking out of the store with her purchase in hand, Kylie made her way back towards the food court and her parents.

The tranquility that she felt while talking to the woman stayed with her throughout the rest of their time at the mall and all the way home. Making her way to her room, she pulled the disc out of the bag and laid it on her bed. Laying on her back, she thought about her experience.

That was so bizarre. I wonder what that meant?

A buzzing on her desk distracted her from her thoughts. Looking at the screen, she saw who texted.

Heath, huh?

> **Can you meet me at the Union in an hour? I really need to talk to you.**

I wonder what he wants...

> Yeah. See ya there.

Rolling off her bed, Kylie made her way out of her room, phone in hand. After passing through the door frame, she paused for a moment before returning back and grabbing the compact disc off her bed and taking it with her.

The drive to school left Kylie feeling confused. *What could he want from me that he can't just text?* At a stop light, Kylie popped the disc into her car's CD player and felt the soothing sounds of the *koto* take her away. Peace washed over her, allowing for her mind to wander. *It seems like today's been a day of journeys lol. Oh God, I can't believe I said the 'lol'. I gotta cut that down some.*

As the parking structure came into view, she pulled her parking permit from behind her sun visor and hooked it onto her rearview mirror. Seeing "her" spot by the stairwell, Kylie parked and got out of her car. Making her way to the union, she saw Heath by the bookstore.

"Hey," he said waving.

"Hey, what's up?"

"Walk with me?"

"Sure."

The two walked in silence for a brief moment before Heath broke the silence.

"Kylie, I don't know how to say this, but Stacy was in an accident this morning."

A gasp escaped her as her hands moved to cover her mouth. "Is she?"

"She's going to be fine, it's just that she's going to be out for the rest of the semester. Kiyumi said she was t-boned by someone running the light. I think she said that Stace's going to need some physical therapy. Her hand and leg were crushed or something."

"Are we going to send flowers or something?"

"Yeah. Everyone in the club wants to chip in to get her some. Caleb and Alisha are going to pitch in some, too."

"I think I can add twenty, if that's okay?"

"That's perfect. Actually, this is only part of what I wanted to talk about. I asked you to meet me today because Kiyumi will be leading practice tomorrow. She's thinking of canceling our end of the year performance. I know you've put in a lot of effort into practice and I didn't want you to be caught off-guard. We'll be voting tomorrow on what to do."

"I see," she murmured. "What are you thinking?"

"I don't think she'd want us to stop."

"Me neither," Kylie agreed. "Will you say anything?"

Running his hand through his hair, Heath sighed. "I don't know. I see where she's coming from and I agree with the premise. I just don't think we should cancel something we've all worked so hard for."

Circling back to the student union, Heath stopped and looked at his phone. "Hey, I have to go to work soon. Thanks for meeting with me."

"Of course," Kylie replied.

"Later."

"Bye!"

As Kylie made her way to her car, she heard Heath's voice calling out to her.

"You know, part of why I told you is because I really think you have something. You pick up the material well. I really hope you decide to solo if we have the concert."

Blushing, Kylie smiled sheepishly and made her way to her car. During her drive home, she listened to the soothing music purchased earlier that day.

I can't believe that happened to Stacy. I'm glad she's okay. Is it wrong that I'm not more upset about this? I'm feeling so... relaxed. How strange...

Stopped at a traffic light, Kylie closed her eyes briefly and took a deep breath. The soft beating of drums coupled with the lilting *koto* music soothed her.

I hope Heath and I can convince Kiyumi to keep the group going.

"I see you're well on your journey," a soft voice said.

Snapping her eyes open, Kylie looked around and found herself on the bridge under the moonlight. The young woman stood to her side, a benign smile on her face.

"What? Where am I?" Kylie stammered.

"The moon is calming, right?"

"I suppose," Kylie replied, confused as to why the woman was ignoring her questions. "But what does that have to do with what's going on?"

Looking over the side of the bridge into the water below, the woman beckoned Kylie over. Large koi swam in lazy circles, moving gracefully through the water. "During the daytime, the smaller fish move chaotically in the lake. Their movements rushed, the water rippling constantly." Kylie stayed quiet, unsure if she was supposed to respond. The woman continued, not noting the silence. "They swim with no real objective, just swimming to swim. Much like yourself. You keep yourself much too busy and disturb the water. I think this is why you are on a journey. You think that you need to swim towards a destination, but perhaps you just need to let the journey find you, like the koi."

Kylie opened her mouth to respond but closed it. Taking a moment, she collected her thoughts. "So, I should slow down?"

Nodding, the woman replied, "Take a moment to find the true meaning of all of your actions. Perhaps you are making too many unnecessary movements."

Kylie blinked and found herself back in her car. Music played softly in the background as the traffic light turned green.

"Weird..." she murmured.

***

Kylie sat in a circle with the rest of her taiko group. Though her mind raced, the beating of the drums was steady, a constant in her hectic life.

The group sat in stunned silence, trying to absorb what Kiyumi just told them. After several minutes, Erica finally spoke.

"So, what are we going to do then?"

"Well," Kiyumi began, "I don't think it's fair to Stacy that we perform her last show without her."

"Yumi, she would want us to go on," Heath said.

"We're few enough in number as it is. Without Stacy, we just have us four," Kiyumi explained.

"How will we continue the group if no one knows we exist?" Heath argued. "The only way we get our name out there is to play shows. We play few enough as it is. With Stacy leaving this semester, it's only the four of us anyway. This will be good experience for us."

Kiyumi sat silently.

Looking around the circle, Kylie saw the mixture of emotions on her friends' faces. Heath's eyes shone with determination, while Kiyumi's were unsure. Erica sat in silence, looking back and forth between the two.

Find the true meaning of all of my actions...

"I agree with Heath," Kylie spoke up.

All eyes were on her. Kiyumi nodded for her to continue.

"I, well, I think that the best way to honor Stacy's spirit in the group would be to play her songs like she wanted us to do. I think you both make good points, but at the end of the day, we're going to be down one member. Let's show all of Stacy's hard work and great leadership skills by putting on a kick-ass show."

The group sat quietly.

Did I do the right thing?

"Kylie's right," Erica finally said. "Let's show everyone Stace's vision."

"Then, it's settled," Kiyumi said with a smile. "We play. Let's get to practice."

***

Mid-May

The dull rumble of voices filled the auditorium. Students, teachers, and family filled the building, chatting happily about finals being over and their summer plans. Kylie stood off to the side, staring anxiously at the growing crowd. She spent the last three weeks listening to her CD and trying to focus on the most important issues in her life. Knowing that her grades were comfortably in the A range, she took the opportunity to cut down her study time and insert a little relaxation into her daily routine. Fifteen minutes of meditation daily worked wonders for her previously stressful life.

Now, all she focused on was her nerves. Breathing slowly, she visualized what she wanted to do. They were playing a short set tonight, just five songs. She'd practice them for countless hours, even in her dreams.

"Ready, everyone?" Kiyumi asked.

"Yeah," everyone replied in unison.

"Stacy is in the audience," Heath added.

"Let's do this for Stacy," Erica said.

"For Stacy," Kylie agreed.

As one, the group walked onto the floor and stood behind their drums. The girls took their place behind the chu drums up front and Heath manned the shime drum in the back to provide the backbeat. Scanning the audience, Kylie saw her family pointing and smiling at each other.

Huh, even Marcus is here.

With a countdown from Heath, the concert started. Butterflies flew in her stomach, but as she went through her first piece she slowly began to settle into the rhythm of the song. By the second song, she found a little comfort in the fact that they'd been practicing the song since September. Her arms moved swiftly as she played the head and rim of the drum. Slowly, but surely, the butterflies in her stomach settled down and she found herself smiling during the song.

Before she knew it, the performance was nearing its end and they began their last song. The butterflies that slowly calmed during the set decided to start moving around again. Closing her eyes and taking a deep breath, Kylie attempted to steady her nerves.

"You got this," Heath's voice rang in her head.

"It's your time to shine!" Ashley's joined in.

"Listen to me, Kylie," Stacy said, *"everyone makes mistakes, but it's how we recover from them that matters. Trust me, no one but you will know if you mess up."*

Opening her eyes, Kylie found her mother and father, beaming at her as she stood on the stage. Loretta's hands were clasped together just below her chin. A mighty *kiai* from Kiyumi signaled the start of the song. As one, the group launched into an upbeat song, Heath playing a peppy tempo in the background. Time seemed to slow down as her solo neared. Before she knew it, the solo was upon her.

With a quick breath, Kylie began. Her solo was filled with booming *dons* and sharp *kas*. Cherry blossoms formed in her mind's eye. The gently falling petals landed around her, comforting her as she played. A small smile crept onto her face briefly before she hit a sour note on the drum. Suddenly, the flowers stopped falling and her nerves got the better of her.

Her strikes were hesitant against the drum. Around her, her group mates were *kiai*-ing in encouragement as her solo progressed. Scanning the crowd, she found Stacy sitting a few seats away from her family. Stacy's eyes were filled with joy as she watched her group's show. Next to Stacy, the pale woman in the robes sat in a seat.

"Look, Kylie," she said, smile upon her face.

Kylie's eyes darted around her and watched as cherry blossom flowers slowly danced towards the lake in the bright moonlight. Somehow, she'd managed to pull her song back on beat and began hitting with strong, confident hits. The koi stopped swimming and appeared to be facing her as she played.

"Your journey has reached its conclusion. This was just the last part."

"I don't understand," Kylie replied.

"You've been living your life at such a breakneck pace. You never took the time to admire the beauty of quietness. Listen to your song. The *ma*, the space between the beats. They are right. You've found your peace."

Blinking, Kylie realized that it was time to move on to the portion of the song to signal her group mates to join her once more to finish the song. With a loud *kiai*, Kylie finished her cue and the group completed their piece with a resounding boom.

The audience erupted into applause as Kylie and her group bowed in thanks to their support. Waving to the crowd, Kylie watched as Stacy hobbled up to them.

"Guys! You were great! I'm so happy I could make it out to see you," Stacy gushed.

Kiyumi and Erica began speaking with Stacy in earnest as Kylie looked for her parents.

"You were wonderful, baby girl!" Vernon exclaimed. "We're so proud of you."

"Thank you," Kylie smiled sheepishly.

"Not bad," Marcus said, trying his hardest not to look too impressed, but failing.

Looking over her family's shoulders, Kylie found the woman in robes standing on the bridge. She nodded her head in approval before slowly making her way off of the bridge. The light of the moon faded as it sunk in the sky.

The cherry blossoms continued to fall around her.

DIRK DARINGMORE
and the Xenubian Queen

Written by

Nicholas Walls

irk Daringmore, Hero of the Inter-Galactic Republic, staggered down the shadowed hallway with gritted teeth and furrowed brow. Each step proved a grueling trial, a contest of will to continue onward and not simply surrender, give in, and let it all go where he stood. Lost in the bowels of a strange and alien planet, he struggled in vain to find the object of his mission.

"Blasted Xenubians, writing everything in their nonsense gibberish. Why can't they just label the bathrooms in Galactic Common like everyone else?" Dirk shuffled down the hallway, legs squeezed tight enough to make his immaculately laundered breeches squeak.

The square jawed hero glanced down at his chrono-keeper. Dirk didn't do so to check the time, but rather because the gold-plated wrist clock doubled as a mirror. Reassured by the ruggedness of his own heroic countenance, the former Captain now turned self-appointed Ambassador inched his way deeper into the stone-tiled dungeon, litany of complaints echoing off the walls.

"I should be hip deep in endless sandy beaches, surrounded by green skinned supermodels, and drowning in exotic fruity drinks! That's the last time I take vacation advice from the Officer's Lounge." Daringmore's erroneous impression of Xenubia, gathered from his fellow officers' gossip, had sent Dirk racing to the stars in his personal cruiser until he alighted on the lush world, located in a quiet corner of Republic space, lured by lurid tales of their Golden Jubilation celebrations.

Had Daringmore bothered to read up on Xenubia, he would have known the quiet, reserved people celebrated their planet's ongoing peace and prosperity with quiet introspection, solemn private gatherings, and public, family friendly ceremonies led by their elder priests.

So it was when the Republic officer first landed on Xenubia, Dirk found the affairs curiously absent of any alcoholic beverages and struggled to reconcile the lack of dancing girls. All through the airport, the red-and-blue uniformed soldier searched high and low for signs of hedonistic abandon. Alas, to no avail. Daringmore passed all through customs and all he got was a lousy, garishly colored, pink and yellow oversized shirt.

Still, a fervent patriot through and through, Daringmore refused to doubt the muttered hearsay of his fellow officers. As such, Captain Daringmore blamed the locals for any discrepancies between his fabricated expectations and the reality of the situation.

At this point, he blamed the locals for just about everything.

After unsuccessfully soliciting local businesswomen for services of dubious repute, mistaking a local high priest for a bagboy, and utterly failing to get drunk no matter the amount of fruity beverages he downed, Dirk had wandered into the large towering ziggurat, figuring there must be some restrooms there.

Now, almost an hour later, the end seemed nigh and Dirk Daringmore valiantly considered dropping trousers where he stood and blaming it on a dog later.

"Always blame it on the dog." Even as he rationalized defecating in public, Dirk found his hands inching toward his belt of their own accord. He froze them in place with a supreme act of will, driven by a sudden and mortal terror.

"No! I'm a hero to millions! Billions! I must press on...for the sake of those poor souls...and my completely deserved reputation. I shall not soil my good name nor my trousers!"

Heroically cross-eyed and whimpering to himself about breakfast cereal endorsements, Dirk tore open a moldering door with a squeak of rusted hinges and pressed ever deeper into the ancient structure.

***

If things previously looked dark for the vacationing Republic officer, things went positively medieval. Torches burned in iron sconces and alien cuneiform scrawled over the weathered red stone of the tunnel floors and walls. It took Daringmore a moment to realize the wall he was leaning against was likely more ancient than the Republic itself.

Dirk stopped in front of a particularly complex mural, its age worn facade depicting figures battling a giant multi-armed evil with burning hair and eyes of fire. The captain studied it for a moment before he flipped the hieroglyphics the bird in frustration.

"You waste an entire wall on your stupid pictures but can't put a sign for the bathroom up there?"

And at that most stoic moment, a feminine voice cried out. "Oh, at last, I am saved!"

Daringmore squawked and jumped at the unexpected sound, very nearly solving his need to find a bathroom right then and there. Finely honed battle skills taking over, he whirled, then whirled again as his half-cape smacked him in the face. Finally free of the cloth, no doubt made too long by a traitorous tailor in the employ of one of the Republic's many foes, Dirk's eyes found the source of the voice.

Dirk gaped. Behind bars of intricately wrought iron stood a green skinned vision of beauty. Looking as decidedly feminine as her voice suggested, she stood as tall as Dirk (counting his boots, which added a good inch or three with the heels) dressed only in gauzy cloth which left little to the imagination.

Golden cuffs adorned her wrists, ankles, and a gleaming collar wrapped about her neck also piqued Dirk's curiosity but decorum prevented the mentioning of such things.

Dirk judged her quite a lovely lady. For an alien.

In keeping with his gallant spirit, Dirk pointedly decided not to mention she was behind bars. Such things were rude while in mixed company. "Apologies miss, I didn't see you there."

She coquettishly batted crimson eyes at the suffering hero. "My savior. Thank you for braving this deep and dark dungeon. Will you help me?"

Dirk smiled wide, the torchlight dazzled off of his pearly whites, with hands on hips and chest and chin thrust outward. The hunch and crossed legs might have undermined it slightly. "CERTAINLY! Though I may require your aid first, good citizen." Daringmore leaned forward conspiratorially. "Could you point me to a restroom?"

The emerald cell dweller blinked slowly. Then slowly again. A third blink nearly passed before raising an arm, golden shackle glinting on her wrist. She pointed directly behind Daringmore where, just to the left of the mural, stood an unmistakable image of a bipedal figure running with hands grasping its midsection. An arrow pointed down the hall.

"Around the corner. Second door. Can't miss it."

"Thank you, citizen!" Daringmore gratefully shouted over his shoulder, already vanishing around the corner as he hurried to find the object of his quest.

***

Quest completed, Dirk returned some time later, feeling much refreshed and several pounds lighter. He gave his pompadoured hair one last comb-through before turning to address the idling maiden, who stood inspecting her nails, one foot tapping an impatient rhythm on the stone ground.

By the groove worn into the stone, it was quite a habit.

"All settled, miss. How can Dirk Daringmore, Hero of the Republic (patent pending), be of service?"

Clasping her hands, which did intriguing things to her décolleté, the captive turned pleading eyes upon the attendant Republic officer.

"Oh, kind sir, no doubt you are here for the Golden Jubilation."

Dirk sniffed derisively. "Indeed. I find the tradition backwards and in poor taste, even by the lowered standards of alien kind. These people can't even write signs in good Galactic Common, much less provide a decorated officer with a stiff drink."

The captive made appropriate sympathetic noises. "It is even worse, I'm afraid. They've trapped me here for so long, all on the words of the tyrannical priesthood. I'm terrified of what they might do to me. Why they might even sacrifice me in some barbaric ritual!"

Dirk's meaty fist pounded into an open palm. "The fiends! I knew they couldn't be trusted. No one who mixes pink and yellow can be on the side of the angels." The Republic officer quickly drew his blaster from its holster. "Stand back, miss. I'll have you out in a jiffy!"

As the humming raygun's barrel leveled at her cell, the jade occupant waved her arms in protest. "No! No, I mean, it is secretly protected! Without the special key, a golden necklace holding a giant emerald, it will, ummm, explode." She pouted sadly, rubbing a sandal across the dust strewn floor, knocking aside bone fragments and not quite faded blood stains. "If only someone, someone strong, brave, and so very handsome, could go and fetch the key for me."

Grinning ear to ear, Dirk struck a heroic pose, followed by several more. Some might have questioned the wisdom of waving a fully charged and primed blaster around but not Daringmore. "Fear not, miss! I'll get it for you!"

The lady-of-the-cell batted her eyes with a breathy exhale, best suited for bad daytime holodramas and poorly written salacious videos. "You will? Oh, thank you, so much! It's located in the Hall of Reverent Memories just a short ways from here." When Dirk nodded and didn't budge, the emerald maiden blinked several times, put her hands on hips, and continued. "Go to the end of the hall, you'll find an elevator. Get off on the top floor. You can grab a map from the guest kiosk."

Directions received, the Republic officer ran off with a triumphant shout. As he left, the abandoned prisoner rubbed the bridge of her nose and let out a small sigh of frustration.

"Who brings a blaster to a peace conference?"

***

Stealthily acquiring a map from the kiosk stand and collecting his change from the tender, Dirk Daringmore planned out his next move carefully.

Five minutes later, he was charging through the front doors of the Hall of Reverent Memories, punching the attendee who tried to halt Dirk's assault with the ancient and universal war cry of "How may I help you?"

The cowardly attendee instantly went down, clutching a bloody nose, feigning confusion. As if he weren't up to no good. "That's for this place's overly fancy title! Just call it a museum like good, honest folk!"

Gallivanting onward, Dirk plunged into the ancient artifacts section, boots squeaking on the polished floor. The fiends likely thought a bit of polish would stop the gallant Daringmore. Devious, but not devious enough.

A gaggle of priests barred his path, looking up in surprise as he burst through the main exhibit doors. Taking this as a clear sign of their overreaching repressive theocracy, Dirk took the initiative and started punching.

"Pitiful flailing and cries for help won't save you. Taste my hammers of justice, you filthy animals." The last elderly man fell with a squawk, holding his midsection after one of Dirk's jabs.

Panting, the conquering hero leapt to the altar holding the key. Though he couldn't read the filthy alien gibberish on it, constant motifs of four-armed, flaming-headed, and burning-eyed creatures adorned the altar. All were undoubtedly and pronouncedly female.

Dirk shook his head in disgust. Clearly propaganda and slander against the fairer sex. Smashing the glass covering, he snatched up the great emerald necklace and turned to wag a finger at the downed priests.

"Your backwards ways are disgusting. All clear thinking men know that women are delicate creatures that ought to protected or rescued. Like this! Case in point!" Leaping over their outstretched hands, Dirk beelined back to the temple, half-cape flapping behind him.

*****

By the time the Xenubians found Dirk he was walking out of the dungeon with a smug grin on his face. Seeing the heavily armed force advancing, Dirk whipped out his blaster.

One could never be too careful when facing a score of bearded old men in robes with ornamental staves and walking sticks.

The valiant officer recognized the bearded villain he'd earlier mistaken for a valet. "Ah ha! Revealing your true colors at least, eh, Balzanar? Well, too bad, because I'm the one with diplomatic immunity." Dirk Daringmore proceeded to triumphantly give them the raspberry, thumbs to his ears and tongue wagging.

Even as spittle flew, the old man hobbled up, leaning heavily on his stick. "Please, outlander, what have you done with the Diadem of Xthc'Chala? It may not be too late to avert the doom of our world."

Dirk stopped mid 'berry, fingers waggling above his ears. Daringmore smirked at the old man. Oh, he smirked as hard as he could. "I assure you, it is far too late. I have already given the, um, thingy of...whatever it was to that lovely girl you have imprisoned."

Gasps of shock and horror rose from the robed bunch. "That 'girl' is the Nightmare Queen of Chala, an immortal creature of fire and darkness, imprisoned here ages ago. Her reign of terror was ended only after terrible sacrifice. She was to be locked away forever."

Dirk scoffed at the ludicrous notion. "Stuff and nonsense, old man. I'll not listen to your superstitious rantings..."

The Republic officer's erudite lecture was cut short by a terrible rumbling from deep beneath the earth in a rising crescendo. As it reached a feverish pitch and intensity, a pillar of green fire shot into the sky, erupting through the highest point of the temple complex. Out of the inferno rose a terrible, shadowy figure, eyes burning balefully as it glowered at all it surveyed. Undeniably female, it raised four arms to the heavens and let out a triumphant bellow and a mocking cackle.

Daringmore recognized both from long experience. He was very good at them.

"At last! After ten thousand years, I am free. A new age of darkness and woe shall be unleashed upon the land. Kneel before your master, worms. Tremble and despair! You will call my name out for mercy and it shall be as sweet music to me!"

Dirk grinned sheepishly at the old man, looking like a child with his hand in the cookie jar. "Oops."

Balnazar gripped Daringmore's sleeve with feverish intensity. "Didn't you read the warnings?"

Dirk brushed off the old man with some difficulty. "That was a warning? How was I supposed to read that?"

"It was a gigantic mural! We even put up pictures and everything!"

"Well, that is all fine and good. I thought it was a metaphor for flood or divorce or something!" Dirk huffed with his arms crossed. "You know, you wouldn't have this problem if you just printed things in Galactic Common like sensible people."

The priest waved his arms in exasperation. "It was printed in twelve different languages, *including* Galactic Common! Didn't you read to the bottom?"

"What's done is done, old man. What matters is the here and now." Dirk turned, jaw set, to look at what he had wrought. The queen was laughing and calling down rains of emerald fire onto the land. The panicked cries of the Xenubians carried on the wind. He nodded, certain what he must do.

***

A brisk jog and several minutes later, Dirk sat at the helm of his vessel, rocketing away from the planet, Xenubia's verdant surface growing smaller behind him. The captain took a moment to sip his fruity beverage before speaking into the recorder.

"Despite the culturally insensitive nature of the Xenubians and their lack of consideration by not providing clearly printed signs in Galactic Common, I have deemed it best to stay out of any local religious squabbles. Yes friends, the Inter-Galactic Republic sticks to its policy of non-intervention and dedication to freedom in all things, including religion."

Cyclops: The Musical

Written by

Estee Lee-Mountel & K.N. Nguyen

A blank darkness lingered in waiting. It waited for a long while; so long, in fact, that it's become downright awkward. If this darkness had been occupying a television screen, for example, it would prompt the television viewer to attempt restarting the device. And just as the viewer reaches for a remote control or power button, something happens. An ethereal voice, more felt than heard, begins to speak.

Then, it quite abruptly stops speaking.

In a far-off corner, the sound of a record player screeching to a halt echoes through the darkness, followed by hurried scuffling. A single spotlight stabs through the emptiness to reveal two shining figures. They are humanoid in form, but perfect in every way. With a confidence that could only come from vast wisdom and intelligence, the darker-haired figure opens her lovely mouth and begins to speak.

"My dear mortal," she says gently, yet firmly, "fear not. Due to, ah, alleged abuse of creative license and the threat of litigation, your original hosts will not be joining you here. Instead, my esteemed and divine compatriot and I shall act as your guides. I am Athena, patroness of wisdom and intelligence."

"And I am Ceres!" the other figure declares, her voice booming across the vast expanse. She strikes a striking pose.

Athena plants her divine face into her divine palm. "I already told you: *Ceres* is a Roman goddess's name. We're telling a *Grecian* tale here!"

"It sounded good in my head, okay? It's all Greek to me!"

"You know, this just isn't working for me." Athena tosses down her famous spear and shield, and begins shedding her divine vestments to the floor. "LIGHTS! BRING UP THE LIGHTS, PLEASE!"

As the lights come up around the two goddesses, a small stage is revealed. Dusty curtains hung askew, as if put up hastily by a couple of harried and annoyed writers. After a minute or two of activity, all that remains are two women in shockingly familiar shirts and jeans; their various props and costuming materials laid about them at their feet. The dark-haired woman speaks first once more.

"I'm Estee," she says, "and this is Kristen. We're the writers of the comedic piece you're about to read."

"We had an introduction and lead-in all setup," Kristen says, "but was told to change it last minute. So..."

"So, what you're getting is us instead. Besides, who better to introduce our piece than ourselves, right?"

"Right. In any case, you're probably familiar with some version or another of Homer's epic *The Odyssey*, thanks to high school English class."

"And one of the epic's most famous scenes is Odysseus' encounter with the monstrous Cyclops, using wit and cunning to escape the creature's clutches."

"This retelling is, well..."

"This isn't it. Not by a long shot."

"We took some, um, creative license with the source material."

"But we hope you enjoy it nonetheless. Sit back..."

"Relax..."

The two women take a deep breath together, and speak in chorus: "As we present to you..."

CYCLOPS: THE MUSICAL

"Mister Ulysses, do you know why you're here?"

Principal Alcinous gazed evenly at the lanky youth. Seated behind his polished oak desk, the school administrator looked stately, almost regal. Alastair Ulysses, on the other hand, had the appearance of someone who had just been washed ashore and dragged into the office by an army of irate sea urchins. The teenager's file was sparse. Aside from his work with the high school theatre group, Ulysses didn't cause many ripples amongst his peers... Which was precisely why the principal was baffled by the allegations brought against the young man and his friends. Everything had an explanation, and Alcinous was eager to hear what the boy had to say.

A minute or two passed, filled with much throat clearing and an assortment of other noises that indicated Ulysses was preparing to speak.

"Well, sir," Alastair Ulysses said, with just the right amount of humble apprehension to add a tiny tremor to his voice, "I would assume that it has to do with what happened over Halloween weekend."

"That's one way of putting it, Mister Ulysses," Principal Alcinous said. "Why don't you start at the beginning? And is it really necessary to have the entire theatre club in here, too?"

Ulysses glanced up at the group of his peers gathered behind his chair. He nodded to the principal. "They're rather vital to the story, sir, as you'll see in a second. Now, for what happened this weekend, it all started when these very same friends and I were on our way to a costume party..."

He let his voice drift off artistically. To Principal Alcinous' surprise, Alastair's friends suddenly leaped into the space between the boy and the polished oak desk, and launched into a short piece of choreography. They splayed their hands next to their faces, shouting, "FLASH...!" Then, they whirled around, thumbs pointed at the space between their shoulder blades. "BACK!" they said. This went on about three to four more times before they settled in behind Alastair's chair again.

The principal stared at the boy in blank astonishment. He proceeded to bury his face in one hand, shaking his head. "Flashback. I get it. Thank you, Mister Ulysses."

"Told you I needed them to tell this story properly. Anyway, as I was saying: we were on our way to Penelope's party when we passed by another house already gripped in the throes of revelry. None of us had eaten dinner yet, so we figured we'd see if the party belonged to anyone we knew and whether we could get a snack. Something small just to tide us over while we continued on our journey..."

***

We were totally fucking lost. *Go straight up Main; hang a left on Whirlpool; take the detour around the clusterfuck construction going on near Blue Water Drive and Stone Island Lane...* This is what I get for listening to some idiot's half-assed directions instead of looking it up myself. Guess that makes me the bigger idiot, though. Oh, I'd turn on the GPS and plug the address in like everyone else, but my family's too cheap to pay extra for data service. All I wanted to do was get to Penelope's and spend Halloween with her. And eat, preferably with Penelope. Maybe dance with Penelope. If I'm lucky, I might get a kiss... *ahem.* Yet, here I am wasting my time getting lost in the labyrinthine— but quite glamorous— subdivision of Cypress Isles.

Behind me, my friends from the theatre club were dutifully following along, if not distractedly. It doesn't help that all of these streets and houses look nearly identical; but that's 21st century suburbia for you. On a whim, I turn down a side street. Why not? When you're lost, you might as well make the best of it, and explore and learn something. Someone grumbles about being hungry. I'm inclined to agree.

Suddenly, a glimmer of hope: I hear the deep, sternum-shaking bass of party music nearby. I glance at the signpost on the corner, but it was wrong street. The music was still a sign of civilization, though. With any luck, it might be some classmate's party and we could grab a quick bite— along with the Wi-Fi password so my phone can be more than just a glorified paperweight. For the first time this evening, I felt like things were looking up.

Our merry band of costumed teenagers crossed the street to what we hoped was an oasis of sustenance and an Internet connection. I waved for everyone else to hang back. Depending on whose party this was, it could go either very well or very, very badly. The thumping music masked my approach to the open backyard. All of my stealth and discretion was apparently for naught. No one noticed me because there was no one around, which was a shame because I can't imagine what idiot would leave such a feast unguarded.

Looking around, my eyes fell on a feast fit for the gods. My mouth watered as I beheld the splendor of a crockpot filled with barbecue meatballs, rolled salami filled with cream cheese, and the salty snackage bounty of Costco. I could practically taste the savory morsels. Stuffing my mouth with a salami roll, I turned and hailed my intrepid troupe of misfits.

This may not have been my best idea. A herd of hungry juniors set loose on such a glut resulted in such a foot pounding that rivalled even the bass. This would prove to be our downfall. Before we could consume more than a few delicate scraps, a heavy hand clamped down upon my shoulder, spinning me around. *Busted... Shit.* Grinning like a fox in a hen house, Jeremiah, football bro extraordinaire, tightened his grip on my shoulder as his band of goons surrounded my crew.

"Well, well, well. What do we have here?" He leered at us as we were herded away from the spread. "A handful of losers, trying to steal my food."

Witty one, isn't he?

"Hi Jeremiah," I wheedled. Might as well attempt to pull out the stops to save us an ass beating. "I'm so sorry, we didn't know that this was your place. We thought it was Costel's place. Just give me a moment and we'll be outta your hair. You'll never know we were here."

My cohorts had the foresight to remain silent as Jeremiah considered my offer. When Jeremiah didn't respond right away, a bit of hope blossomed in my chest. *Maybe he's in a good mood today...*

Motioning to his lackies, Jeremiah smiled a devilish grin once more. "No can do, I'm afraid. See, you guys ate my food." He waved his hand over the table, pointing out a barely noticeable dent in the smorgasbord. That bastard. "I can't let you eat my food and bounce without an invite. It's rude to steal, you know?"

I can't believe I'm about to do this.

"Jeremiah, please..." Begging does not become me.

"You must suffer the consequences."

Snapping his fingers, two of the goons made their way directly behind my crew and grabbed the hapless victims by their underoos.

Lifting like a deadlifter, you'd never believe it, but they hoisted Anthony and Craig above their heads in a couple of wedgies o' doom."

***

"Excuse me a moment, Mister Ulysses," Principal Alcinous politely broke in. "Did you really just say 'wedgies of doom?' Isn't that a bit overdramatic?"

"No, no, it's 'wedgies *o*' doom,' sir," Alastair said promptly. "And, honestly, what did you expect from the Theatre Crew? Drama is kinda our specialty, sir."

The administrator once again buried his face in his hands. "I'm sorry I asked. Please, continue."

***

Crying out in agony as their nether-regions were assaulted by their underwear, the brutes began laughing. Once they decided to finally return my comrades back to the ground, the two slunk into the center of our group to hide their shame. Jeremiah and his gang high-fived each other and made their way to the drinks, watching us out the side of their eyes. They were not going to get away with this.

One thing I've always been good at was thinking on my toes. Probably because my older brothers were such cockwombles, and I needed to adapt to survive. My gears began turning and I took in my surroundings. Heavenly feast... A table filled with a variety of sodas... Garish punch bowl... Nectar of the adults... Candy for the trick-or-treaters... Wait! Nectar of the adults! If I can get them to drink some of that adulterous ambrosia we might be able to get that damned Wi-Fi password and escape this hell with a bite for the road.

I casually strolled towards the beverages and grabbed a bottle of something clear. Keeping an eye on the jock flock, I upturned the bottle into the punch bowl, pouring a generous helping of whatever it is into the unadulterated beverage before stashing the bottle under a bar stool at the counter. As subtly as I could, I stirred the concoction with the ladle, praying to the gods that my plan would work.

At this point, all I wanted to do was see my darling Penelope and our little boy.

***

Principal Alcinous suddenly sat up, his typically unruffled demeanor gone. Sheer alarm took its place. "Wait, you and your girlfriend have a *son?!*"

The teenager blinked in confusion for a moment, then laughed and shook his head. "That's just how we refer to Penelope's dog. We found him abandoned as a puppy over a year ago. My folks can't stand dogs, so he got to stay with her. It works out, though. Penelope's place has a huge yard where Telly can run around."

"Telly?"

"It's short for Telemachus."

"That's an interesting name."

"We got it from Homer's *The Odyssey*. And seeing how he's Penelope's fur baby..."

"Yes, Mister Ulysses," Alcinous said, his voice cracking as he pinched the bridge of his nose. "I get it. Wish I didn't, but I get it. Very clever and all that. Now, please, move on."

***

Having stirred the punch vigorously, I took a deep breath. Time to set this sucker into motion.

"Hey guys," I called out in a mock whisper. Thanks to my training, I knew it would carry, despite the body-wracking throb of the bass. "Let's grab a quick drink before we go. I don't think they're looking."

Jeremiah perked up. Bullseye.

Untangling himself from his fellow bros, he excused himself and made a beeline towards me. Time to steel myself. O Blessed Nerves, don't fail me now.

"Oh, hi Jeremiah." A touch of quiver, just to bolster his already oversized ego. "I wasn't doing anything. I was just leaving."

"With a cup of punch in your hand?" His raised eyebrow emphasized his amusement. Snatching the cup from my hand, he downed it.

Bingo!

"I just got a little thirsty, man. No harm, right?"

"I thought I told you earlier, no stealing from me." He cracked his knuckles menacingly. "Why'd you even come inside in the first place? You're not stupid. You knew it wasn't Costel's place."

With a sigh, I decided that a bit of truth wouldn't hurt. "I just wanted to find out the Wi-Fi password so I could grab some directions real quick. My data's almost out for the month and, well, the others don't have smartphones." I point at my crew for emphasis.

"Tell me your name, nerd, and I'll give you my password." God that smirk on his face was starting to get on my nerves. "I want to know who I'll be getting lunch money from for the rest of the year. After all, I haven't been paid back for the food and drinks you guys stole."

"Oh, you don't want to waste your time with me. I'm just Nobody."

"Nobody?" His eyes looked a little glazed.

Has he not eaten in a while? Is it taking effect?

"Yeah, Nobody."

Smile, nice and big now. Show him you're no threat.

"So... about that Wi-Fi password?" I placed a hint of hope in my voice. Let him think that he's got me over a barrel.

"My Wi-Fi password?" he bellowed.

"Oh, it's 'goodiefoodie,' all lower case," an older woman, presumably his mother, replied as she walked by to grab a soda.

"Thank you," I stammered.

I tried to walk away, but Jeremiah grabbed my jacket. Once the woman returned to her group of friends, he yanked me into him. I could smell the "punch" on his breath.

"You're getting on my nerves, nerd. Let me make this quick for you."

Rearing back, Jeremiah balled up his fist in preparation to hit me. I've never been an athletic person, but by the grace of the gods, I was able to dodge his attack and land a clean blow on his eye. Chaotic mutterings broke out from my crew. Variants of "The eye, the eye. Nobody socked him in the eye!" could be heard. Bless their hearts. They overheard my cover name.

***

The older man started in surprise when Alastair's entourage of theatre geeks jumped into action once again. Their faces were deadpan, hands held up with fingers ready to snap out a beat: an artifact of muscle memory from last year's production of *West Side Story*. "The eye, the eye," they chanted in a monotone *voce sotto* as they traversed the office in a processional line, snapping their fingers as they did, "he punched him in the eye! The eye, the eye, Nobody punched him in the eye!"

Then, just as it looked like they were done, a lone member from the group dashed out in front and sang out, "Nobody's going to pay for this! He punched him in the eyyyyyeeeeeeee!" and proceeded to rejoin the group.

Principal Alcinous simply stared at the youth across the desk from him. Ulysses opened his mouth to speak, but stopped short when the principal held up a hand.

"Just... finish telling your damn story, kid."

***

Jeremiah roared in rage, alerting the room. Time to make my grand escape. Flipping on Google Maps, I quickly found the right street to take to get to Penny's and then made a dash to the door, posse following suit. Stopping at the food table, I grabbed the plate of salami rolls, spooned a handful of meatballs onto the platter, and made my way out into the night.

The evening ended with me finally making it to Penny's house, where we cuddled with Telly on the couch and watched *Scream* on Netflix. My colleagues enjoyed a spirited marathon of *League of Legends* in her basement, ganking the preteens who were too cool to go out and trick or treat.

***

Alastair Ulysses sat back as his story concluded. Awkward silence coalesced in the dusty office.

"Well, seeing as how this 'Nobody' was the one who threw the punch that busted Jeremiah's eye, I can't understand why I needed to call you into my office, Mister Ulysses," Principal Alcinous said. The youth was about get up, thinking he was off the hook; but stopped when he saw the look on the older man's face. "Except that, during the rather artistic retelling of your misadventures here, you confessed that *you* were this 'Nobody' who threw the punch."

The color drained from Alastair's face. "And," Alcinous continued, "we have multiple witnesses from the neighborhood and party who heard you yell, and I quote, 'It was not Nobody who blinded you, but I, Alastair Ulysses, who put out your eye! Take that, you stupid ass motherfucker,' unquote, as you left."

If the silence earlier was awkward, the one that hurried to settle in now was downright obscene. Ulysses stayed very still until the principal spoke again.

"Needless to say, Jeremiah's uncle— who happens to be on the city council and coaches the swim team, among other things— is quite unhappy with you."

Ulysses tried not to groan in despair.

About the Authors

Estee Lee-Mountel

Estee began writing professionally as a journalist, during which she published narrative non-fiction stories with *Sacramento News & Review*. Now, she is a quasi-librarian (or "library services assistant," as the HR department puts it) for the Public Library of Cincinnati and Hamilton County by day; writer and artist by night. She is the lead writer and editor for indie mobile game developer Advenworks, headquartered in the startup campus Station F in Paris, France. The iOS app game *Birdy Party*, which was released late 2016, features her campaign story. They also recently completed a Kickstarter for their current project, *Slashrun*, that was born from her story concept.

New Adventures is Estee's second dance with writing and publishing fiction.

She's a native Californian currently living in Cincinnati, Ohio with her husband, the Orc, and their two kids, the Whelpling and the Broodling.

You can still follow her oft-punny and nerdy musings on Twitter @Toriah_the_Mom (now with 50% more art!).

Photo/art credit: Caricature self-portrait by the author.

T. M. Lowe

T. M. Lowe was an aspiring writer from Jacksonville, Florida, when her mother took her own life in 2012. Mrs. Lowe stopped following her lifelong passion while trying to figure out how to cope with the sudden, unexpected loss. Four years later, she determined to take up writing again in her mother's memory.

Her first published works were "What Makes a Man", a science fiction short story and "The Lady and the Dragon", a fantasy short story. Both appeared in DragonScript's first anthology, *New Beginnings*. She is currently working on more short stories as well as a full-length novel.

Mrs. Lowe is 33 years old and currently resides in St. Augustine, Florida, with her husband and household of rescued animals. When not writing, her hobbies include playing video games, watching her beloved Florida Gators play football in the fall, reading, attending medieval and renaissance faires in full knightly costume, fishing, and shooting pool while drinking whiskey in smoky dive bars.

To catch updates on her current writing projects, follow her on Twitter at @TiffanyMLowe or visit her Facebook page at www.facebook.com/AuthorTMLowe.

K.N. Nguyen

K.N. Nguyen is a fantasy author and the co-founder of DragonScript, a group that offers an outlet for new writers. Growing up, she often found herself immersed in some imaginary world, conquering enemy nations, and saving the day. As time went on, her love for horrible puns and nerd culture pulled her out of these worlds and brought her back to reality.

It wasn't until she started working at her office job that she felt the itch to begin writing. Her debut novel, *King's Blood*, was released in 2018. It is the first of a high fantasy series drawing on her love of ancient Mediterranean mythology and epic fantasy.

A native of Sacramento, California, K.N. Nguyen spends her time singing karaoke, playing taiko, enjoying rhythm dancing games, and travelling with her friends and family when she isn't writing.

C. Red

Avid cosplayer and comic reader, C. Red is the newest writer to join DragonScript. She got her start from fanfiction, in which Red has contributed many different works to the community. Since then, she has branched off to her own original material  and is looking forward to the release of her first book, *Divine Disaster*. It is the story of an impassive and violent drug dealer who goes to collect on a debt from an addict. Entering the dilapidated trailer, he finds an eleven-year-old girl. When the dealer sees the atrocious conditions of the child, he feels compelled to take her away from the neglect, abuse, and squalor to try and give her a better life.

You can follow her on her Facebook page through that journey at www.facebook.com/c.redwriting.

Nicholas Walls

Nicholas Walls has always been a charter of the fantastic, telling stories with friends on the playground even at a young age. A long-term enthusiast of sci-fiction and fantasy, if a story had a fantastical element, Nick would devour the story. A historian by training, Nick also brings the past to life through the Facebook page History-In-5. He is now ready to release his debut novels, *The Butcher's Tale* and *Primal Real Estate*.

Johnny C. Vid is a man fallen from glory, a burnout living in the shadow of gleaming high-rises and neon signs in the sprawling metropolis of the Heap. A false-life junkie, Johnny scrounges for shards of memories, living stolen snippets of other people's lives through Vicarious Reality just to avoid the horrors in his own mind. As Johnny desperately chases his next escape from life, he runs across death itself, a nightmare creature of blood, gristle, and rusted iron. Now Johnny must run not only from his past, but also from the brutal attentions of the Butcher in *The Butcher's Tale*.

There are things that go bump in the night and sometimes they need legal counsel. Jon Doe, newly minted Harvard Graduate, learns that some things are too good to be true when he gets roped into a shadow war between two rival houses of shapeshifting monsters. They've been going at it tooth and claw for centuries and Jon is the latest pawn in their game. Now the lawyer will have to rely on his silver tongue and quick wits or his blood will stain the sands in *Primal Real Estate.*

Acknowledgements from Estee Lee-Mountel

For Jim "Piles" Phillips

Readers, I'd like to introduce you to a kind soul. A wonderful, luminous soul. You know those wise, sometimes eccentric mentors who help the protagonist in a heroic epic? That's Jim.

I had the honor of meeting Jim through *World of Warcraft*, where he played an Orc hunter named Piles. He joined our guild during a time when we quite literally needed him the most. Not because he was tricked out in high-level gear or a seasoned raider: we needed him for his presence, and the lessons he would eventually teach us with his very existence. We were in a rut and hurting because we'd gone through a series of recruits who used us, took advantage of us, then left us. Jim restored our faith in ourselves, in the community, and led us to find our guild's true mission of fostering a warm, welcoming gaming family. The only thing he ever asked for was a guild invite. For years, he would farm materials and play the in-game auction house for gold to support our raiding endeavors without asking anything else from us.

"You humoring an old man in this game is enough for me," he'd say.

Jim had a way of building bridges with people. If there was some way to build common ground with you, he'd find it and do it with apparent ease. We loved him like the doting uncle that he was to us. He happily harmonized his love of traditional tabletop RPGs, science fiction, and fantasy with his Christian faith. Being a generous, hard-working man was his way of living out that faith— in addition to being an old-school geek.

In 2011, when Blizzard announced their writing contest, I hesitated. I hadn't written anything worthwhile in years. That part of me was buried underneath a mountain of responsibilities, anxiety, and depression. Jim, on the other hand, encouraged me to do it. He was the first to sign up to help proofread and edit my story. His critique was even-handed and constructive, as you'd expect from a man like Jim. But, more than that, he reached beyond the manuscript to bolster my confidence in my writing. He called me "Wordsmith," a title I strive to honor. He was my blog's #1 fan and cheered me on when I started writing pieces that mixed geekdom and faith. He would repost my work to his friends and family, introducing me as a "budding apologist."

It was right after the new year of 2012 that we found out Jim's absence from WoW wasn't because of the holidays. He had passed away from complications with diabetes.

Through that grief and in missing Jim, I also found myself galvanized. I wasn't about to let my writing go again.

He'd probably scold me for writing another five hundred words about him, you know. "What, the first 1100-plus words weren't enough?" he'd ask with his trademark virtual chuckle.

No, Jim, they aren't enough. The rest of the world deserves to, needs to, know you and the legacy of good you've left with us. As long as I can type into a word processor and put pen to paper, I will tell them about a man named Jim who approached me under the guise of an Orc hunter in a virtual world— the man who helped me rediscover my passion for writing; my mission of loving my fellow human.

For the original tribute I wrote following Jim's passing, it's archived at https://mommyjenkins.wordpress.com/2012/01/17/a-man-named-jim/.

Acknowledgements from T. M. Lowe

To my husband, Jason Lowe. He drinks, and he knows things. For which I will always be grateful. His wit, his tenacity, his toughness… his patience, his kindness, his support and belief in me. I wouldn't want to do any of this without him by my side, the jigsaw piece with the weird, curvy edges that fits my own. I'm not sure I can throw any more pop culture media references at this that are more fitting, so we'll leave it there. He'll get my meaning, and that's all that matters.

To my father, Rick Myers. Always.

To my late mother, Holly Myers, who was my first cheerleader and my biggest supporter. I wish she could be here in the flesh to see this now. But wishes are as fragile as butterfly wings.

To my late grandparents, Anne and Thomas Darby, who encouraged my creativity from a very young age. I miss our fried chicken lunches together.

To Estee, for being my friend, for introducing me to this writing group, and for faithfully checking in on me and encouraging me. Thank you for being one of the few who regularly checks up on "the strong ones". It's appreciated more than you know.

To K.N. Nguyen, for welcoming me into this group and letting me be a part of the anthology adventures.

To C. Red, who inspired the original "The Lady and the Dragon" from our first anthology. I treasure you so much as a friend and wish our states were closer together. I am exceedingly glad you decided to join us on this adventure.

To Melissa Rhinehart and Kimberly Reese. The two ladies who literally save my sanity on a daily basis and regularly talk me down from the ledge at the location of my non-writing career. Blessed be.

To Megan Keyes, for being my medieval faire ride or die. So happy we've reconnected.

To everyone else who has touched my life, be it family or friends; I love you all dearly and each of you has had an impact on me and my writing.

Acknowledgements from K.N. Nguyen

To my loving husband, Francis. I am eternally grateful for all that you have done to help me achieve my writing goals.

To my parents, Kaylyn and Earl, I would like to thank you for always encouraging me to reach for whatever goal I set within my sights. Even when I fell short, you always motivated me to pick myself up and move forward instead of give up.

Acknowledgements from C. Red

To my husband, Stephen. Who puts up with my face buried into a bright screen at 2am, and all my other lovely idiosyncrasies. My writing takes a lot of time from us. Time we both know that we can't get back. You know how much it means to me, and you never once get frustrated. Not once. You're the kind of man that I could only hope to be with, yet I have you. I'm the most difficult and controlling person, but you never let it bother you. I love you unconditionally. Are we havin' chicken or what?

To my mother. You've put up with more than anyone I know, and you shouldn't have had to. You always think of others. You are the most selfless person I have ever known. I love you. In case you're wondering, I probably still haven't cashed that check yet.

To my sister. You've grown into such a beautiful woman. Your positivity is something that everyone should learn from. Going to see you these last few trips have been the most fun I have ever had. You are a wonderful mother. Oh, and I'm sorry I threw that volleyball at your head when you were a baby.

To my brother. The one person that I can be livid with, yet we're playing Final Fantasy the next day like nothing ever happened. Some of my best memories are with you. I don't say this enough, but I'm proud of the man you've become. Sorry I made you take the fall for that volleyball, man. (Well, I'm like fifty percent sorry, ok?)

To Allison. You mean so much to me. I can honestly say that I wouldn't even be writing if it wasn't for your message encouraging me to. I wanted to give up, but you wouldn't let me. Just like all the times I have wanted to delete my stuff and you calm me down. You know we're going to be ninety and still talking about Lord Dingus, right? Please continue to create because you have incredible talents that need to be shared.

To Stephanie. I remember when your heat went out and just that awful feeling of waiting for your text that you're ok. It made me realize in that short time of knowing you how dear you were to me. I know that I can be ridiculous and you never judge me for it. I can talk to you about anything. MADORI for life!

To T. M. Lowe, even though you'll always be Dragon to me. DRAGON! Thank you for this wonderful opportunity. From that day you left me the review it's like we've always known each other. Who I know will protect me in the apocalypse. We're Trish and Alice, after all!

To Julia, who levels me when I can't seem to figure out what's going on in my own head. You always make time for others and ask nothing in return. You tell me how it is, even if it might not be what I want to hear. It's what I need to hear. I wish I could return half of the advice you've given me. I am so glad to have met you and your beautiful family.

To Krystal, the Deadpool to my Cable. Dude, you are the funniest person I have ever met in my life. We just have this understanding in each other that I love. You are supermom, but you still make time for me. Thank you for all the support you have given me.

To Penny. LOL. I can't tell you how much I appreciate the extra pair of eyes on my stories.

To my fellow writers in DragonScript. Thank you for letting me be a part of this. For all your critique and encouraging words that have helped me become a more efficient writer. I wish all the luck to you guys.

To my fanfic readers who better know me as 217. Your reviews inspire me to keep going.

To Ghoulmask, Jaime, Damsel, and Mom 2. You guys mean the world to me!

To my family and friends.

To everyone who has supported me on my journey, thank you.

I need to stop now because my eyes are sweaty.